THE

Jackass

CALAMITIES

Perfidious Nick

by

PERFIDIOUS NICK

Contributing Artist (Cover): Penin Eenk
copyright 2022

Contents

Author's Notes

ometimes the world of politics is so messed up that the old Russian proverb "A Little Revolution Now and Then is a Good Thing" is the only response that makes any sense. In 2016 that was exactly what happened and a second (counting the Civil War, really third) American Revolution took place. American politics had become so corrupt over the years that there really was no difference between Republicans and Democrats – it was no longer a question of which candidate was the best for the country but which establishment politician you preferred to get screwed by. Politics was a business and virtually everyone was on the take, scamming us and doing the bare minimum to "get by". It was all about re-election and promises were just empty words. Americans had become so jaded we expected our leaders were lying to us.

But then came Donald John Trump. A successful businessman and accomplished negotiator this non-politician knew what was wrong with our country and how to fix it. He was brash, unpolished, blunt and ballsy – the spitting image of the Founding Fathers of the United States of America. When Trump was a Hollywood Democrat he was the toast of the media, appearing in films such as *Zoolander* with his wife Melania, being referenced as a success story in movies like *Lethal Weapon 2* and even hosting the popular long-time TV show *The Apprentice*. All that changed when "The Blue Collar Billionaire" put the interest of the American people above the profits of the career politicians. The political elites joined forces to attack him and the lies peddled by the major media outlets and internet moguls were merciless. Overnight Trump was branded a racist, a rapist and a traitor – there was no such thing as a lie too big for the political machine to try and sell the public and no limit to how much they were willing to re-write history.

When despite all this false negative press (as well as a biological attack from China in the form of Covid-19) the American people chose in 2020 to re-elect Donald Trump, the political establishment committed the ultimate sin: they threw aside the will of the people, fixed the votes and installed one of their own into the highest office of the land. The outrage was real and there was (and is) good cause for it. Our ancestors called out to us from the grave for liberty and justice. Those who had given their lives in service to this country watched from above with anxiety as a second Civil War loomed threateningly in the background.

But President Trump was wise enough not to repeat the mistakes of the past. The American Civil War was destructive and did not really hasten the end of slavery or the establishment of universal equality and suffrage. Democracy is based on the power of the will of the People to command our government and what is wrong and what is right is ingrained in the DNA of humanity. Election fraud only succeeds when the margins are razor thin – and the voices of the American people have become legion. There is no hope for those who have violated the cherished values we hold dear and they will be held accountable; the American Revolution part Three has already occurred and will continue. Had Democrats and Republican-in-Name-Only establishment politicians exited the field or reformed themselves they would not presently face the merciless wheel of Justice they now face.

A few other short notes are in order before we begin our celebration of what it means to be an American. This book is quintessentially protected First Amendment free speech: the well-deserved mocking and lampooning of the ridiculous political establishment, criticism that is essential to the health of our Republic and is being squashed on "town hall" social media platforms like Twitter and Facebook. It is largely a work of fiction (KFC was never involved with Bernie Sanders nor has he recently worked at McDonalds) and I'm sure there are lots of other incidental references to popular establishments and events that simply never happened in real life. This novel is also graced with many factoids that are completely true, however. You may notice a particular turn of phrase coming out of the fictional mouth of some a-hole politician within this book that sounds quite familiar. This is by design – real life quotes have been sprinkled in with the dialogue whenever possible and when germane to a scene. Some sections (such as the one concerning corrupt Congress-fool Nancy Pelosi) are composed entirely of quotes provided by Fancy Nancy herself – dialogue taken almost verbatim from sound bites this mental midget has actually made in public in front of the cameras "representing" the State of California. The rest of the story *"Just Desserts"* is made up – but let's face it: it's still more truthful than anything you'll ever see or hear concerning politics on Google, CNN, MSN, Yahoo news or Wikipedia.

Lastly, the author wishes to acknowledge that the character of "Quintuple Jay" in *"So This is Earth"* was heavily, heavily inspired by master comedian Jeff Dunham's puppet "Bubba Jay". John-Jay Jasper Jefferson Junior is a perfect example of how even the least intelligent Deplorable is smarter than the smartest Progressive. I'd also like to acknowledge Mr. Dunham for creating a caricature of Joseph Robinette Biden before the rest of us knew what a cantankerous mentally-absurd dumb ass the former Vice-President really is. "Walter" is clearly the intellectual superior of the two.

This book was written to laugh at the corrupt political establishment and ridiculously drunk-on-notoriety radical left newcomers like AOC who don't know their head from their ass. Their "policies" are so absurd they don't deserve to be taken seriously; they are jokes – and laughter is healthier for the soul than anger and far more powerful. So get comfortable and be prepared for a good time! Celebrate our country; we are back and we are cleaning house!

Now no more speeches! Prepare to laugh your jack-ass off! America the beautiful is back!

Let's Go Brandon
Means
Let's Go America!!!

The *Jackass*

Calamities

Outside the Square Room

The two men standing in the antechamber looked pensive. The occupant inside the square room upon who's person they were duty bound to protect hadn't made a sound in quite a long time.

Ear pressed to the door Agent Dell McKinley turned towards his partner Rudy Hayes. 'What do you think? He's been in there a long time.'

Hayes scoffed, stifling a yawn. 'What do you expect? It's the "Porn Room".'

His partner shrugged. 'Well, at least he's out of our hair.', he replied gratefully.

'Yup.'

McKinley nodded to himself. After a brief pause he shook his head and palmed his face. 'Remember last week?', he bitched. 'When the old fool hit the damned panic button?'

Remembering what confronted them upon entering the Square Office, Hayes grimaced. 'Yeah. Man, that really sucked.', he growled, shaking his head in disbelief.

McKinley's expression turned to one of exasperation. 'I don't know why he even watches that stuff! At his age and crappy health it's not like he can do much! I mean – it was a pathetic half-stiffy!'

Not wanting to think about it Rudy shrugged. 'I think he naps in between. Dude needs Viagra.'

Still in disbelief at the horrible scene, McKinley abruptly started chuckling. 'He was beating off to Stormy Daniels!', he exclaimed. 'Stormy Daniels!! I mean – talk about being a wannabe!!!'

Joining in the mockery of the decrepit old man they were forced to protect, Hayes snorted. 'I remember the video.' His smooth forehead wrinkled as his eyebrows shot wryly skyward. 'She was taking it right up "S-Hole Country".'

Enjoying the play on words the two agents burst out laughing.

1

After their chuckles died down McKinley's eyes became wistful. 'You know, the President bagged some serious hotness back in the day. He kept it clean while He was here but, man....'

Rudy nodded. 'Yeah, He did some babes. Which one was the playboy model again?'

Dell shook his head. 'Shit. Can't remember her name now. It was just on the tip of my tongue.

Rudy Hayes tried to remember who the model was he was referring to. He could see her face and knew she had an incredible body but her name escaped him. 'She was chasing him around. When he ditched her she stalked him. Tried to get a hit piece published in *The National Enquirer*.'

McKinley nodded. 'I remember that. It was during the election.'

'Yup.', Hayes snarked, rolling his eyes. 'That magazine with such an upstanding reputation – *The National Enquirer*.'

Dell McKinley sneered. 'It's not like the *New York Times* is any better these days.'

'True dat.'

After a brief silence the really tall agent went on. 'He definitely picked the right one to marry, though. I mean the First Lady is a total gem. She's gotta be the sweetest of all the women who've ever come through here.'

Rudy agreed. 'Definitely. Smart too. Total package.'

'You ever heard her on the phone? Five languages. Fluently.', replied Dell wistfully.

Hayes nodded. 'Incredible woman. And the fucking press crucified her like she was a rabid dog! Couldn't go after her so they went after the clothes she wore!'

'The press are a bunch of mother fucking douche bags.', scoffed McKinley. 'They'd never have done anything like that to the First Lady when old Chicago-Shelly was here.'

'Nope. And you can't tell me it wasn't a serious upgrade!' After a quick check to make sure they were alone he leaned over towards his partner. 'You ever seen the pictures of Her? I mean, the ones on the internet?'

Dell's brows lit up. 'The modeling stuff?'

'Yeah.'

'Yeah is right.', McKinley replied with a nod. 'Damn.'

'Damn.', Hayes agreed wistfully.

Stuck momentarily on the images burned into their brains of the charming legal immigrant model who'd graced the hallowed halls they were sworn to protect the two bachelors paused reverently. No more regal matron had ever wandered through the corridors of the White House than Lady Melania. The secret servicemen had felt like knights-errant guarding her. Now, though....

'McDougal!', Hayes suddenly exclaimed. 'That was it! Katie... something.'

McKinley's brows knitted. The name sounded familiar but was still a little off. 'I thought it was Karen?'

Not really caring, Agent Rudy shrugged. 'Whatever. She was old news when they hooked up anyway. If she was all that she wouldn't have become such a stalker.'

'Totally trading on the Big Guy's fame.', Dell quipped with a nod.

His partner nodded in agreement. After a sec he tilted his head thoughtfully. 'Kind of a feather in his cap, though. I mean, a porn star <u>and</u> a playboy model both bragging they got dicked by him.'

McKinley shook his head. 'I never really got what the fucktards in the press were going for with their whole supposed "scandal" story line. I mean, people **pay money** just to *watch* Stormy get fucked! She gets paid for this shit! And the Big Guy stuck his dick up her ass!'

'Allegedly.', Hayes reminded his partner with an impish smirk.

'Yeah, allegedly – ', Dell seconded. 'According to *her*.'

'Totally trustworthy.', Agent Hayes chuckled sarcastically.

'Yup, totally. Porn hos are known for that.' McKinley cleared his throat. 'What was the big deal, anyway? So, he banged another hottie. Big-fucking-deal.'

'Back when she *was* hot.', Rudy noted wryly.

'Yeah, back in the day when she was still hot LOL.', nodded Dell. His smile faded. 'Too many fucking drugs. And hanging out with stupid people.'

Hayes dismissed the whole issue with a wave of his hand. 'Banging hot chicks is bragging rights stuff. Ask anyone.' He thumbed his nose towards the closed door. 'Hell, "Mail In" here falls asleep watching porn!'

Dell grunted. 'When the old bastard's not shittin' himself.'

Disgusted that they were protecting a "leader" who was incontinent as well as incompetent the two highly trained secret service agents fell silent for a time. It was boring work, standing outside the room while a dirty old man did his business. What had this country come to?

Bored to tears Rudy finally broke the silence. 'Ha-ha!', he exclaimed with a sudden cackle. 'After the lawsuit lil ol' Stormy's gonna have to get her saggy ass back to work! She'll be doin' granny-porn to pay off her bills for decades!'

'I saw that her lawyer just got jail time.', McKinley crowed.

'I know. Started crying!' Hayes shook his head. 'What a mother-fuck-ing bitch.'

Agent Dell's eyes twinkled mischievously. 'Oh, he's gonna be some-body's bitch, alright.'

The abrupt sound of a door opening came from down the hall. McKinley and Hayes both turned and a moment later two agents, Guy Guildencrantz and Emily Rosenstern, appeared. The day shift relief troops had arrived!

'Hey, dudes!', Rudy greeted.

'Hey.', Guildencrantz replied with far less enthusiasm than his soon-to-depart coworker.

Put out, Emily Rosenstern gave Hayes a look. 'Dude?', she scoffed.

'Dude and dudette.', Rudy corrected. 'Feel better now?'

'Careful, buddy – ', snarked Dell as he gathered up his stuff. 'Don't let the PC police hear ya say that.' Annoyed, he looked towards Guy and Emily. 'They want us all to use "non-binary" terms from now on.', he informed his coworkers with a disgusted frown.

Ignoring his partner's rebuke Rudy fluttered his eyes exaggeratedly like a silent film ingenue. 'Yeah. Calling a man a man and a woman a woman is "offensive" now.'

'I'll remember that next time the "POTUS" tries to grab my ass.', Rosenstern quipped. Turning to more professional matters she queried, 'Where is ol' "Mail In"?'

Dell McKinley pointed towards the closed door. 'Takin' care of per-sonal business.'

'Jerkin' lil' Joey again? Shit.'

Agent McKinley shook his head. 'Not this time. I think he's havin' a nap.' He rolled his eyes. 'It's that "time of day".'

Guy Guildencrantz blinked then stared blankly at the closed door that housed the free world's supposed "leader". Gee, wonder why Russia felt emboldened enough to invade Ukraine? 'An hour after he woke up and he's already having a nap. Christ Jesus. "Democracy" at work.'

Ready to leave, Hayes shouldered his bag. 'Yeah – if you count millions of "ballots" all with the same name, same address, same birthday and no verified signature or photo ID as "Democratic".'

'Oh, they were "Democratic" all right!', his partner retorted as he started towards the exit.

Pausing, Rudy Hayes shook his head. 'I still don't get why the Guinness book of World Records isn't looking for all these people! I mean, the oldest recorded living person was 115 years old! If all these supposed ballots have January 1, 1900 listed as a birthday that means they're all over 120 years old!'

'They're not looking because they know it's bullshit!', declared Dell, slowing his escape. 'Everybody knows it's bullshit!'

'You wouldn't know it by the media.', Guy Guildencrantz remarked. The big man scratched his chin. 'They keep repeating "Biden Election Victory" over and over.'

McKinley shook his head. 'Media don't tell us anything that they don't want us to hear. If they're not telling a blatant lie, they are covering something up.' He shook his head. 'Oh, the books we could write...'

'None of us will, though.', Emily Rosenstern reminded him sternly. 'Part of this job is keeping our mouths shut about all the stupid bullshit we see. It's Code.'

'Yup.', her partner agreed. 'Anybody who believes any of these so-called leaks just doesn't get that. If it's bad and true we're not gonna talk to the press about it. Even if it's good we're not gonna talk to anyone. Silence is golden.'

Hayes scowled morosely. They all knew the drill. As much as they hated it they had to keep the American people in the dark about all the incompetence going on around here. It was part of the job. 'Well folks, it's been nice shootin' the shit with ya but that's all the time we got for today.', he said, glad he could finally leave this hellhole. 'Me and Dell are outta here. Ya'll take care now.'

Guildencrantz waved. 'Have a good one, Rudy. Bye Dell.'

'Bye guys.', seconded his female partner.

Hayes and McKinley headed out the door while the day shift replacing them settled in. In preparation for protecting herself from unwanted advances Emily Rosenstern plopped herself in the chair against the wall. In far less danger of being groped by "sleepy-creepy" Guildencrantz took the one opposite. It was a good tactical position with clear view of both entrance points. 'Fuck. Country is going straight to hell.', he breathed to the air. Already bored he thumbed his nose towards the closed door. 'What do you think? Should we try and wake him up?'

Rosenstern shook her head adamantly. 'No. Leave him be. He fucks less shit up when he's comatose. Safer for the country to just let him sleep.'

Guy nodded. Emily wasn't just protecting the country – she was literally covering her own behind. 'The ones actually running the show behind the scenes aren't any better.', he complained.

Knowing what Guy was saying was true his partner quietly cursed. Concerned for the trajectory the nation was on and looking for something to do she examined her nails. If she was undercover instead of being stuck on protection duty she could grow them out again. She preferred having longer nails. It made nights with Chad more fun.

Bored, Guildencrantz turned the clock on the desk so he could see it.

'Why you gotta do that?', Em groused. 'It'll just make the day go by slower.'

Guy frowned. 'Every hour we get closer to when our relief shows up gives me hope.', he asserted.

'Dude, we just got here.'

Lamenting that fact, Guy sighed. 'It's gonna be a long fucking day.', he breathed.

'Yeah. Long fucking day.', his partner-against-crime agreed.

The secret service agent twosome sat quietly for about half a minute. Though it was digital you could almost hear the ticking of clock-hands in the air.

'Remember when things used to happen around here?', Em asked suddenly, breaking the silence.

Guy Guildencranz nodded fondly. 'Yeah. Good times. Meeting after meeting, energy and prosperity. A lot of good got done. America was back.'

'Wouldn't even *have* any vaccines if it weren't for the President.', she noted.

'Yeah. The bastards don't give him any credit, though.'

Knowing burying the truth was all the current inhabitants of the White House knew how to do Emily Rosenstern turned and glanced idly at the portraits hanging on the wall. George Washington and Abraham Lincoln dominated the eastern side. Giants walked through these halls once. Not Washington, of course, because the White House hadn't been built yet, but other great leaders. The whole entire city was named after Washington. It had since turned into a Swamp. The First would be ashamed of what his namesake had become. 'I still have a hard time not calling him the President.', she remarked wistfully.

'Well, he is still President Donald John Trump.', Guy replied. 'They just stole his office out from under him with a bunch of fake ballots. Fake News, Fake Ballots. They are all fakes and liars.'

Rosenstern nodded. After a thoughtful pause she replied: 'You know, I don't see how the press and – ', she thumbed her nose towards the creepy old fart taking a nap in the room beyond, 'Can refer to it as "The Vaccine" and be on this push to force everybody to take it while still trying to pretend their predecessor isn't the one 100% responsible for it. It's not "The Vaccine" – it's the "Trump Vaccine".'

'They're disingenuous as hell.', Guildencrantz agreed. 'Still trying to pretend Pfizer made it up all by themselves! Got paid for it – but "didn't take any money from the government" LOL! And they wouldn't have had a fucking clue where to start if it weren't for all the research that got shared with them!' He shook his head ruefully. 'It was a team effort but they want to pretend it wasn't. And it happened in record time! They said it would take five years, minimum! Trump got it done in months!'

Emily vigorously nodded her assent. After a momentary pause, she chuckled. 'I want to get a tee shirt made with the legend: "Two seconds before a liberal's head explodes". And underneath it is this picture of some dorky tied-dyed wearing chick with pro-choice tattoos running up both arms and tacky GBLT rainbow socks pulled up to her twat carrying a sign over her shoulder that reads, "People who don't get the Covid Vaccine kill children!" And at the bottom it says: "When you remind her that she just volunteered to get a big ol' shot of Trump into her body!".'

'Oh, that'd be fucking hysterical!', Guy chuckled. 'You should totally make that! I'd buy one!'

'Yeah, it'd sell. Libtards would probably call it "hate speech", though.'

'Yeah, California would.' Guy shook his head. 'Those people are seriously fucked in the head. Everybody's got free speech – except those who disagree with them.'

Emily nodded. 'There's another one I want to do with the word DEMOCRAT in stone letters and a big hammer like the one Thor uses coming down on it with the letters MAGA emblazoned on the side crushing the word "Democrat" to pieces.' She rubbed her hands in anticipation. 'Twenty-twenty-two is going to be crushing.'

'God-willing! If the votes aren't tampered with again, it will be.'

'I'm still hoping we'll get justice for twenty-twenty!'

Guy sat back in his chair. 'In hindsight this will either be when Democracy ended or when America cleaned house and Democracy was restored. China has got to go down. It's either that – or we're gonna have World War Three. They keep stealing our technology and it's only a matter of time.'

Rosenstern bit her lip. As a government agent she really wished she could do something about that shit but her job prohibited her from taking action. It was so frustrating! 'I have another one I wanna make that reads "Democrats Hate Democracy", or "Democrats are the Enemy of Democracy" – something to that effect. Maybe we should just start calling them DEMONcrats?'

The burly man opposite her gritted his teeth like a dog struggling not to bite. 'Can't say that, though. We're supposed to be "non-political". Can't put anything out to the public.'

Em shook her head. 'As long as we're not using our government position to support a political agenda I think we should have the same free speech rights as anybody else.', she asserted. 'The dickheads of years past certainly used that excuse when they kept reporting all these "anonymous" leaks to go after the President.'

Guy bared his teeth but there was no mirth to his smile. 'Ah! Good ol' "Anon Ymous" again!', he bitched. 'Funny, I've worked here for ten years and I've never met the guy.'

'Or girl.', quipped Rosenstern, shaking her finger crossly. 'Or gender-neutral "them". Can't be sexist or "binary"! Powers-that-be wouldn't like it!'

Guildencrantz flipped the bird to show exactly what he thought of the word police. Country was going to fucking hell but *their* priority was taking common sense words out of the English language. 'Oh no. Can't have that. "They" might get "offended".'

'When are these pricks <u>not</u> offended?!', blanched Rosenstern, not caring if anyone overheard her using a curse word that distinctly referred to male anatomy. It was funny how calling someone a dick was not a problem but referring to someone who had a penis as a man was!

Liking that his partner-in-law Emily was a bit foul-mouthed Guildencrantz grinned in reponse. After a brief pause his smile faded. 'You know I have this theory – and it seems to make sense. You tell me if I'm wrong: In the 1930s when Hitler came to power he used the Jews as a focal point for hostility to unify the country, to give people an enemy to focus on.'

Rosenstern nodded. 'Yeah. And?'

'And all these social justice warriors – these Black Lives Matter people – they seem to be doing the same thing. Everything's all about "white privilege" and "systemic racism", even though studies prove beyond any doubt that those things don't actually exist in this country. Sure, occasionally someone – an asshole, some individual – breaks the law, but how is that any different than a Muslim terrorist blowing up a supermarket? It doesn't make all followers of Islam bad – it's just one individual criminal who committed a crime.'

Emily's brows knitted. 'So what are you saying? You think BLM is planning to blow up a supermarket?'

He shook his head. 'I'm saying that equality for all is something I can get behind – I think everybody can. But making Caucasians out to be the bad guys is just plain racist! It's making white people – and white men specifically – out be villains just because of the color of our skin. It's like all this "non-binary" crap. It's nuts! The majority shouldn't have to change how we refer to ourselves because someone else is different from the norm.' He cleared his throat pointedly. 'Anyway, I'm saying that I think BLM and the Progressive movement are using white people like the Nazis used the Jews.'

Emily blinked. Pausing to really consider her partner's theory, her brows furrowed worriedly. 'You know, I never thought of it that way. But I think you may be right – they are creating a villain to blame everything on to distract everyone from their agenda. And their agenda IS pretty fucked up! Hell, the booming economy they've destroyed proves that.'

Guildencrantz nodded. He was hoping he was wrong, that his friend and partner could find some flaw in his logic. It was disturbing to think that any political party in America was using the same tactics as the ones used by Nazi Germany. Wanting to escape this place he looked at the clock. Only ten minutes had passed. Damn. 'Hey, maybe we should play a game? To pass the time?', he suggested.

'We're on duty.', she said with a shake of her head.

Guy frowned. They were babysitting an old fart sleeping in the next room! What the hell was there to pay attention *to*? 'I could use a distraction to keep me perky. Otherwise I'm afraid I will fall asleep – or die of sheer boredom.'

'What you got in mind? Checkers or something? Now that the Big Guy's gone they've taken all the Chess boards.', she reminded him pointedly.

Guildencrantz sat back in his chair and smirked. Games like Chess were too intellectually advanced for the current occupants of the White House and they'd removed them from the premises out of shame. He and Emily would have to find something else to do to pass the time. 'Okay, how about this: since we can't break out a board game, I tell you a story about our favorite group of people – some macabre tale where they end up finally getting their just deserts. Then you tell me a different story about someone else.'

Em pursed her lips. 'So...you mean kind of like "I Spy"?'

'Well, no, not exactly. I mean, like, a story. So-and-so gets cancer and dies and isn't that so sad, hee-hee. Some ironic calamity or catastrophe befalls one of these a-holes.' He waved his hand in the air, encompassing the totality of their surroundings. 'Some crooked joker who desperately needs to finally get a comeuppance finally gets it in both ear-holes.'

Emily stroked her chin thoughtfully. 'Hmmm. Well, it can't be anything violent.', she noted. 'We're here to prevent our elected officials from assassination, not plot it.'

Guildencrantz let the obvious issue every thinking American had with 2020's voting integrity pass. As secret service agents they had to protect whomever occupied the office whether they were legitimately elected or not. 'No, of course not – absolutely no assassination.', he agreed, setting an important ground rule. 'The story needs to be more creative than that anyway. An Act of God, some poetic natural disaster.' He chuckled. 'Something that would make a fitting end for these butt monkeys.'

Rosenstern paused thoughtfully. After a moment a smile slowly graced her pretty face. 'So...we judge each other's stories based on creativity <u>and</u> irony?'

'Yes, exactly.'

'And the winner gets?'

Guy shrugged. 'How about the loser buys the other one lunch tomorrow?', he suggested.

'Oh, you know that's not fair – ', his slender partner-in-law blurted, giving him a look. 'You eat like a horse! And I just started a keto diet!'

'You're always on a diet!', he complained with a huff. Realizing he would have to propose something more egalitarian if Emily was going to go for this "Game of Stories" idea Guy paused to think. What would make for good stakes? What would entice her to play? 'Okay, okay – how about this: loser takes the other one out for a couples dinner? You bring Chad and I'll bring Veronica. Winner picks the place.'

Emily paused to consider this new proposition. She would love to have a night out on the town as a foursome. It'd been a while since she'd gotten to hang out with Veronica. 'Why don't we let our significant others be the ones who pick the place?', she countered, wanting to chat it up with her girlfriend and also spoil her boyfriend rotten so he'd finally get off his ass and propose to her.

Accepting her terms Guy gave a nod. 'Okay, I'm down with that. And we'll both get brownie points for making the night special for our squeezes.'

'Oh, I make sure every night with Chad is special.', Em winked, wagging her eyebrows suggestively. Her competitive juices flowing she rubbed her hands together. 'So....how do we start this thing?', she said eagerly.

'I'll go first, then you try and Trump me.', Guy offered.

'Trump me?', she laughed. 'No pun intended?'

'Oh, all possible puns.', assured Guildencranz, settling into the game with a smirk. 'But it's about the ends and the means...justifying...the end and the means. It's the journey straight to heck that counts.' He rubbed his hands together happily. 'Oh, this should be fun...'

'Just don't get us caught doing something that'll get our asses in a sling.', Emily needled. She wanted to make her work day bearable but didn't want to lose her job in the process. Trump was going to run again in 2024; she wanted to still be here so she could protect the First Family when he won.

Eager to play Guy held up his hands in surrender. 'Hey! We're just two friends shooting the shit! It's not like there's anyone else here.'

Rosenstern eyed the walls suspiciously. 'These paranoid people probably got the whole place bugged.', she whispered. 'You know they stab each other in the back behind closed doors. It's only when it comes to voting that they all go one way.'

'Probably because they've got dirt on each other.', Guy agreed with a nod. 'But, hey – we're just two coworkers telling fanciful bullshit stories to pass the time. No law against that.'

Emily bit her lip. 'Just so long as nobody ends up accusing us of treason.'

Guy gave her a look. 'Mocking douche bags isn't treason. We're just trying to have a laugh and pass the time while Uncle Joe has his post-jerk off session nap.'

'Okay.', Emily said, giving in. 'But let's keep it somewhat clean. No AIDS or Covid deaths.'

His first inclination poo-pooed Guy frowned in disappointment. 'Aww. You sure about that?'

'Yup. Those are my rules.', she declared firmly, setting a condition of her own. 'If you want me to play your little game you have to agree to those terms.'

Guy beamed a wry little smile at her. 'Or you're taking your ball home?', he sassed.

'Something like that.'

Letting her have her way, Guy sighed. Ah, home sharing a bottle of wine with Veronica – the end of the work day couldn't get here fast enough! 'Okay. I'll agree to those terms.' Stretching his arms to get the blood flowing he scratched the back of his head. 'How many tales shall we tell?'

Emily bit her lip. 'It's got to be an even number, doesn't it? We're taking turns.'

Guy nodded thoughtfully. 'Okay – six a piece then? We'll need a scoring system. How about this: one point for being ironic and another for good story telling? The one with the most points at the end wins. And the end of our shift has to be the time limit regardless.', he said, unwilling to delay leaving this swampy shit hole any longer than he had to. 'Any interruptions pause the game.'

'Deal.', she agreed. Ready for the show to begin Rosenstern tucked her legs more comfortably around the chair. 'I'm all ears, big man. Make me laugh.'

Sensing their day was about to go by more quickly, Guildencrantz twiddled his fingers happily. There was something deliciously sneaky about mocking "the boss" when the shit-stained jerk-off was out like a light in the next room. He glanced at the closed door. 'Oh – one other rule I want to put out there before we start: "Sleeping Beauty" is off the table. He's enough of a joke all by himself. It doesn't feel right to mock somebody just for being a decrepit old fart.'

Thwarted, Rosenstern's face pained. Biden was the first asshole she was planning to skewer! '"Sleeping Beauty" was a total creep before he got old and decrepit!', she complained crossly. When her partner didn't immediately give in she glared at him. 'You're not the one who keeps getting your ass grabbed!', she bitched.

Genuinely sympathetic to her plight Guy's face softened. Biden had gotten away with groping women for more than forty years; his horrible behavior wasn't new. Of all the things for the senile old limp dick to remember from his youth...! 'I'm sorry, Emily.', said Guy to her remorsefully. 'Really. But he's *got* to be off limits. He's the guy we're assigned to protect. Our hands are tied on this.'

Knowing her partner was right, Em's scowl deepened. 'I wish his hands were tied.', she complained.

Guildencrantz nodded. Twenty twenty-four couldn't come soon enough! Maybe, God-willing, the Republicans would grow some balls, retake Congress and Impeach the bastard?! There was certainly enough evidence to warrant it, what with the charges of that $900,000 bribe from Ukraine proven in court, Hunter Biden's laptop and the Durham report slapping indictments on everybody...

He banished those serious thoughts for now. It was time to turn their frowns upside down. 'Okay! Let's get this party started!', he said, rubbing his hands. 'Lemme see if you like this one...'

Show Me the Wampum

*I*t was a small crowd. The poor attendance wasn't due to the rainy weather but rather because the keynote speaker Senator Elizabeth Warren simply wasn't very popular. Her primary numbers during the 2020 election had been abysmal and nothing she'd done since had elevated her status. She was a minor cog in the wheel of corruption, a bit player hanging on just so she could suck on the teat of the public dole. In many ways she was a welfare case. She contributed nothing and took resources from the commonwealth that could be better spent building sewers and improving the roads. Her only achievement to date had been to convince a few saps to vote her into office.

'Now I know we're here to talk about environmental issues.', she said to the twenty or so assembled guests. 'But I want us all to take a moment to appreciate the beauty of the Earth. Let us all sit down in the grass here.'

Though it was wet Warren plopped her behind on the grass. The people looked to one another in confusion. Did the alabaster-skinned woman not realize it was raining?

'Come on. It's only a little water.'

Gradually those assembled around her bent down. Most of the spectators simply crouched, however, rather than got their pants or skirts soaked.

'Feel the land. Feel the Great Spirit between the trees, the breeze blowing the leaves...all of nature in balance.'

Huddling under their umbrellas a few of the younger people nodded.

Warren picked up a hefty patch of weeds. She examined it carefully, then tucked it behind her ear. Unsatisfied with her new adornment she ripped a tuft of grass out of the wet dirt. Brushing off the bottom she stuck the whole wad in her mouth and began to chew it into cud. 'Mmmm. Taste the green.'

One or two of Warren's followers followed suit and plucked an edible stray dandelion stalk to suckle between their teeth. The rest of the onlookers looked at Senator Warren like she was nuts, however. She was chewing a wad of grass like she was a cow.

'And Donald Trump wants to fuck this all up!', she screeched, cursing like a sailor. 'He wants to poison you and your children! He's a monster! We have to end his evil rule once and for all! Take back the land that is ours! By my Native American heritage I promise to do this! The tomahawk will be stained red with his blood and the blood of all his followers!'

About half of the assembled mob – the crazy half – cheered. The others paused, realizing how violently insane the words coming out of Warren's mouth were. Did she not realize this was America? This was the land of Free Speech and civil debate! True, the tech companies were censoring their opponents and universities were promoting a liberal agenda rather than offering different ideologies and allowing students to choose from among them freely, but none of this had directly affected them yet and they didn't realize the danger this Nazi intolerance posed.

As if on cue a bolt of lightning flashed across the sky silencing Warren's calls for blood. 'Okay folks! The senator hates to cut this short but lightning is no joke. It's time we best get inside!', her staffer Melly Sykes announced fearing a bolt from above might strike her or her boss dead.

The small listless assembly began to disperse. Those few foolish enough to sit in the grass left wiping their wet behinds. The seats of their new hybrid cars were about to get a permanent nature stain on the drive home.

'There was no need for that Melly! It's only a little weather! A brave has no fear of nature! It's only the lightning spirit come to lend its support to our cause!', Warren roared, shaking her fist at the thunder.

Thinking her boss must be on drugs again Sykes took her by the arm and ushered her away. 'Come on, Senator. Let's get in the car.'

The old woman reluctantly shuffled into the limo and her driver closed the door behind her. Her clothes thoroughly soaked she stripped off her blazer. 'It's too bad we have to move around in this hearse instead riding a horse.'

'It would be more environmentally friendly.', Sykes jokingly agreed. In spite of their horseless carriage there had certainly been no shortage of horse shit on this trip! 'We'd have a hard time selling that to the public, though. The proverbial slippery slope to Amish country!'

Ignoring the jab Warren began stripping off her wet pants.

'Here, senator. Let me get you a new pair.', her aide offered. 'There's a change of clothes in the stowaway compartment.'

The pale-faced woman in the back seat regarded the polyester slacks with disdain but reluctantly put them on. 'From now on I want no more of this prefabricated fashion.', she declared, thrusting her foot into the leg. 'It's time to embrace my heritage. I want clothes made of natural materials: leather and homespun cloth! It's time to embrace nature again.'

'Whatever you want, senator.', Melly Sykes placated.

They drove the remaining five miles it took to reach headquarters in silence. The driver opened the door and held the umbrella so Warren wouldn't get wet but the senator wouldn't stay under the rain shield and with an uncharacteristic burst of energy raced from the car into the lobby. Sykes tried to catch her at the elevator but the old woman charged for the stairs instead. 'Senator? It's six flights!', her fat personal assistant breathed, out of breath and trying to slow her down.

The old bat scampered up the stairs like she was running cross country, though, and Melly lost sight of her in the chase. Warren greeted her staff on the fly then made a b-line for her private office, slipped inside and closed the door.

Hobbling up the stairs fat Sykes at last reached the sixth floor. 'Where'd she go?', she gasped.

'Senator Warren went to her office.', informed the secretary.

Winded, Melly nodded. After taking a full minute to catch her breath she knocked on the door. 'Senator?'

'You may enter into my teepee.'

Sykes blinked at the strange greeting but opened the door anyway and went inside.

What confronted her was a sight no one wanted to behold. Senator Warren was in the process of stripping off her polyester slacks. Her top was already gone. 'Ms. Warren?! What – what are you doing??'

'I told you – no more false clothes! I will cover myself in the fruit of the trees and the skins of the animals! Bring me my moccasins and my loincloth!'

'What? But – but – Senator, you don't have those kinds of things!', Melly stammered, averting her gaze. 'You have a meeting with Marc Kline-Jefferies in one hour!'

Ripping off her underclothing Warren turned and stomped her feet. Confronted by her nakedness Sykes shut her eyes tight. The old woman's saggy breasts were dangling all the way down to her navel! 'Then go to the market!', challenged Pocahontas. 'Take trade goods and make exchange with the other tribes! Bring me what I need, brave Melly! Bring it quickly! I am your Chief!'

'Um...um....okay....Senator. If that's – if that's what you want...'

'And bring me a headdress!', demanded Warren, thrusting her fist defiantly in the air. 'I am the Chief here and I will be properly adorned!'

Frightened, Melly Sykes withdrew quickly and closed the door behind her. Her boss was most certainly on drugs! That had to be it!

But insane or coked out of her mind she was her aide and had to fulfill Senator Warren's bizarre request. Melly had to make several phones calls to costume shops that specialized in theatrical custom-made wardrobe to get what she needed then delegate three staffers to act as couriers to get the items back to the office in under an hour for the meeting. The apparel arrived just in time. Warren accepted her new clothing with zeal and immediately kicked her chief of staff out of her office so she could get dressed.

When Kline-Jefferies arrived five minutes later Sykes was almost afraid to knock on the senator's door. 'Senator? Mr. Jefferies is here to see you.'

No answer came from within the chamber and she was forced to knock a second time. The door was slightly ajar and this time it rolled open. Fearful of seeing her boss naked again Sykes peered inside with trepidation. What confronted her was almost as bad. Senator Warren was decked out in authentic Native American dress from the beads in her hair to her new tan moccasins. Mercifully the buffalo hide tunic she wore concealed her sagging breasts but it did nothing to aid her androgynous figure or swelling waistline. Worst of all was the imitation feather headdress: cheaply made it was a mixture of mismatched fake feathers in all the vibrant colors of the gay rainbow – including fuchsia – and had the most ridiculous ostrich plume sticking out of the middle. Warren looked like a rejected wannabe applicant for a Village People tribute band or the drunken drum major for a transgender-gay rights parade.

Kline-Jefferies didn't realize it wasn't a joke, though, and thought Warren's get up was hysterical. 'Wow! Getting tricked out for Halloween early I see!', he exclaimed.

Warren rose stoically. 'How, white man.'

Jefferies' smile broadened. 'How you, red woman?', he chuckled with a wink, playing along.

Warren held up her hand for silence. 'Pale face not understand. Medicine woman is great chief. Need much wampum for trade.'

So it was down to brass tacks already! Kline-Jefferies straightened his tie and dropped his smile. 'So...how much money are we talking here, senator?'

'Much wampumpeag. Many shell beads.'

'How about....five?', he threw out.

'Must have more.'

Kline-Jefferies' breath caught. 'More than five million?! That's very steep, Senator.', he objected with a shake of his head.

Warren folded her hands over her sagging chest and puffed it out. 'Must have wampumpeag. Make Chief Shitting Bull very important. Slap-a-hoe tribe dominate other tribes and nations. From Ohio valley to Mississippi delta, all will know her importance.'

Kline-Jefferies frowned. 'Give me a number. How much gold and green, senator? Or do you want it in Bitcoins?'

Chief Shitting Bull shook her head. 'Wampum. White man money unimportant.'

The opposite party in the bribe blinked. 'Wampum.', deadpanned Jefferies. He'd already directly mentioned money! What was up the code words? 'How much money, Senator? Give me a figure!'

Warren again shook her head. 'No money. Wampumpeag.' She held her arm out and made a sweeping gesture with it. 'You bring Chief Shitting Bull wampum. We make treaty.'

Taken aback by her bizarre behavior Kline-Jefferies took a half step backwards. He turned to Sykes. 'Do you know what the fuck she is talking about?'

Baffled, Melly Sykes shook her head. 'I have no idea.'

Oblivious to the two standing just inside her door Senator Warren suddenly whooped a war cry. When the two interlopers failed to move, despite the storm raging outside she then began to dance the rain dance.

'Has – has she gone insane?', the man offering her a bribe stammered.

'I wish I knew, Mr. Jefferies.', Sykes replied truthfully. 'I wish I knew.'

* * *

Excerpt from the Trump MAGA rally held on September 19th of this year in Ohio:

'Well, ol' Pocahontas is back in the news. Well, not the Fake News – but the real news, the real news. Seems little Miss Pale Face Pocahontas...has retired from public life....and gone to live in the woods, just like her dear departed high cheek-boned ancestors. Instead of living in a house...she'll be living in a teepee from now on. It's no Mar-A-Lago, I can tell you. No running water, no toilets. She's changed her name to Shitting Bull and wears nothing but a loin cloth. I don't know about you but that's not something I ever want to see! Elizabeth Warren in a loincloth! She told me once that I hadn't seen nasty yet, but please, no thank you! DNA tests confirm that Pocahontas is only 1/1024th Native American, despite all her protests and assertions to the contrary. But there are new tests now that are more important than DNA tests. Psychological tests performed by doctors... doctors who confirm what the rest of us have always known: that Senator Elizabeth Warren is positively one hundred percent bat-shit crazy. So sad, so sad! Goodbye Pocahontas! We'll miss you. May the trees....and the berry plants....and all the animals of the forest provide for your needs. We hope you are happy with your new life. Our government....and our country is safer now...that you are living in your new outhouse out in the woods....'

*　*　*

Guildencrantz finished his tale with a smile. 'And that was how dear old Elizabeth Warren met her political end.'

'Oh, God! That was fucking hysterical!', giggled Emily, stamping her feet. She clutched her middle in laughter. 'Do another! Do another!'

Guy shook his head. 'No, no – it's your turn now!'

'But you sounded just like the President at the end! "So sad, so sad! Goodbye Pocahontas! We'll miss you!"', she chuckled with glee.

Agent Guildencrantz joined his good friend, sharing a hearty laugh at the faux-Native American political hack's expense. Guy didn't have another story prepared, though, so he demurred and insisted his partner give it a shot.

It took a good minute before Rosenstern could calm down enough to think straight and another before she could regain a stoic demeanor. The handsome young woman paused, thinking. What could she say? Who should she pick on? Who really deserved a good thumping? She wanted to do Biden so badly but he was off-limits! 'Okay...okay....lemme think. Who deserves to have something bad happen to them? Okay, let me try this one out...'

Who's the Chinese Spy Again?

*I*t was a banner day for Senator Diane Feinstein. She had just spoken at a gala event, raking in hundreds of thousands of dollars for her campaign. The saps who donated to her wouldn't receive a thing in return, but thanks to grandfathering like all elected officials when she finally retired she'd be able to transfer the money to her private accounts.

Obscenely wealthy, she tapped on the glass separating the back of her limo from her driver. 'Mr. Yang, head up north. I have an important briefing to attend.'

'Yes, ma'am. Will we be going to the "Black Building" or the offices?'

'Black.'

The personal driver who had ferried her around for five years and acted as her gofer for the last twenty glanced down and removed his wallet from his pocket. Squeezing the listening device to turn it on he placed it in the crease between the back of his chair and the seat cushion. Chinese Intelligence would certainly want to know about this.

Unconcerned, Feinstein got on her phone. As Senate Intelligence Committee Chairwoman it was time to text the principals, appraise them of the situation and send out the intelligence packets. The transmission would be secure as long as she texted from within the confines of her vehicle; the roving tower imbedded in the limo's frame would take all the steps necessary to scramble the transmission from would-be hackers trying to intercept it so she could communicate safely.

Finishing the upload, she dialed the office. 'Yes, hello. Mr. Yang is currently taking me on site. I've sent out the encrypted packets and will be returning this afternoon around 1 pm. Please have lunch waiting for me.'

'Yes, ma'am. You have several meetings scheduled.'

'When?'

'A Mr. Wang at 12:30.'

'I might not be back by then. Please ask Mr. Wang if he wouldn't mind waiting in my office.'

'Yes, senator.'

Her itinerary set Feinstein secreted her phone and set the proximity alarm. Russian intelligence would love to get their hands on the briefing she was about to receive concerning America's latest 6th generation stealth fighter and the alarm was set to go off if the phone got more than five feet from the wrist watch on her person. Any more than fifty feet and the phone was set to automatically delete its own memory card. As the senior official on the Intel committee it was vital she keep the United States' military secrets intact.

She checked her watch and found she was running behind schedule. She knocked on the window and her driver lowered the screen. 'Pick up the pace, Mr. Yang. I don't want to be late.'

'Yes, Senator.'

The Chinese operative floored the accelerator and the limo scurried through the light just as it was about to turn red. Secure in the back Feinstein wasn't concerned. With her credentials, traffic stops were optional. If Yang got pulled over a call from one of her flunkies could get any ticket removed.

*   *   *

With all the sensitive information the Intel Committee had to discuss at the Black Site the briefing took longer than expected and Feinstein returned to her office famished. That was no excuse for not being cordial, however, and as a public figure it was in her best interests to be courteous to her staffers. The receptionist behind the desk to the entrance was a junior level employee but the Senator felt it was important to remember the names of everyone who worked under her. 'Hello, Miss Li. How are you this afternoon?'

'I'm quite fine, thank you. As you requested, Mr. Wang is waiting for you in your office. You also have messages from – ', Li paused and shuffled nervously through her papers. 'A Mr. Jiang and Mr. Chen. They wish to speak with you about possible investment in semiconductor technology. We also got a letter from Dean Zhang at the Chinese People's Republic branch of Pacific Tech Institute. He was wondering if you had time to look over the information he sent regarding student loans.'

The old Senator shook her head. 'No, I afraid I haven't had time to read it. I'll take a look after my meeting with Mr. Wang.'

'Yes, senator.'

Feinstein's stomach rumbled. 'Did my lunch arrive?'

'Yes, ma'am. It's waiting in the break room. Should I have it sent up to your office?'

'No. I'll grab it up on the way there.'

'Yes, ma'am.'

Feinstein wiped her brow and strode towards the break room. Such a busy day! She had to carry her own food back to her office instead of dining out!

*   *   *

It took the better part of two hours to meet with Mr. Wang. Fortunately the phone calls with Jiang and Chen proved brief, and Feinstein was able to free up enough time to read through the materials Dean Zhang had sent over from Pacific Technical Institute. The senator could see the potential benefits the institution could gain by admitting more Chinese-born students, but she couldn't sign off on granting them access to the student loan program. If China wanted to send more of its citizens to the United States for their education they would have to do so through scholarship programs – and grease the wheels of Democracy by offering the right people the right choice stock opportunities at discount prices. The People's Republic of China had more than enough money; she should get her fair share of it.

With her afternoon business concluded it was time for the well-tenured Senator to engage in more leisurely pursuits. Though she'd had to eat lunch in house her staff had called ahead and placed a reservation at Lu Chan's restaurant. A very exclusive and expensive destination, the authentic cuisine was one of her favorites. It also provided the opportunity to mix a little business with pleasure.

Arriving at the restaurant Senator Feinstein was greeted by the host and with her security detail at a discreet distance was immediately ushered to her VIP seat. Four men were there waiting for her: Aiguo Zhang of the Chinese Patriot Society, Bambang Hang, formerly a Colonel in the Chinese People's army, Chuanli Leung, a lawyer specializing in intellectual property transfers and Chao Kuang, nicknamed "Victor" of the Bank of China.

'Ah! Senator Diane! Welcome!', Victor Kuang greeted.

'Senator.', bowed Col. Hang. Zhang and Leung did likewise.

Knowing she was among friends, Feinstein smiled. 'Gentlemen. It is good to see you all.'

The lawyer Chuanli Leung shooed away the waiter and gallantly held the chair out for Feinstein himself. Treated like royalty the octogenarian gracefully accepted and sat her plump well-cushioned derriere down on the well-cushioned seat.

'It feels like a celebration. We took the liberty of ordering wine. Would you like some, senator?', Victor the banker queried with a smile.

'Please.'

All their glasses now full the quintet raised them for a toast. 'To prosperity!', intoned Victor.

'To prosperity and global cooperation!', seconded Chuanli Leung.

The assembled gleefully sipped their wine then set it down beside their ice waters. 'I understand the dean has made you a proposal on admitting more students to his fine institution.', Aiguo Zhang began.

The old Congresswoman nodded. 'He has. I am giving it due consideration.'

As expected, when Feinstein said nothing more Chuanli Leung spoke up. 'Continued advancements in Chinese technology will only strengthen the global marketplace.', he lobbied.

'Yes. All will benefit.', Victor Kuang added, adding the weight of the Bank of China to Leung's suggestion. 'Trade brings prosperity.', he noted pointedly.

'And rising wages in China means more purchases of American made goods.', Zhang added with zeal, ignoring the fact that in reality forced technology transfers did little except increase the trade deficit. 'More purchases will increase the prosperity of American companies and in turn benefit American workers.'

'It is why so many of our trade agreements must continue to include the transfer of the processes used to manufacture goods.', added Leung the lawyer. Eager to maintain his bread-and-butter source of income and continue the gravy train of benefiting from American innovation and technological advancements without paying for the cost of the research and development used to create the new technology, he went on: 'Without the knowledge of how to make the things America purchases China will enter into Depression. Such a thing would be terrible and cause the Markets to plummet. Wouldn't you agree, Senator?'

Faced with the possibility of another Black Friday, Feinstein shook her head. 'Of course. No one wants a Depression.'

'Exactly.', nodded Victor Kuang with emphasis. 'It is unthinkable. The financial toll would be catastrophic – to both countries! As a banker, perhaps I am jaded – but in truth I believe all conflicts have their root in economics.'

'I am not sure I agree with your assessment, Mr. Kuang.', Col. Hang replied coolly, his jaw set. As a soldier he believed conflicts were settled on the battlefield, not in the boardroom. The enemy must be destroyed without mercy! All is fair in war! Death to America!

'But surely prosperity eliminates the need for conflict?', suggested Zhang zealously. Unlike career politicians President Trump understood what he was saying implicitly. As a patriot Zhang could not allow China to continue to suffer under the weight of America's tremendous economic might; if the tariff's continued the totalitarian regime might be forced to actually have to resort to Democracy! 'People who are safe and secure have no need to covet another's things. There is no need for war when all people are "Shiny Happy People Holding Hands".'

'And is not technology and the money necessary to create the weapons the military uses essential to a soldier's success?', added Chuanli Leung soberly. While China had a solid manufacturing base it had no designs anywhere near as sophisticated as that of the United States – at least not yet. 'As a former military man you must acknowledge this.'

Bambang Hang's expression turned deadly serious. 'I will fight the enemies of my homeland with whatever weapons are at hand.', replied the colonel belligerently.

Seizing an opening Zhang perked up. 'I believe that China is best served if brave soldiers like yourself have only the best weapons and the best technology. Disparity in technology only creates instability, heightening tensions and escalating conflicts.', he lied flatly.

Trying to keep the argument from getting out of hand Victor Kuang turned their attention back to their target, Senator Feinstein. 'Which is why I hope with all sincerity that the United States and China are never in conflict. You are our friend, Senator. I hope you will do everything in your power to insure that no "disruptive elements" interfere with our mutually beneficial relationship. How is the expression – "To upset the apple cart"?'

Well into her eighties, Feinstein had no interest in disrupting the arrangement that had for years been padding her pocketbook. A belligerent totalitarian nation like China gaining technological parity with the United States increased the likelihood of World War Three considerably – but that (like the collapse of Social Security) was a problem for future generations. The elderly Democrat placed her hand atop the banker's. 'Of course, Mr. Kuang. I assure you that I want our countries to remain friends. I have considerable wealth in the Marketplace myself. I would never do anything to, as you say, "Upset the Apple Cart". It would be against my own best interests – and that of my partners. Congress in committed to maintaining our cordial relationship.'

'We are all glad to hear this, Senator Feinstein.'

From the shadows the waiter rolled out a cart overloaded with scrumptious but obscenely overpriced food. Dumplings, fried shellfish, desserts – it was all authentic Chinese cuisine that only the wealthiest Chinese elite could afford.

'It looks as if our dinner has arrived.', Chao Kuang "The Victor" of banking announced with a smile. The task appointed to him by the High Command now completed it was time for the quartet of Chinese spies to celebrate with their asset. Americans were so delightfully stupid and their political leaders so incredibly easy to corrupt! 'Let us talk no more of politics. This meal is too delightful to waste on such serious matters.'

With that the quintet dug into the delectable food. Prepared here in United States the Chinese feast was a delightful taste of home and the operatives found it far preferable to any of the Mexican, French, Japanese, Indian, Thai, Polynesian, Italian, Greek, Egyptian, Mongolian, German, Russian, Cajun, Madagascan, Namibian, Lebanese, Peruvian, Scandinavian, Spanish, Filipino, Moroccan, British, Caribbean, Serbian, Armenian, Hungarian, Tanzanian or any of the other exotic non-Chinese cosmopolitan restaurants one might go to in intolerant, racist, "White-privileged" America.

***

Emily Rosenstern frowned. 'I'm sorry. My story sucked! It wasn't funny like yours.'

'It's sad, but it's totally true.', Guy Guildencrantz nodded soberly. 'And nothing has been done about it! Nothing at all! Makes me sick.'

His female companion looked at him with sad eyes. 'I just don't get how the people in her State keep electing her! It doesn't make any damned sense! I mean, she was warned way back in 2010 that she had a spy in her staff! The guy was her driver for twenty years and definitely spying for China for at least five of those! And this was while she was the Chair of the Senate Intelligence Committee!'

'I'm guessing people just don't know the facts.', was all Guy could think to say.

Agent Emily wouldn't let it go. 'Ignorance isn't bliss – it's just ignorance! How is this not plastered all over the news!? This got leaked in 2017! Why doesn't everybody know about it?!!! How does Feinstein still have a job???! She's got financial interests in China! Serious financial interests! Why are we not interrogating her to find out if she's a traitor?! Why is she getting a free pass on this?!'

Guildencrantz shook his head. 'California is one-party rule. It's how someone that corrupt gets in and stays in.'

'It's not right! This is treason we're talking about!'

Agent Guildencrantz couldn't agree more. 'No, it isn't right. She should be grilled in front of the whole country! We should be asking her hard questions under oath – like you said, finding out if she's a traitor! It's what would happen to anyone else!'

'And the driver wasn't even prosecuted! He was simply "asked to retire"! How do you spy on the Senate Intelligence Committee Chairwoman and not get charged with outright treason! He was spying for a foreign country, for Christ's sake! Spying for China!!!'

Utterly outraged, the pair simmered in silence for a while. Neither agent knew what he or she could do about Feinstein's behavior. It was totally, utterly reprehensible. How could even the Deep State turn a blind eye to something this serious?

Trapped within the bureaucracy of Washington DC, Guy held up his finger. He wanted to regain a lighter tone before their conversation became too depressing. 'Speaking of "not right", I guess it's my turn again. And I know just the asshole I want to skewer...'

Out for blood Emily gritted her teeth and quipped, 'Go for it.'

Wanting to regain a more jovial mood Guildencrantz cleared his throat and began to sing softly in the style of the Beverly Hillbillies. 'Oh, let me tell you a story bout a Dem middle named Mark, who was so stupid ordered sick people in nursing homes on a lark. They got the Covid and ended up dead, but that didn't stop 'em voting in twenty-twenty so everybody said: "Go fuck yourself, Cuomo! We're gonna make your life suck! To the home you go, with Mrs. T., enema-style..."'

Smiling again, he motioned Emily closer. 'Gather round, my friend, because this one's guaranteed to please! I give you a tale about "the end" of former Governor Dumb Ass himself from New York: Andrew...Mark... Cuomo!'

Private Nurse

Old corrupt Cuomo had taken a nasty tumble down the stairs and broken his leg in four different places. The hospital had mended his ailing limb and surgically placed three screws in his femur and one in his tibia to aid in the healing process, but for the next six weeks he was not ambulatory and wouldn't be able to get around and take care of himself. Forced to convalesce that meant 24/7 care – at least for a little while.

Wealthy from his governorship (and the many perks he'd acquired during his "service" to the State) Cuomo could have hired a private duty nurse to take care of his many needs, but with all the allegations of sexual misconduct he was fighting his attorney advised him to keep a low profile and check into one of the many private nursing homes in New York rather than give the other side the opportunity to gather more evidence against him. The Sweet Dreams Convalescent Home had a solid reputation and was rated highly so Cuomo was ferried there following his stint in the hospital. The director of the home was a Dr. Henry Stein.

'Welcome governor.', Dr. Stein said. Wearing gloves, a face shield and a N95 mask the little Jewish doctor quickly shooed his staff out the door and closed it behind them. He turned back to Cuomo. 'I just got the latest test results from the hospital and I have some rather distressing news. It seems you've caught the Coronavirus. Everyone who's been in contact with you now has to be quarantined.'

'What?', stammered Cuomo. 'But – but the pandemic is over!'

'Well, not really.', replied Stein. 'In states like ours Coronavirus goes on forever and is never ending. In other states, the Midwest and such, Coronavirus seems to have been eradicated. But for whatever reason the Coastal areas seem to have a new outbreak every other day, ahem, excuse me, election cycle. And the border states along Mexico seem to be overrun with new cases. It seems hospitals in Texas are filled almost entirely with illegal – excuse me, *undocumented* persons – who are Covid positive.'

'What do you mean?! You're saying I've really caught the Coronavirus?! But I'm here because I broke my leg!'

The doctor cleared his throat. 'Yes. Well, it seems you must have been exposed at some time during your hospital stay. Not uncommon, really. And because all Coronavirus cases are paid for by the Federal government it's standard procedure to diagnose a patient with Covid-19 until private insurance kicks in. Only when payment is received from a private source is the diagnosis removed. In your case the tests seem to have come back positive. There's always the chance of a false positive, of course, but to be on the safe side we're going to have to quarantine you – just as a precaution.'

Not wanting to be shut away in a tiny little room like a prisoner Cuomo turned apoplectic. 'But diseases like this don't go on forever! They die out! The people who catch them die and then the disease ends! That's how it works! I don't even have a cough! I don't have any symptoms!'

'Well, we need to protect the public from your cooties so you don't spread any germs. The infections coming across the border seem to be almost exclusively affecting those who've been sheltering in place. And because this plague seems to just keep mutating...'

Cuomo's jaw fell open. 'But that doesn't happen – my advisers, my medical advisers – they told me that couldn't happen! It's science fiction! Coronaviruses only mutate once every million years!'

Dr. Stein shrugged. 'Well, medically speaking that's true – but according to the CDC there's apparently all these new "variants" now. There's Gamma and Lambda and Epsilon, and of course the Delta, Omicron (which came from laboratory mice experiments) and Omega stains – and now the "Z" variant and the "Q" strain too! There's the pinko version and the polka dot version, there's a paper cut version transmitted by using paper products instead of electronic communications...I've even seen a new report warning parents to keep their kids at home in October so they don't catch the Halloween mask Covid! And just last week they identified a Biker Patriot strain and a Capitalism strain too! It seems there's a Coronavirus variant to attack any unruly population not following orders – basically anyone who wants this plague to end and who's trying to go back to regular mask-less life.'

'But – but none of that is true!', the former governor exclaimed feeling like he was about to pass out. 'I'm – I'm in the "know" on this! We – we only went to the media to scare people about new strains so we could keep people away from the polls! To continue mail-in balloting for the next election cycle! It – it was voter suppression, plain and simple! Voter suppression! It was never real! None of this is real!'

Stein shook his head. 'Well, I'm afraid it's personally very real for you, Mr. Cuomo.'

Trapped like a spider in its own web, the deposed Governor rubbed his temples. 'So what are we going to do about this, doc? What's the cure? How do we treat this?'

'Well, since no new treatments have been developed since Mr. Biden took office we'll have to use the remedies the Trump administration came up with. They have proved highly effective – in most cases.'

Stein paused. When the pregnant silence lingered the handsy former governor spoke up. 'I sense a "but" coming on here doctor...'

The physician nodded. 'Well, Mr. Cuomo....according to the lab tests, you've caught ALL the strains. Every last one, from Alpha to Omega.' Dr. Stein shook his head. 'I've never seen anything like it before.'

Faced with this devastating news the former Governor of New York broke out in a flushed sweat. Every one!? He'd caught them all??!! How??? 'But I just came in here because of my leg! I broke my leg and needed rehab! How in the fucking hell did I catch the plague?! How did I get diagnosed with Coronavirus?!'

'Coronaviruses – all the CV-19 variants.', Doctor Stein corrected. 'Well, I can only speculate, of course....but it seems Governor that because of your executive order infected patients are still exposing uninfected at-risk individuals. Normal healthy people shouldn't worry about this virus anymore but immuno-compromised patients will always be at risk for any number of infections. I believe you came in contact either in the hospital or when one of your staff members inadvertently passed it to you while investigating our facility here. As you know, we have been sent infected patients before. Then there's the fact that the World Health Organization said back in 2020 that 1-in-10 people worldwide were infected. With your younger brother Chris on CNN breaking quarantine when he was infected, mixing with so many people in spite of testing positive...well, there's no telling where you got all these strains. I tend not to take the WHO at their word – it *is* run by China and doesn't really serve America or the world's interests – but 1-in-10 is a good baseline and seems reasonable. If the data was accurate, it was certain everyone was exposed before the end of 2020.'

Cuomo's face turned beet red. 'You mean the fucking hospital gave this shit to me???'

'I don't believe we will ever know for sure how you were exposed.', Stein replied. 'It's one of the many reasons why contract tracing is utterly useless in stopping fast spreading diseases – though your own decree seems to have been a significant factor, I must add.'

Stunned, for a moment Cuomo sat in silence absorbing this terrible news. After a few beats his volatile temper surfaced and his face screwed up. 'No! No! You people fucked up and gave this shit to me! You fucked up and gave me the China Virus, you son-of-a-bitch! Why weren't these sickos isolated!'

Insulted, Dr. Stein became stern. 'We run a clean facility here, governor. I can not and will not take responsibility for what is beyond my control. I just do what the law demands. It was your order, after all.'

'That's fucking bullshit!'

Stein eyed Cuomo a moment, then shook his head. 'Instead of arguing about how you *got* "the Invisible Enemy" let's discuss your treatment options. About the only effective treatment known that seems to have some success against *all* the mutated strains of CV-19 is hydroxychloroquine. Despite what you may have heard in the corrupt non-scientific media there are almost 1000 peer reviewed studies at present on the subject and it most certainly works. Regular enemas seem to help too.'

Cuomo swallowed. 'Enemas?', he answered meekly.

Doctor Stein nodded. 'Yes. An enema every three or four hours seems to benefit some patients who've acquired multiple strains.'

'But – but it's a respiratory virus!'

'These treatment protocols work, Governor – and unlike mass media as a physician I am going to follow the science.' Ready to escape from the blustering former civil servant Dr. Stein walked to the door and peeked his head out. 'Mrs. Teacup? Could you send in Nurse Ratchet? Governor Cuomo requires an initial treatment before we can get him settled in to his room. He'll be staying with us for the foreseeable future.'

'Nurse Ratchet?', bleated Cuomo.

Stein nodded. 'Yes, Governor. She is my very best nurse. Very no non-sense. She'll get you straightened out.'

Cuomo grabbed Stein's arm. 'Look, doctor...I know we may have got off on the wrong foot here...'

The little Jewish doctor brushed him off. 'It's very important you follow the treatment regimen, Mr. Cuomo. Your life is at risk here – as well as the health of the rest of my residents and my staff. You've contracted every known strain of Coronavirus – and maybe some new ones we've never even seen before. You need to take this seriously – I am taking this seriously! We can't let you become a super-spreader! I have to protect the rest of my people.'

Cuomo's voice turned small. 'But....it was just....the mail-ins.', he stammered. 'The votes we needed....we don't have to...'

Cuomo's blustering whine faded into the background. Dr. Stein turned aside just as a towering nurse dressed all in white walked in. Garbed head to toe in PPE the hulking woman smiled thinly at the doctor. 'Ah, Nurse Ratchet!', Dr. Stein announced with glee, patting the nurse's bulging arm. 'Please take special care of the Governor here! He's our VIP patient!'

'Yes, doctor. Of course.', she replied, her voice deep as a well.

Dr. Stein slipped past Nurse Ratchet and exited the room. Six foot seven and three hundred twenty-five pounds the burly nurse gave Governor Cuomo a once over. With a little smirk she walked to the sink and began to prepare the enema bag. 'Now you relax and do as I say and we'll get along just fine, Mr. Cuomo.', Ratchet said evenly.

About to get a nozzle shoved up his ass Cuomo studied her movements with trepidation. Nurse Samantha Ratchet was menacingly huge but it was her prominent chin and adam's apple that put him ill at ease. 'I'm used to my nurses being blondes...', he joked, trying to calm his frayed nerves.

'Oh, yes, I've heard. I've heard you've got some roaming hands on you, Governor. I trust I won't have any trouble with you – I know just how to take care of troublesome patients who can't keep their hands to themselves.' Nozzle in hand the hulking health care worker turned and faced him. 'You see, before I became Nurse *Samantha* Ratchet I used to go by the name *Samuel* Ratchet. Before I transitioned I enjoyed shoving things up other men's rectums. *Roughly.*' The gigantic male-turned-female nurse smiled faux-sweetly. 'Now you just drop those pants and get on all fours, Mr. Governor. It's time to start your procedure.'

Cuomo backed away hurriedly. 'Wait a minute! Wait a minute, here! You're not putting that in me! I demand another nurse! Dr. Stein! Stein! Get in here!!'

'Oh, no Mr. Governor! You know we can't do that – ', Ratchet said, shaking her gigantic head. 'You know of all people should know it's illegal to discriminate against someone just because they've changed genders! The State of New York doesn't allow that.' She smiled. 'You're all mine.'

'But – '

'Now Mr. Cuomo, am I going to have to put you in restraints?! Believe me, I really don't mind getting rough and man-handing you...hee-hee....I don't mind at all.' The big woman leaned closer. 'It would be *my* pleasure.'

'You wouldn't – '

Ratchet's calloused hands found her hips. '*Try me, honey.*', the trans-sexual man-turned-cosmetically-into-something-more-female taunted with a hiss. '*I dare you.*'

Her smile broadened but the glint in the burly nurse's eyes promised she would make Cuomo take his enema no matter how much he protested – and if he continued to defy her she was going to purposely make it hurt so he wouldn't give her any more sass in the future. Doctor Stein's orders said Andrew Mark Cuomo was to receive an enema every three hours – and for his own good that was exactly what Nurse Samantha Ratchet was going to make sure happened.

*　*　*

'Oh – if there's ever someone who needed an enema, it's Cuomo!', Emily Rosenstern exclaimed with joy.

Guildencrantz smirked. 'Well, he was always talking out of his ass...'

She slapped Guy's leg laughingly. 'The moron's brain was totally in his butt! What a dumb ass! Putting sick people in nursing homes to infect all the people there! How stupid do you have to be to do that?! Shoving a nozzle of hot water up the dip shit's fat ass would finally give his brain a wash!'

'Brainwashed!', Guy chuckled. 'Film at eleven!'

Emily joined him in his laughter, then shifted in her seat to get more comfortable. 'Okay, okay – my turn! I got a good one for ya this time!', she promised.

Guildencrantz sat up attentively. 'I'm all ears! Lay it on me, little sister!'

Silent But Deadly

The girl sitting opposite Maxine "Mad Max" Waters was an absolute doll. Of Latin ethnicity and only ten, Alicia Iglesius Cortana had a bright smile and a cherubic voice. The old Congresswoman hoped speaking with this Junior High School student translated well with the twenty-something hipster voters she wanted to woo. After the trouble Waters faced in the last election the senior Democratic black woman in the House of Representatives hoped a fluff piece like this one could bolster her image with the youth vote. She'd lost several percentage points among the Hispanic community and after Biden's epic Afghanistan debacle her rating with female voters had plummeted. The continuing crisis at the Southern Border, the escalating Ukraine-Russia war and the horrible state of the Woke economy was weighing down the Democratic party's chances across the board and even with constant media propaganda and the rabid environmentalist leaning of her state she worried about whether or not she would be re-elected. Mail-In ballots wouldn't be available to nudge the results and if she was going to maintain her extravagant lifestyle she would have to rely on misdirection and disinformation to stay in Congress. Any shift in power could lead to a real investigation of all their behind the scenes dealings – and that was serious trouble they absolutely could not afford. The unrestrained Durham probe was already issuing Indictments and working its way up the proverbial political food chain.

So here Mad Maxine Waters was at Martin Luther King Junior elementary sitting at a table in the cafeteria about to be interviewed by a nobody ten year old little girl. It was a stupid waste of time – but delivering media content for the sheep often was. Re-elections were work, about the only time Waters and her comrades actually did anything resembling the word. How she actually voted was determined by Nancy Pelosi, who in turn got her marching orders from billionaire globalist enslaver-of-the-masses George Soros. Like the 2020 Election Fraud the decisions were all mailed in before hand.

Oblivious to the old swamp creature's maleficent schemes the naive young girl sitting opposite Waters nervously shuffled her handwritten papers across the desk. Trying not to puke up the butterflies fluttering around in her stomach Alicia Iglesius Cortana – A.I.C. for short – did her best to ignore the camera pointing at them. She didn't want to mess up and appear stupid in front of her friends; like all kids School was her world and becoming a social pariah was her worst fear. The knots in her stomach made her want to run to the bathroom, throw up in the toilet then hide out in the janitor's closet until everyone left. Panicking like a spaz was the stupidest thing she could do, of course, but the precocious ten year old couldn't help it – this was her first big interview with a grown up and the whole thing was being taped for YouTube! Congresswoman Waters might not know it but this Social-Death-Defying stunt was being streamed live on Rumble!

Trying to keep her teeth from chattering the little girl swallowed her butterflies and opened her mouth to ask her very first question. Asking the old lady about something stupid *she'd* said in public might calm down the preteen's own frayed nerves. 'So –', Alicia began, trying hard to remember to breathe as she raced into her first query. 'I read on the internet that you – Congresswoman Waters – publicly called President Trump a racist. I was wondering Congresswoman...how do you explain that? I checked – and according to my sources Black unemployment, Latino unemployment and women's unemployment were all at historic lows during the time Trump was the President. How do you, um, reconcile those...things....with say-ing...with calling the President of the United States a racist?'

Surprised by such a serious question coming from a child, Waters used a magician's trick and waved her hands to distract her audience's attention. Though she was expecting to be treated with "kid gloves" by the ambitious youngster she'd been navigating difficult political non sequitur faux pas like this one since long before AIC was born. 'Donald Trump claims he's bringing people together but make no mistake, he is a dangerous, unprin-cipled, divisive, and shameful racist. The proof is in his ridiculous public statements. Any improvements in the unemployment numbers were the direct result of his predecessor, President Barrack Obama – a black man.'

Expecting honesty instead of another lie from the old woman Alicia Cortana frowned. 'But – but what about Joe Collins, your challenger in the last election? Wasn't the man running against you an African-American man?

A *Black Republican*? Why would Joe Collins link himself to President Trump if the president was really against black people? I mean, you can't try to say that an African-American man is against black people, can you? And if President Obama really was the cause of those good numbers how come they only happened *after* President Trump changed all of President Obama's policies? Why didn't they happen earlier, during President Obama's, um, eight years in office?'

Waters shook her head, refusing to concede these obvious points. 'Joe Collins lost the election because he was a poor candidate.', she declared with a smile. 'Linking himself to a proven racist like Donald Trump was one of the many reasons why he lost. And sometimes, young lady, it takes time for the positive economic policies of a President to take effect. President Obama was a clearly superior President to Donald Trump. Some people don't think Donald Trump was ever really elected.'

Waters' double-talk made absolutely no sense at all to young Alicia Cortana. She pressed on anyway, though and segued into her next question. 'But didn't you say things about your challenger – about Joe Collins – that weren't true? Didn't that change the election?'

Deflecting the question like the professional politician she was Waters smiled and leaned towards the girl. 'All candidates say things during an election to sway the electorate.', she breezed. 'It is how our political system works. Criticizing your opponent is simply part of the election process.'

Starting to get flustered, Cortana blinked. Knowing that not saying anything made her look stupid she untied her tongue. 'But what you said – '

Not wanting to rehash a sore spot the elderly black representative interrupted by gently patting the girl's hand. 'It's just an exercise in free speech, young lady. I told my side of the story and Joe Collins had the opportunity to tell his side of the story. The public just didn't believe him, which is why he lost.'

Becoming distressed AIC shuffled through her papers to give herself a chance to gather her composure. As she stalled she spied the paper that contained the substance of her dilemma. 'But you said that Mr. Collins was *dishonorably discharged* from the armed forces.', she quoted, pointing out Waters' very explicit lie.

Practiced in the art of deception without batting an eye the elderly politician nodded in agreement. 'Yes. In a written news letter I directly referenced a judge's statements to that effect.'

It took a moment for the young girl to decipher what all the congress-woman's fancy words and doubletalk meant. When Alicia Iglesius Cortana was finally sure the old woman had just agreed with her, her jaw dropped open. Congresswoman Waters just admitted she'd told a bold-faced lie to win the election! 'But Mr. Collins was released because he was disabled! He wasn't dishonorably discharged! He got hurt! You said something that wasn't true!'

Prepared for her young inquisitor's objection, Waters' shrugged. 'If that was really so then why did a judge say he had been?', she replied, leaving the rhetorical question hanging in the air.

Before AIC could answer her the silence was suddenly interrupted by a popcorn snap of gas. Eighty-something Representative Maxine Waters had inadvertently just broken wind.

Trying to maintain her composure in front of the camera and upset by Waters' casual admission of dishonesty, Alicia Cortana grinned but tried not to laugh. She managed to hide her smile by locating her primary source. Farts were so gosh-darned funny! 'According to this – ', she said, waving the paper around to disperse the awful stink. 'Collins was accused of "dishonorable conduct" for making a website saying he was going to run for office. He successfully, um, won against the – the – the people who said he'd done something wrong by trying to run against you, and – and – his lawyer sent you a letter with proof – <cough> – and told you to stop saying it anymore.', the girl said, her voice rising shrilly as she tried to escape the growing wave of flatulence invading her personal space.

'Young lady – ', the elderly woman said condescendingly, using a firm authoritative tone to bully the girl. 'Because we all have free speech the rules say that it's perfectly okay to quote someone in a piece of election literature. In this case, I quoted a judge. At the time we began the advertisements we believed them to be correct.'

'But you kept saying those...*things* – ', AIC challenged, unwilling to call Waters' lies lies because that was impolite and she'd been taught to be polite to older people even when they said things that weren't true and farted loudly on camera. 'Even after Mr. Collins proved that it was wrong for you to say that! He showed you his army – I mean his navy – discharge papers! And the whole reason the judge tried to say Joe Collins had done something wrong was because he wanted to run for office against you!

How – how can you say that's bad? How is it bad for someone to run for Congress?'

Representative Waters opened her mouth to reply – and got silenced by her very own derriere. Unlike her earlier opening salvo this cannon blast was a rapid fire twenty-one gun salute.

Embarrassed by her on camera public fanfare flatulence Mad Maxine momentarily lost her cool. 'Look, just cause a ni – just because a black person runs for office and has a military background does not make them the better candidate. I have great respect for the honorable people who serve in our military. The people in my district just thought I was a better candidate than Joe Collins.'

Alicia Cortana tried her very best not to laugh but she just couldn't help it! The old woman had just ripped one big time! 'But – but – hee-hee – what you said about him – what you said about him was wrong! He was wounded in service to our country – ha-ha – not – not dishonorably discharged!'

Flustered by her own churning bowels Waters gave the girl a distressed look. 'And I have great respect for that.', she declared, though based on how she'd abused Collins reputation it was obviously not true. 'It's all a matter of perspective, Alicia. What the judge said was true when it was said, even if Mr. Collins was later on able to reverse that ruling. That's all there is to say about it. If there was anything wrong with what I said about Mr. Collins his lawsuit against me wouldn't have failed.'

If Waters had been a child her own age ten year old Alicia Iglesius Cortana first thought would have been to reply that there was something very, very wrong about her stinky farts. But she couldn't say that on camera and was deeply disturbed that the Congresswoman had been able to get away with such a terrible lie so instead she said: 'I – I don't understand. How can you say something about someone that's not true? Aren't you supposed to do what is right and set a good example?'

Clamping down on the latest offering she felt pushing the boundaries of her gas chamber Waters patted Alicia's hand and smiled like the Cheshire Cat to cover her gastric distress. 'Politics is all just a game, young lady. You'll understand that when you're old enough to vote. You shouldn't worry about stuff like this right now. You're too young to understand it. Don't worry. Some day it will all make sense.'

Wrinkling her offended nose and upset that the truth had been so badly abused Alicia pushed aside her stack of papers. It seemed so wrong for someone to lie about someone else like that! Her stack ajar she spied a quote from President Trump about Congresswoman Waters that seemed to make her point. 'So, if that's okay – if it's okay to say what you said about Mr. Collins – ', she suggested, seizing it with a wave she hoped wasn't too obvious to disperse the Congresswoman's lingering odor. 'What do you have to say about President Trump calling you a "Low IQ individual"?'

Taken aback by the question, Waters recoiled. The girl had just quoted the President of the United States calling her a poo-poo head and then asked her opinion about it! 'See what I mean?', the old woman sneered, baring her teeth. 'Typical Trump bullying behavior! I told you he's divisive and unprincipled. There's no room in school for bullies! He sets a very bad example for children – excuse me, young people – like you!'

So strident were Waters' accusations that the churning A-bomb up her butt could no longer be denied entrance into the world. It hissed out in staccato like a machine gun: p-p-p-p-p-p-p-p-pah!

Trapped in proximity to the blast AIC could no longer contain her mirth. She doubled over, waving her arm to protect her nose from the terrible stench! 'Oh-my-God!', the little girl who'd skipped a grade exclaimed, flushing beet red. She wished Waters' butt was over a toilet so she could flush away the stench! Pee-yew!!!

Knowing the storyline would all be about her breaking wind facing off against a schoolchild Waters face screwed up. This was terrible! She'd come here to court the youth vote – but her incompetent butt-trumpet had just made a laughingstock out of her campaign! She had become a YouTube fart farce!

Seeing the bullying Congresswoman as a silly farter now instead of a mean scary old lady, AIC laughingly rifled through her papers again to gain time. She couldn't find the exact quote she was looking for but they'd just talked about it. Congresswoman Waters didn't seem to like it when someone stood up to her – it made her toot her own horn, hee-hee!! 'But wasn't the President – wasn't the President saying that about you because you had just said bad things about him? Didn't he say that to respond to you saying he was a racist and a bad person?' Before Waters could answer the ten year old sixth grader mercifully located the right paper and vigorously fanned her immediate vicinity with it so she could breathe freely again.

When the air wasn't so foul she read word for word what she'd printed out. 'Didn't *you* say: "You see anybody from that cabinet (the Trump cabinet) in a restaurant, in a department store, at a gasoline station, you get out and you create a crowd. And you push back on them. And you tell them they're not welcome anymore, anywhere!"'

Losing her smile the watery-eyed preteen looked Congresswoman Mad Maxine Waters square in the eye. 'Didn't the people who support you do *exactly* that? Didn't they <u>bully</u> Trump supporters? When you said that weren't *you* telling people to *bully* other people? To *bully* anyone different than you that belongs to a different group or has different opinions? How is that not – ', the little girl paused to find the unfamiliar words she had circled in yellow marker from another paper. '"Inciting Insurrection?"', she quoted. 'Isn't that kind of bullying behavior what really caused what people in the Democratic party – your party – are calling the "Capitol Riots"?'

The microscope pointed at her and her evil party the old woman vigorously shook her head. 'No, no, no!', Waters denied adamantly. 'Trump and Republicans are to blame for them Riots! It would be totally wrong to blame anyone else for what *they* did!'

Sensing she'd finally gained her first real victory the brilliant schoolchild leaned back in her chair away from the source of the ill wind. 'What makes you sure Trump and Republicans are the cause of what happened in the Capitol, Congresswoman Waters?'

Feeling she was getting fenced in by a ten year old school girl Waters paused a beat to collect her thoughts before she answered. This little brat was grilling her ten times harder than any CNN reporter ever had! 'We've subpoenaed the phone records of several individuals. I'm sure that when those records are released it will prove they were directly responsible for the Riots.', she asserted, accompanying her statement with a low squeaker.

Becoming used to the old woman's butt-fireworks AIC wasn't about to take Waters' answers on faith. 'So it's just like what you said about Mr. Collins, then – you *say* the other team did something bad but can't show us anything to prove you are telling the truth.', Alicia Cortana countered, feeling more confident now that she was finally starting to understand how Democrats played the game. They said tons of stuff in front of the camera but when it came down to it it was all just hot air. It was like her classmate Mellie Chalke saying her family was close personal friends with Tom Brady – it was just a made up story! Mellie didn't even have any pictures of them together – not even anything posed on the sidelines after a game! 'Don't you think the belief that cheating happened during the 2020 Election is what caused the protests in the Capitol? And isn't it true that the FBI said these "rioters" didn't have any guns with them? Isn't it true that votes were tampered with in the middle of the night in "Purple" states? Don't citizens have a Constitutional Right to protest when something stinks?!'

Incidentally called out for her flatulence Waters slammed her hand down on the table, making the little girl jump. There would be no talk about Constitutional rights or fairness! Citizens must submit to Democrat rule! 'Absolutely not! There is no excuse for what happened on January 6th! Joe Biden was elected President fair and square! Trump lost! He's the loser! And I resent you trying to place the blame for what he did on us – for – for – what those crazy Trump rioters did in his name! If the Republican party had any backbone they would have gotten rid of that con man and voted for Impeachment! Like I said before, he is divisive! He is a dangerous racist! He's inciting Insurrection!'

Feeling physically unsafe around Mad Maxine the ten year old sat as far back in her chair as she could. Scared of the stinky old bat again she managed to stammer: 'But Congress-Congresswoman Waters – how can you say it is wrong to say – to say – that Democrats might have done something illegal and that it should be investigated when you are saying that you are sure Republicans and Trump – President Trump – are to blame for what happened in the Capitol without showing us any evidence? Isn't that wrong? Isn't it – ' Filled with emotion and feeling lightheaded because she'd been repetitively gassed the young girl searched her brain for the right words – and came up blank. 'Isn't it "Double Jeopardy" or something? Shouldn't Democrats and Republicans be treated the same way?! Isn't that the law?!'

Punctuating her words with butt-blasts, Waters slammed her hand down again repetitively. 'There is <u>no</u> <u>double</u> <u>standard</u>, young lady! Republicans and Trump are just guilty and sometimes you just have to say it that way! You have to call out obvious bad behavior!'

Not knowing whether to laugh in her face or feel stupid that she'd said Double Jeopardy instead of Double Standard, ten year old Alicia Iglesius Cortana blushed. Double Standard – so that's what it meant when you treat someone unfairly but say you aren't?

Feeling like the farting Congresswoman was doing exactly that to her in a flash of insight the preteen suddenly remembered the question she had really, really, really been wanting to ask. 'Isn't it true that the votes in the 2020 election – the last election – didn't have the names on them verified?', she challenged. 'Isn't it true that California law says they have to be verified for the election to be legal? If we don't know that the names on the votes are right how do we know that you – or any other Democrat in California – wasn't cheating?'

Fired up but caught flat-footed Waters' ruddy skin turned slightly green, mirroring the rank feces threatening to explode from her rump. Her media propaganda allies had been very careful never to raise that thorny issue. 'The election commission takes care of details like that, not me.', answered Waters lamely. 'And the election was certified.'

Irritated that the Congresswoman was dodging again, AIC was undeterred. 'But how do the people know it was for *real*?', she pressed. 'How do we know it wasn't all *fake*?'

'Because the commission certified it.', repeated Waters.

'But don't Democrats control the government in California? That's like – ' AIC blinked and searched for the best way to express what she was thinking. 'That's just like having students grade their own tests!', she exclaimed triumphantly, hitting the nail right on the head.

Waters shook her head. 'It may seem that way, but the commission is bipartisan.'

'But they didn't follow the law!', bleated Alicia. How could something be said to be legal when it didn't do what the law said to do?! 'How do we know you weren't cheating if you are allowed to break the rules? To break the law?!'

Waters smiled condescendingly. 'Young lady, this has all been challenged in court. The courts threw it out. It was so silly the Supreme Court refused to even hear it. That's how certain we are that Democrats won the election.'

Hearing that Alicia Iglesius Cortana sagged in her chair, speechless. How could this happen?! It was the law! How could they say that it was *okay* to break the law?! The video tapes she'd watched in Georgia *showed people cheating*! And cheating by a *lot*! And there were over two hundred people who *swore in court* that election fraud happened! If they were lying, why weren't they charged with lying in court?! Isn't *lying in court* a crime?

Why didn't Congress investigate that? Why wasn't it all over the TV?! Why do people like Congresswoman Waters want to blame the people in the Capitol for being angry and do all sorts of investigations on them but <u>not</u> investigate the reasons *why* the people were protesting??? It wasn't right!!

She was just about to say so when her principal Mrs. Garcia stepped in. Embarrassed she hadn't offered a pause so Congresswoman Waters could take a bathroom break the ardent Democratic supporter (and President of the local chapter of the Teacher's Union) said: 'It looks like we're out of time today. We'd all like to thank Congresswoman Waters for taking the time to come here and speak with us. I'm sure we all learned a lot about how our government works.'

Smiling for the camera Maxine Waters tipped her phantom cap to Ms. Garcia and the rest of the staff who put on this little theatrical show to further her campaign. Feeling better now that she wasn't being grilled by the preteen she stepped off the platform. Her churning bowels made for a terrible performance but any rough spots she might have had fencing with the sharp little girl would be smoothed out before the tape aired. 'Thank you, Ms. Garcia, for having me here today at Martin Luther King Elementary. And thank you Miss Cortana for posing such bright and challenging questions! I'm sure you'll make a fine reporter for CNN some day!'

Praised by a flatulent old woman she didn't have any respect for Alicia forced a smile as she was ushered off stage. In spite of the fact that the difficult interview was over and the air didn't smell so foul the little girl felt a dull ache in her stomach. None of what Congresswoman Waters said sounded right! How could Americans be sure about anything if their elections weren't safe? How could she be sure her rights would remain protected if the Courts wouldn't even listen to what witnesses say happened?!!

Eager to get back to her office and take a dump Maxine Waters hurriedly shooed her entourage out the door. The parking lot outside Martin Luther King Junior Elementary was swarming with children at recess. Curiously the normally boisterous children were not busy scurrying around on the playground equipment or kicking a ball to one another. Surrounded by their friends the kids were glued to their phones.

A boy about nine years old suddenly looked up and recognized the congresswoman. 'She's over there!', he shouted.

'Hi, children!', Waters automatically responded with a wave. All around her smiling faces turned to look her way. Mad Maxine's heart swelled. The youth vote was hers! They loved her!

Beaming, she strode into the crowd of kids – and someone began to snicker. A few other chuckles joined in and then a group of young girls pointed in her direction and burst into laughter.

'Clear out, everybody!', a boy about twelve shouted abruptly. 'She may let one go!'

Surrounded by laughing children the blood slowly drained from the eighty-three year old Representative for California's 43rd District's face. Everywhere she looked the children were mocking her. Black, White, Asian and Native First Settlers, Hispanic and Pacific Islanders....they all were pointing at their phones then at her. Feeling pressed in by the crowd Maxine Waters suddenly felt the air grow hot and her heart turn to lead. The interview! Someone in the room had been taping it! *It was already posted* – **unedited** – *to the internet!!!*

'Get out of my way!', she barked angrily, banishing the disobedient little brats from her sight.

But the mirthful children did not part. Laughing at her expense they continued to mock her.

Feeling shamed for the first time in years Maxine Waters' elderly heart stuttered – and she ripped a gigantic splatter-fart big enough to soil the inside of her underwear.

The kids surrounding her roared. 'Omigod! That one was a killer! Run away! Run away!!'

Feeling like she'd just discovered she'd been walking around with a long stream of soiled toilet paper hanging tucked from the waistband of her slacks Waters fell into one of her aides. She wasn't a divisive force – she had unified the young people of America against her! They believed in being civil and hated her for all the terrible things she and her party had said about the President! They knew her arguments were stupid! They knew the Democratic party was stealing their candy! She was just one big giant FART!!!

Choking on her own stink Waters couldn't breathe. Dizzy, her own fateful words fluttered back to her: "Show up where ever we have to show up! Create a crowd and push back on them! Tell them they aren't welcome anymore! You see anybody...you get out and you create a crowd!'

The elderly old hag from the slums of St. Louis sagged to the ground. She had come to California from East St. Louis and turned her district into the same kind of dump she grew up in because that was all she knew how to do. She had no clue how to fix things and had only run for office to get rich. Like the rest of the Democratic party she touted her poor upbringing and promised to help the downtrodden but had never done anything but enact policies that made it harder for the poor to get ahead. She furthered the interests of her wealthy donors and used the money to pad her extravagant lifestyle so she could live in a posh neighborhood away from the impoverished people she was supposed to serve.

None of that mattered now, though. Mad Maxine Waters was in her eighties and could not take the heat of an honest debate – not even one against a precocious ten year old schoolgirl. Like the Grinch her heart was many sizes too small to take it. Mocked by the sounds of children laughing at her the ancient swamp creature finally at long last vacated her Congressional seat. Coronary heart disease, like the rancid fart she let out upon her passing, was a silent-but-deadly killer.

*   *   *

'P-p-p-p-p-p!!!', Guy Guildencrantz sounded, putting his lips to his forearm to add sound effects to the end of Rosenstern's tale.

Very pleased with her effort Emily palmed her hands. 'What? You didn't like it?'

Guy shook his head exuberantly. 'Of course not! I loved it! Farted to death!!', he chuckled with appreciation, clapping softly. 'Very appropriate way for Waters to go!'

Glad her friend was pleased Em smiled. 'The old bat's nothing but hot air anyway...'

The big man nodded. 'I gotta give you that round. Yours was better than my Cuomo story.'

Rosenstern beamed proudly. Winning on points now she crossed her legs and bounced in her chair.

Guildencrantz held up his hand. 'But the game's not over!', he said sinisterly in a passable Khan Noonien Singh via Ricardo Montalban accent. 'It's time for....drum roll, please....the chicken dance!'

Emily blinked, then tilted her head to the side. 'The chicken dance?'

'Yup!', declared Guy. 'Here we go! As they say, it's time to get real!'

The Chicken Dance

*I*n consideration of the crime and with due understanding of the nature of the offender's long standing service to this country, the court hereby sentences former Congressman Bernard Sanders to 200 hours of community service.'

Sanders looked at his attorney and smiled. Better than they had hoped for!

Judge Reginald P. Tarrament III went on, however. 'In lieu of the circumstances the defendant is also ordered to make full restitution to the injured parties in the amount of twenty-eight million dollars. In payment of this debt Mr. Sander's assets will be seized immediately. Such forfeiture to include real estate assets, personal property including vehicles, financial entities such as bank accounts, stock equities, business ventures and any and all acquisitions made in pursuit of higher office. This sum shall include all properties held individually and jointly in any form and instruments used for campaign finance.'

Sanders gasped. His entire fortune! The government was going to seize it – seize it and distribute it to the Masses! All he earned taken away and given to the People! The Horror!! The Injustice!!!

His head snapped over towards his attorney Jade Chen. The young woman was just standing there mute. She had to do something! Appeal this theft of his property! Have it voided somehow! They couldn't do this to him! They just couldn't!!

'Additionally, the defendant is ordered to personally pay an additional $1 million dollars for the pain and suffering inflicted and an additional $5 million dollars in punitive damages.'

Trapped in a surrealistic nightmare the blood drained from the former Congressman's face. This could not be happening!!! Another six million dollars! Sanders wiped his face. He – he would have to reach out to the party – otherwise he'd be living on the streets like a pauper! Speaking

47

engagements – he could make a living doing speaking engagements! Speaking out protesting this absurdity! Obama still drew crowds willing to pay to hear his lies! It didn't matter if he was guilty or not!

'Furthermore – ', the industrious Judge went on. 'Understanding the dishonest nature of Mr. Sanders' crimes he shall be barred from fund raising events, both virtual and in person. Mr. Sanders is not allowed to create a "Fund Me" page or accept monies obtained by third parties. He is not allowed to accept gifts, whether political in nature or personal, nor is he allowed to obtain loans in payment of these debts. Such a loan would no doubt present a further temptation to the former Senator to misuse high office again in yet another quid pro quo scheme.' The long-tenured African-American judge cleared his throat and stared "The Bern" in the eye. 'Mr. Sanders, it is the judgment of this court that to pay these debts you must.....actually get a job.'

Already suffering from a heart ailment the ex-Senator from Vermont swooned and clutched his chest. A – a job!? A REAL JOB!!! NO!!!!! Send me to prison – send me to a minimum security prison instead!!! One with air conditioning and 200 television channels!!! One with internet and tennis courts and conjugal visits!!! Send me someplace where I'll be taken care of at tax payer expense!!!

'Your honor – ', Chen finally interrupted.

Judge Terrament III cut her off with a slicing motion. 'If you wish to appeal the sentence you may do so – as is your right, Ms. Chen. However, should you do so your client will be spending his days in a proper *maximum security* penitentiary until such an appeal can be heard. The correctional facility in Jefferson county should serve nicely.'

'But – but your honor! This is a former US Senator we're talking about!'

'And the law must be blind to that, young lady!', barked Terrament. 'Your client has vast financial holdings and tremendous political influence. In my judgment he is a potential flight risk.'

Chen could barely find her tongue. In China this was unheard of! How could this judge be treating her client like a common criminal?! He was part of the elite! The same rules did not apply to him like they did to other people! 'Surely a man of Mr. Sanders stature in the community could be remanded to the custody of another responsible institution?', she began. 'Could he not...stay with a colleague until this matter is settled amicably?'

The patriotic American judge pointed his finger at the young woman. He knew her services were being paid for by China and he would have none of this "Yellow" Privilege in his court room! Stay with a "colleague" bah! This hack deserved to be treated like the criminal he was! 'And another thing Miss Chen: your client Mr. Sanders will be getting a real job, not some cushy little office arrangement where he lays on a couch all day watching TV and collecting a pay check. Your client is finally going to learn the value of an honest day's labor! He's going to work just like every other American works!'

'But your honor – this is Involuntary servitude! Slavery!!'

'Which – if you understood the Constitution of these United States correctly, Ms. Chen – is perfectly legal in cases where a citizen has broken the law! Mr. Sanders has been legally convicted of the crime and the state has the right to dictate the terms of his confinement and restitution. I could sentence your client to work on a chain gang – but because of his heart ailment that would constitute cruel and unusual punishment.', Judge Terrament III conceded, thumping his gavel. 'In light of this – and because of Mr. Sander's obvious political influence and contacts – this court feels obliged to insure that the defendant actually receives the punishment for which he has been sentenced. As such I order that Mr. Sanders work for minimum wage at a restaurant for a minimum of two hundred hours time. This arrangement will satisfy Mr. Sander's obligation to perform community service and allow him to better understand the value of a dollar.' Judge Terrament III smiled beatifically. 'Of course, Mr. Sanders will be paying taxes on the money he earns.'

The Bern could stay silent no longer. 'You can not actually be serious!'

'Your honor – !', Chen objected simultaneously.

'Oh, I assure you both I am very very serious. Following completion of this two hundred hours of real labor Mr. Sanders will be free to seek gainful employment at a higher wage. He will need to as he has a considerable debt to pay. However, such employment can not be any speaking engagement or political consultant job – Mr. Sanders is barred from being a political entity and anything connected to the political world in any way, shape or form is forbidden. This includes working as a consultant or as an employee for *any* business or business interest connected with the Senator's former life in Congress. Anyone the senator dealt with either directly or indirectly during his career in office is off limits. Any violation of this clause will send Mr. Sanders to the maximum security prison previously mentioned where the former Senator will be doing *hard time*.', the judge threatened ominously.

Stunned, Jade Chen stared at him like she was the one who'd been sentenced to the gallows. This was unreal! In her country she had never heard of such a thing! A member of the political elite actually held to account by the courts?! Where was the special treatment?! How could this judge do this without fearing he would be taken in the middle of the night to a cell for "re-education"?! 'Your honor, surely a more equitable solution can be reached? In the interest of amity?'

Looking down from his bench, Terrament smiled. 'Young lady, justice in the great sovereign State of Mississippi is not dumb or deaf but it is blind to color, creed, sex *and* political influence. This is not Vermont, nor is it California or New York or any other locale where your client's political connections outweigh the law. Your client has broken our state laws with impunity. And while it is Mr. Sanders' right to appeal this verdict in a higher court, continued outbursts by you or your client will be dealt with harshly. Any more contemptuous behavior and I will order that he perform additional community service holding the Confederate flag beside a historical monument – or sentence him to act in a civil war reenactment! I warn both of you: Don't test my patience any further.'

Muzzled, the foreign agent at last observed her right to remain silent. Her superiors would be most displeased to learn of her defeat; she'd failed in her obligations to protect the openly communist senator. When she returned home the high command might be so angry with her they might invent some charge to levy against her and sentence her to be caned!

Oblivious to her consternation Judge Terrament III continued. 'Now, Ms. Chen...here are some appropriate business entities located within twenty miles of Mr. Sander's summer beach home that will satisfy his debt to Mississippi society. I remind you that this secondary residential property will be seized in payment of your client's outstanding debts in the next 90 days so alternative arrangements should be made when that event occurs. I understand that several low priced apartments are available close to the place your client will be working, so it would be wise to investigate them. As Mr. Sanders has for decades openly championed Socialism – ahem, excuse me "Progressivism" – I can not think of a more appropriate punishment than making him learn the value of an honest day's labor. Perhaps Mr. Sanders will finally appreciate what Capitalism has done to improve his life (and the life of every other citizen as well) now that he actually has to contribute to the common good for once.'

The criminals in his court room stunned into silence the wise old judge smiled. 'This judgment is so entered into the record on June 26th, 2022! The Case of the People of Mississippi v. Bernard Sanders is now closed!'

*   *   *

As a particularly lazy US Congressman Bernie Sanders believed wholeheartedly that the word "Work" was indeed a four letter word. He had failed at every business enterprise he'd ever attempted and had never gotten his hands dirty before doing anything besides putting his dirty dishes in the sink. Bernard considered such things beneath him. He had found a profitable niche providing an endless series of quirky soundbites to a dishonest media hungry for anything that they could sell to gain attention (and therefore market share). The empty talking heads on CNN happily regurgitated his heavily disproved Marxist ideas as new and improved "Progress", pretending for politics sake they were not radical, ridiculously ruinous, utterly absurd garbage. Sanders' entire political career had been to be the champion of a system that lead directly to economic catastrophe and the media elite were happy to sell it if it could gain their shadow masters access to the gold in Fort Knox. Sander's ailing heart was in the wrong place but as long as it had any chance of gaining them power the DNC cabal ran with what they thought they could sell.

When he was a nobody Sanders' insane ideas had been no threat. But as the mis-education of America's youth took hold his foolishness began to gain traction like a cancer. It didn't matter if it was stupid – it sounded good to the Democrats' target voter: the indoctrinated, woefully-ignorant jobless woke youngster. What votes they couldn't get they would manufacture in a paper mill.

But that was before Judge Tarrament threw the proverbial book at him. "The Bern" had been convicted. He was in the service of the state now and there was going to be no cushy job talking smack. He was going to have to work for a living for the first time in his life.

Sanders' first attempt at holding a job was at McDonalds. Commensurate with his feeble intellectual abilities the old crone was placed first at the cash register. Memorizing the menu and pricing proved too taxing, however, and he was soon demoted to fry chef. He lasted only two hours at that, though; lifting the boxes of frozen spuds proved more than his shrunken stooped body could take. Working for minimum wage at McDonalds was beyond Sanders' physical and mental capabilities.

His next stop on the road of involuntary servitude was at Walmart as a greeter. This employment did not last long either. Bernie's gravely eastern tones proved too curmudgeonly for the people of Mississippi and there were soon complaints and a loss of business. He was shuffled around to other departments but his lack of math skills and frail body made him an impediment to the rest of the staff. Sanders' repelled customers and screwed everything up. Faced with an employee who was hurting the bottom line he was once again let go.

Running out of options Sanders was on the verge of being held in contempt of court and getting remanded to the penitentiary to do real hard time. This "work thing" was something he was simply not suited for! His only skills were in conniving people to buy failed ideas and convincing them history would not repeat itself! He might have used those skills to work as a used car salesman but selling pre-owned vehicles was paid on commission and not a minimum wage job! What could he do?! He would end up in prison sharing a cell with Bubba Joe Henry if he didn't think of something soon!

It was then that his good buddies in the fictional arts came to his rescue. "Minimum wage" was a term that could have a different meaning than the State of Mississippi's legally dictated "floor" minimum wage of $7.25 per hour – if one argued that "minimum" was defined as the least a person could be paid for the particular industry in question. By the Hollywood standard actors with speaking parts were required to be paid at scale regardless of which state or country the shoot was actually taking place in. Although this was clearly not the intent of Judge Tarramont's order this could be stretched in court to meet the standard of "minimum wage" – if the shoot was done within the borders of the State of Mississippi. It wasn't the Federally dictated minimum wage, but it would work (no pun intended). If he was forced to actually keep trying to work at a fast food restaurant "The Bern" was sure to die of exhaustion.

But what could a bland talentless personality like Bernie Sanders actually do in front of the camera? He wasn't allowed to do anything political or use any of his campaign resources. He couldn't do political ads or sell anything with a clearly diabolical Democratic bent.

Name recognition was his only card to play. There was only one real option...and it was sure to poke a finger in the eye of the good ol' boys from Mississippi...

*   *   *

Dressed in the clean white suit of Southern gentry Sanders did his best to stand up straight. His stooped elderly posture wouldn't allow it, however, and he remained the shriveled bent up old buffoon he had become over the years. Leaning heavily on the prop cane he threatened to snap the little thing in two. 'Some mashed potatoes and...corn will do your heart good.', he went on, mangling his lines badly. 'So....so come on down and get....try...some Kentucky fry. It's finger....licking...finger good. You'll be mightily...mightily....glad you did.'

'Cut! Cut! Jesus Christ!', director DJ McKay barked. The young up-and-comer slapped his forehead in exasperation. This was their fifth ruined take! How could he work with such a bad actor? It was unprofessional – Sanders couldn't even remember his goddamned lines! 'Finger licking good! It's finger licking good! How can you forget that? Kentucky Fried Chicken has been using that tag line for years! And what is with that stupid accent? Can't you at least *try* a southern accent? Dammit! Where the hell are you from?'

Not used to being unrecognized Sanders looked at him, aghast. 'Vermont, of course! I'm – I'm a former United States Senator! I ran for President of the United States! I'm Bernie Sanders! Don't you know who I am?'

McKay made a face like he gave a shit about some former congressional loser. 'I don't fucking care who you *think* you *were*, you jackass! On this set you are supposed to fucking play Col. Sanders! Colonel Sanders! Col. Sanders from fucking Kentucky! Ken-tuck-y!!! This is a spot for Kentucky Fried Chicken! KFC! He's way more famous than you, you dickhead! Now get your shit together, play the character right and stop wasting everybody's fucking time! I'm the mother-fucking director here! Me! Ray "DJ"-fucking-McKay! Get it right! Either play the scene as it's written or you will end up out of a job! Do you get me?! I will fucking fire your ass! Jesus-fucking-Christ!'

Itching to give the director a scathing tongue-lashing Sanders bit his lip. One more strike and he'd end up back in court – or worse, have to get back behind the fry counter. This was slavery! And the taxes they took out of his paycheck to pay for all these social programs like medicaid and welfare! 'Alright. I got ya. I'll try to get it right this time.', he harrumphed, scratching his balding scalp. 'Just an old guy, I guess...'

Not caring about any of The Bern's excuses DJ McKay turned away from him. He was used to shooting music videos filled with shapely dancers clad in skimpy barely-there clothes, not wrinkly old has-been buffoons. Who the hell's cheerios did he piss in that he ended up working a gig like this with this loser? He must have pissed off somebody. It was probably some Weinstein-style producer that had his eye on one of the models he'd dipped his wick in. 'Okay, people, from the top.', McKay said, trying to master his anger to salvage what was left of his career and get it back on track. 'Places....and action!'

'Hi – you all know me. I'm Sanders – Colonel Sanders. Here at KFC we make the best fried – fried chicken in the business. Come on down and try our family deals. A bucket of chicken, some mashed potatoes and corn will do your heart good. It's finger food licking good. So try – '

'Oh, for fucks sake! Cut! Cut! Cut!', screamed McKay, slapping his forehead. Listening to this talentless dick was like listening to Sister Mary Clarence raking her nails down a chalkboard in *Sister Act 2*! This whole shoot was a disaster!

'Can't you just fire this asshole?', Jonesy the cameraman growled only half under his breath.

McKay shook his head angrily. 'No. Our "friends" upstream don't want him fired. I have to use him.'

The frustrated camera man and director were setting up for yet another pointless take when a pretty dark-haired assistant suddenly approached them. 'Mr. McKay, sir....I think I may have a way out of this mess.'

The director looked her up and down. It was the new intern he'd hired on last week. He didn't remember her name. 'Yeah? Well time's money, honey.', he quipped.

The girl cleared her throat. 'Well, sir, we know Bernie can't play the Colonel.'

'That's for sure.', Jonesy smirked irritably. He gave the young intern a once over. 'Your "female intuition" give you that little tidbit of information, Captain Obvious?'

McKay made a chopping motion to silence his camera man. 'He's complete shit.', he agreed. 'Hearing him tying to sell the product I'd think KFC mashed potatoes are filled with maggots.'

'Well, does he have to play the Colonel?', the girl asked pointedly.

'It's a KFC spot. What the hell else can he play?'

Hoping she was on to something the intern gestured to The Bern. 'Well, he's obviously no actor – so maybe we can use that to our advantage?'

McKay scratched his nose. The new girl had a point. What they were doing was getting them nowhere. 'Okay, I'm listening. What's your idea...Miss?'

'Chambers. Jessica Chambers.', she said quickly, flashing a winsome smile. She pointed her thumb towards the curmudgeonly former Senator. 'So this old codger here's name is Bernie Sanders. But he's not Colonel Sanders – he's a washed up politician. And...'

*   *   *

'Places!', yelled McKay to silence the commotion. 'And....action!'

The youthful new actor in the white suit and beard playing Colonel Sanders took a few casual strides forward. 'This is the Colonel here. As you already know, at KFC we make the best fried chicken in the business. So come on down and try our family meal deals. A bucket of chicken, some mashed potatoes and corn will do your heart good.', he promised using a passable but clearly inviting southern twang.

'That's right – ', the man in the giant chicken suit beside him said cheerfully, pulling off his head-mask to reveal ex-Senator Bernie Sanders' gnarled face. 'You don't have to wear a mask like this one to stay safe from Covid-19! Don't be a chicken! Come on down to KFC for deals so good you'll swear they're government subsidized!'

'We've got bucket deals from $25 on up – ', the actor chimed in. 'And our chicken is always hot and fresh!'

'That's right!', the dancing buffoon in the rubber chicken suit seconded. 'So take it from one Sanders to another, KFC is the place to go for your next outing!'

'It's finger-lickin'-good!', promised the Colonel, placing his hand upon Chicken Sanders's shoulder like they were bosom buddies.

'Keep smiling...keep smiling....', Ray DJ McKay directed, stretching the moment out. 'And....cut! That's a wrap!', he said with relief. 'Cut and print!'

Safely out of the shot behind the cameras Jessica Chambers beamed proudly and bounced on her heels.

Manning his station next to her Jonesy turned and gave the girl an appreciative thumbs up. 'Stellar idea, kiddo. You might have a place in this business. Care to get a drink later after work?'

The girl responded with a coy little shrug. 'Maybe.', she promised noncommittally, keeping her options open. Seeking someone higher up the ladder than the camera-guy she sidled up next to the director. 'So what do you think Mr. McKay?'

'Not bad, not bad.', he said with a relieved smile. 'And it's DJ from now on.'

'Yes, sir – DJ.', Jessica replied, accepting her promotion up the Hollywood social totem pole with glee.

Standing in a rubber chicken suit looking like an imbecile Bernie Sanders cleared his throat loudly. 'Would someone please get me out of this damned thing? It's hot in here.'

'No – stay there. We have to do a few more shoots to make sure we've got a good print.', McKay ordered, turning back to the clever young intern who'd saved their collective bacons. This Jessica Chambers didn't have a bad figure. If the rest of her was as ambitious as her brains the girl might be worth taking back to his trailer for a test drive.

'Ah, Mr. Sanders?', a woman asked.

'What?!', snapped Bernie irritably, turning in her direction.

'I meant the Colonel.', the make up artist answered with a sour look. Offering the method-acting "star" of this little production a cup of ice water the little blonde took his prop cane from him so he could sip his drink comfortably while she reapplied make up to whiten his brows.

Left standing in his ridiculous rubber chicken outfit Bernie Sanders attempted to scratch his itching chin. His arms were like flippers, though, and he couldn't reach. 'Hey! I need to scratch my face! Somebody help me!', he demanded.

'Social distance, please!', another low-level assistant sneered. Like most of the working class in Hollywood she was secretly a Trump supporter and hated what the Woke Democrats had done to the State of California and the rest of the country. She couldn't even voice her displeasure at how ridiculously expensive everything was on social media for fear of getting blacklisted like beautiful, intelligent sexy bad-ass star Gina Joy Carano! 'Put your mask on, you old fool! You want to give everyone The Covid!', she joked, tormenting the old establishment coot with glee.

Trapped by his party's own cyclic propaganda of never-ending plague Sanders did as she asked and put the mask back on. Without a microphone in front of him to babble his sales pitch to he was just another parasitic old politician scratching out a living doing the only thing he was qualified to do: making an ass out of himself for the whole world to see. At least this time he was selling chicken instead of economic catastrophe. Raising the nation's cholesterol and blood sugar levels was a lot better than crushing the American Dream and ballooning the National Debt!

* * *

Emily Rosenstern could not contain her mirth. 'Oh, that was freakin' hilarious!', she said, doubling over with laughter.

'Was it finger-licking-good?', Guildencrantz replied, flapping his arms like a chicken. 'Bawk! Bawk! Bawk! Ba-caw! Bawk! Bawk! Bawk! Bawk! Bawk! Ba-caw!'

His boisterous antics only made his secret service agent companion laugh harder. 'Making a socialist like Sanders finally get a job!', she bleated, trying to catch a decent breath. 'Holy shit! And making him dress up in a chicken suit and try and play Colonel Sanders! Sanders to Sanders! What a hoot!' Em wiped the corner of her eye with a tissue and it came back dirty. She was going to need to touch up her makeup before she went home to Chad. 'Where do you come up with this shit?!'

'Just like The Bern – I pull it straight outta my ass.', her partner answered with a wink.

Emily wadded up the used tissue and tossed it in the trash like she was playing hoops. 'Oh, man...that....was the shit!'

Guy sighed merrily. 'If only that "shit" would happen for real...'

'Yeah! Wish all Congress had to finally get a job.'

'True dat.'

After another lengthy pause Emily finally got her breathing under control. She giggled happily. 'Damn. Almost passed out there.'

'Need a break?', queried Guy.

Em shook her head. 'Naw, I'm good.' She sighed then gave her partner-in-law a look. 'You set a high bar! I gotta get my ass in gear and catch up! Don't wanna have to take your ravenous ass out to dinner – you eat like a whole freakin' team of horses!'

Feeling confident now that his partner had just admitted he was ahead in the game Guy grinned back at her and taunted her with a little good-natured trash talk. 'Veronica likes our nights out to be really memorable. She always orders something nice – and always gets dessert.', he warned jokingly.

Rosenstern rubbed her forehead worriedly. 'Oh, shit.'

'Oh, shit is right!', he replied with a nod.

Concerned about how much a night out on the town might cost in this new Biden inflation-based economy, Rosenstern sat with her head bowed, thinking. Who could she skewer? The Democratic party was literally filled with assholes...

'Okay – ', she said suddenly, knowing who she had to talk about. If you were gonna ream the Dims in the butt there was a couple of serious assholes you absolutely <u>had</u> to go after. 'I got it. You did your chicken and dumplings, bud – now it's time for shit to get real and dig into the main course. It's grilled hamburger time!'

'Veronica likes prime rib...and lobster...and bacon-wrapped filet mignon...', wise-cracked Guildencranz.

Ignoring his jabs, Emily Rosenstern cracked her knuckles. Time to finally get down to business! Dinner with all the trimmings was at stake!

A Double Epstein

William Jefferson Clinton rolled over in bed. Rubbing his bloodshot eyes he reached for the glass of water waiting on the nightstand. In preparation for the after-effects of his Friday night revels a pair of aspirins were already sitting on a small saucer beside the cup. He swallowed the pills, chugged the water until the glass was empty then rolled onto his back to let the pain reliever do its work on his hangover.

Sinking comfortably back under the soft sheets he noticed a warm body was beside him. The lecherous old man smiled. Being an ex-president (even one that had been Impeached and should have been successfully removed from office for outright perjury) had its perks. If Starr hadn't committed a gross act of prosecutorial incompetence and informed him prior to going under oath about the stains on Monica's dress – stains he was completely unaware of – he *would* have been removed from office. Instead he created the fiction of a one-off act of fellatio and claimed: "I did not have sexual relations with that woman", which under the letter of the law of the State he was testifying in *would* have been technically true if he and Lewinski hadn't in reality been engaged in a full blown affair. The undeniable proof that he, President William Jefferson Clinton, had perjured himself didn't come out conclusively until decades after his terms of office were over and Lewinski finally admitted publicly that their tryst wasn't just a single act of head.

In many ways he should have just confessed to the whole affair from the beginning instead of being stuck on 1950s-style politics; the American people didn't really give a shit about the sex lives of their leaders only how competently they did their jobs – well, Democrat leaders that is. Being prudish was only acceptable when used to attack Republicans and this double-standard was in full display when the press tried to go after Trump for his supposed (but still uncorroborated) many years prior-to-campaigning booty call dalliance with a porn star – even though he was a private citizen at the time and even if proven meant absolutely nothing. As it was if Starr hadn't been so completely incompetent, according to the Constitution Bill Clinton *should* have been forced to resign like Nixon had over Watergate. The perjury was pretty clear; even if the public didn't care about the subject matter he *had* explicitly committed a felony.

To deflect public attention from the truth Clinton "wagged the dog" on the day of Monica's testimony and ordered the military to launch a bunch of million dollar Tomahawk missiles to blow up empty $10 tents in some shit hole third world country. His allies in the press front page news-ed his pointless misuse of government resources and buried Monica's damning testimony. This media malpractice was standard operating procedure and nothing new. The heavily biased liberal press had been spinning his failed policies to take credit for the economic boom directly caused by the technological revolution of the internet Clinton's entire presidency. As Hillary once said in an email to her colleagues: "The average Democrat voter isn't too bright."

But that was all water under the bridge and about as important to former President William Jefferson Clinton as a used condom. These days he spent his time gallivanting around with his rich well-connected buddies bedding under-aged girls. The media kept their escapades out of the public eye because it served their own interests – they were the propaganda arm of the Democratic party and could move the line whenever a member of their faction crossed it to protect the brand. Sleeping with whomever he could was simply a powerful well-connected man's right; it was part of human nature and consent was just a matter of money – or if he get away with taking what he wanted without serious repercussions. Hell, he'd gotten away with taking over twenty-five trips with Jeff Epstein on his private sex plane and lying about it, for shit's sake! The aircraft was a flying juvenile halfway-whorehouse! The lovely young underage thing beside him was no doubt inebriated to the point of being comatose and was probably even more hungover than he was.

The aspirin started to take effect Billy Clinton yawned. Coming to his senses he looked around for signs of a condom wrapper and was distressed not to find one. Hopefully his revels hadn't resulted in yet another trip to Planned Parenthood. Taking care of the results of using women as cum-dumpsters was what abortion centers were there for but he still didn't want the added hassle of having to cover it up. Unless a repeat performance was warranted the hit-and-run sign was on – and it was time for the umpire to throw this bitch out.

Curious to see if he'd bagged Major League talent or yet another star-struck junior high-school player William Jefferson Clinton peeled back the covers – and to his absolute horror discovered the last female in the world he expected to find inhabiting his bed. The nasty bitch laying beneath the covers was of disgustingly fat proportions, a rancid piece of fetid meat that smelled like three month old ham – Hillary Diane Rodham Clinton!

Ready to vomit Billy Jefferson sprang from the bed like he was covered in fire ants. What had he done?! Had he blacked out??!! Had he gotten so goddamned drunk he'd actually fucked "HIS WIFE"???!!! What-the-Mother-Fuck!!!!!!!

'Uhnnn....', murmured the duplicitous fat cow cratering the far side of the bed.

WJ backed away from the she-beast defiling the sheets of his play pen like she was Lilith herself. The woman who stalked through his nightmares was the Devil's ugly step-sister! She was the Queen of Cock-Blocking, the Cunt of Cunts! And he'd slept with her! Slept with her! Oh-My-God!!!! He'd had unprotected sex with the Rug-Muncher!! With the HAIRY PITTED H-A-R-P-Y!!!

Unable to contain his churning stomach Slick Willie grabbed the nearest trash can and heaved. Whatever came up was vile but it was a pretty sight compared to what he saw in his bed. My eyes! My eyes!! My eyes!!!

Hearing stomach splatters hit the can the Beast slowly stirred. Moving like a hippopotamus Hillary Rodham Clinton slowly sat up in bed. 'Where are my clothes?', she grumbled, looking down to find her ugly chest bare.

'Not – not – where they – need – to be!', Billy hacked out. Catching full sight of her hideous top half he jammed his face back into the bucket. Oh, sweet Jesus! Let me drown in my own puke rather than see that again!

Rubbing her eyes, Hilly lifted the covers and found the rest of her was nude as well. 'William Jefferson Clinton! Did you undress me?!', she exclaimed, aghast.

'No...I didn't! <Hack!> Honest! <Sweet Jesus, huuugh!> I – <choke> – I <gasp!> <gasp!> <gasp!> huh-huh...I was <gag!> drunk!'

Hillary screwed up her face like a pouting fat kid denied her third dessert. She picked up the vase laying beside the bed and threw it at him.

'You're always drunk! Always drunk and sticking your dick into anything you can! Your fucking around is what cost me MY PRESIDENCY!', she declared.

Wanting to get out of the room before he caught full sight of her hideous figure, Bill Clinton ducked and hid behind the vomit filled trash can. Oh, sure – being stupid enough to get caught buying fake information from Russian spies or selling classified information to the highest bidder through their foundation had nothing to do with losing! It was his raping and whoring around with under-aged girls that fucked up her failed 2016 campaign's chances! 'I – I didn't do anything! <Spit!> Honest! I'd never touch you like that! I promise! I did not have sexual relations with you, woman!'

Hillary thrust her hands on her hips. Barely able to find her ham hocks amid the fat, she shouted: 'Well, I popped out our daughter so you must have!'

Reminded of the greatest mistake of his life William Jefferson grimaced. 'I never touched you! I swear – I did not have sexual relations with you!'

'Then where are my clothes, Billy?! Where are all my clothes?? I want to have clothes on!'

'I want you to have clothes on too!', he retorted, his Arkansas-tinged twang fading as he almost retched again. 'You have no idea...'

Hillary felt through the folds of her fat and to her disgust found them slick with goo. 'If I've found out you've fucked me...!', she roared, pointing her finger at him like a pistol.

The thought that he might actually have stuck his dick into the post-menopausal she-beast was enough to make Bill Clinton fear he was going to shit himself. Concerned the trash bucket wouldn't be enough to contain what might come out of his bowels the 43rd President made a mad dash for the bathroom. Hilarious Hillary threw another piece of glassware at him as he retreated, missing his head by an inch. Ignoring the projectile he plopped his wrinkly rump on the face of the porcelain goddess. 'Knock it off, you fucking bitch!'

'Rapist! I want you dead!'

Squeezing out a saucy new piece of legislation the former POTUS grunted in reply.

'I want you dead!', she repeated.

Fanning away the stench filling the bathroom Billy Clinton coughed. 'Oh, you wanna a piece of me?', he hacked. 'You want a piece of Slick

Willie?! Do ya? Well come on, you old bitch! Come on! I'll smother your fat ass in shit!'

Safely out of the gas zone Hilarious Hilly hailed the shitting chief of under-aged sex with a double-fisted one-finger salute. 'I want you dead! Fucking rapist!', she screamed.

'Come on, then!', he grunted. 'Let's do it! Come on, you old hag!'

'Fuck you!', she retorted.

'Fuck you too!!', he roared back.

If it weren't for Billy-boy's churning stomach and loose bowels they might have strangled each other then and there. The political hacks were screened by a bathroom wall (and the stench of vomit, shit and rancid ham), however, and could not bring themselves at that time to engage in a battle to the death. Every time Bill thought of Hillary's naked girth it was enough to send him retching over the trash can and he was forced to shelter in place until he had emptied himself and regained control of his digestive tract. For her part Hillary's sensitive nose found the stench of Billy's bullshit too repugnant to risk approaching for an attack. In this way the two former politicians remained separate-but-equally-asinine and when Billy was finally able to pull his wrinkly ass off the pot the she-beast he hated so much had already slithered away. He prayed that where ever she went off to Hillary was finally clothed.

Their mutual hatred did not end there, however, and the substance of their malice only increased with time. Having finally reached the breaking point over the next twenty-four hours the pained pair made several unsuccessful attempts on the other one's life. There was an aborted poisoning, a stair push, an attempted stabbing with a table knife – their spirits were willing but the intellect and ability to do the other in was weak. Try as they might the Clintons could not turn the spouse they hated so much into the not-so-dearly departed.

At his tits-and-ass addled wits end the former forty-third President finally pulled out his smart phone. The proliferation of technology is what had saved his presidency from the inevitable financial ruin his capital gains tax hikes would have caused and he figured it could save him from his beastly bitch-of-a-political-partner wife now as well. 'I'm disgusted.', he typed, his fingers flying over the touch screen. 'I can't live like this. I'm tired of all the lies. Let's end this.'

Hillary's reply was almost instantaneous: 'It IS time to end this. Once and for all.'

Slick Willie: 'Downstairs.', he challenged. 'Just you and me. I'll send the maids and secret service away and we'll finally do this thing.'

Hillary: 'Done. No reset button.'

Slick Willie: 'About time.'

Hillary: 'Food for the worms.'

Slick Willie: 'Pushing up daisies.'

Hillary: 'Perfect. I'm ready to go.'

Slick Willie: 'You have no idea how ready I am to go.'

With the staff shooed away the respective combatants were finally left alone in the house by themselves. Like all 2nd Amendment antagonist neither owned a gun and they had to improvise hand held weapons for their final battle. Slick Willie's weapon of choice was his golf club and his first swing knocked Hillarity's roast carving knife from her grasp. Disarmed, the post-menopausal bitch picked up a nearby metal lamp and bashed him with it, bending his golf club nearly in half. Both weaponless now the crabby old dyke retreated towards the stairs that led to the second level to get a tub of acid bleach-bit. Bleeding from the scalp it didn't take Slick Willie long to catch up to her. The 43rd President rapidly overpowered his portly wife and began choking her. Turning blue, in desperation Hil fumbled for one of the long spokes lining the stairwell and tore it from its moorings. Running out of air she stabbed it through Willy-boy's back. His lung punctured Bill staggered backwards.

Gasping for breath haggish Hillary crawled up the stairs for the second level. Slick Willie hated the evil cunt too much to just let her go, though, and grabbed for the leg of her designer lesbian-inspired cream pant suit before she could make it. She kicked him off and despite the stake in his side he was forced to rise to his feet to catch her. Struggling at the top of the stairs he once again over-powered her. Unable to free his hands from around her throat Hilarious Hillary slammed her fist into the wooden spoke. His already terrible wound now made fatal Slick Willie grabbed her in a bear hug and together they tumbled over the rail. The mismatched partners-in-crime plummeted to the first level's unforgiving marble floor with a crash.

Cushioned from the fall by Bill's plump body but impaled on the very spike she'd thrust through his chest, former Secretary of State Hillary Rodham Clinton shuddered for a moment then breathed her last. Repulsed by the shit filling the seat of her cream colored pant suit (and by the rancid ham-smelling she-beast he hated so much) William Jefferson Clinton tried feebly to pry the dead hippo off his body. His strength failed him, though, and the former President's heart stalled. As he faded to black he tried one last time to get Hilly off him but his arms gave out and came to rest across her back.

***

Inspecting the crime scene one last time Special Agents Beckman and Tolver stood at the edge of the room and gazed at the carnage.

'This has got to be the weirdest one I've ever seen partner.', Tolver mused incredulously. 'Double-suicide, sure, but usually the people offing themselves use a gun or poison – something quick. Why in the hell would you stab yourself with a piece of wood?! If you're gonna do yourself in, why not do it with a knife or a sword? There was a goddamned kitchen knife only a few feet away! Makes no damned sense.'

Beckman scratched her head. 'Maybe they thought they were vampires? Maybe it was some kind of weird-ass cult thing?'

The FBI agent shrugged. 'Maybe. It just seems like am awfully painful way to go.'

'Yeah, I guess.'

'Any sign of drugs in their systems? What was the toxicology report?', the FBI agent asked.

Beckman tilted her head. 'Oh, you know, the usual for people who live like this. Autopsy report came back relatively clean – a few prescription narcotics, antidepressants, Viagra and Cialis for the former President, seizure meds for the missus for her mental health condition. Nothing we didn't expect to find.'

Tolver cursed. 'Damn. At least if they were coked out of their minds or on PCP or meth or something that would give us some kind of a motive! All we've got to go on is those vague texts they sent each other before they sent the staff away.' Sighing, he fidgeted with the keys in his pocket. 'Back in the day we would at least have had a suicide note for psyche to go over.'

'Forensics did find poison in one of the waste receptacles, but neither of the victims had any in their systems.', Beckman noted.

'Jesus! Why the hell didn't they just use *that*, then? Why impale each other on a goddamned spike?!', Tolver groused. 'Suicide is always stupid, but I gotta say – this one is totally stupid as fuck!'

Grasping at straws his coworker shrugged to show she hadn't a clue. 'Maybe they wanted to, I don't know..."go out together"?'

'Poison works just as well as a damned stake through the heart! Makes no fucking sense to kill yourself in a painful way when there's a quicker and easier way to go!', the male half of their professional partnership bitched, scratching his scruff out of habit. It was well past five and though Tolver's hair was light enough not to show it he could feel the stubble. A sudden thought came to him. 'You don't think, well...that they were actually, you know, together? Like, still a couple? Could that, I don't know, explain why they were...why they both felt the need to be...pierced? To, I don't know, share each other's blood? To hold onto one another as they died?'

Pursing her lips, Beckman paused to consider Tolver's theory. Raising her eyebrow she shook her head skeptically. 'I don't know. It's possible, I guess. But the Coroner says no signs of sexual intercourse. Said the Missus' nethers were collecting dust – there was nothing but cottage cheese down there.'

Forced to consider that image Tolver shivered. 'Well, that was a lot more information than I needed.', he replied, consciously trying to banish the disgusting thought of the former S-o-S's infernal regions from his mind. He'd always assumed their daughter Chelsea was the product of artificial insemination. He didn't even want to think about what the Clinton's might have looked like actually engaged in coitus.

'Look – ', Beckman said with a dismissive shrug. 'If there was a spark between 'em, I suspect it died out years ago. Must've been why they were depressed enough to kill themselves. Maybe the guilt about all the shit they pulled got to be too much for them to handle, maybe it was something else. I don't know. But for whatever reason they decided to kill themselves – that's all there is to it, partner!'

Tolver sighed, then after a moment scratched his chin again. 'I still can't shake the feeling this wasn't a double suicide. Why did they do it together if there was nothing left between 'em? You'd'a figured they'd've been fucking or something to go out together like this.'

Beckman shrugged again then shook her head side to side. 'Can't say. I gave up trying to figure out this kinda bat shit crazy stuff years ago.'

Tolver emitted another protracted sigh. After a moment he got a strange look on his face. 'What – what if this was some kind of "Epstein" thing?'

'You thinkin' this was staged?', his partner replied, her eyes widening. 'Worth a look see.'

His senior on the force by three years, Sarah Beckman sucked a deep breath in. She did not want to go down that type of rabbit hole. Once they did there was no telling what they'd find – or how many snake-bitten bodies they'd unearth. 'What's the point?', she countered with a cynical shrug. 'You know if we turn up any leads it's just gonna get squashed by the DOJ. Besides, what good would poking around do? There's gonna be a state funeral and a bunch of hullabaloo but nobody in their right minds is really gonna miss 43 or thank God, not-45. Best leave the bodies where they lie unless somebody up the food chain makes us go digging.'

Realizing she was right, Tolver exhaled with a sigh. After a moment he bobbed his head up and down. 'Yeah, you're probably right.'

Beckman nodded her agreement. Case closed – they wouldn't pull on any loose threads. 'I say we wrap this up and go get some dinner. You game?'

He thumbed towards the adjacent bathroom. 'I gotta go take a quick Democrap, first.'

'I'll meet ya at the car then.', she answered, beating a retreat. 'Dibble Dobbers work for you? Or do you wanna go someplace fancier?'

'Nah, DDs sounds good. I need a beer, burger and some fries.'

'Cool. Meet ya at the car in say...five?'

'Five's good.'

'K. Later-gator. I'll be in the car.'

*   *   *

'Oh, you fucker! I was gonna do the Clintons!', Guildencrantz kvetched.

'Awwwwww.', Agent Rosenstern cooed, happy to have one upped her partner and stolen his thunder. 'Did I beat my Guy to the punch?'

Thwarted, her friend stuck his tongue out at her playfully. 'You suck.', he said.

Emily beamed but let the obvious juvenile retort about the prowess of her tongue dancing skills pass unsaid. Deciding turn about was fair play she began teasing him about the amount of money she planned on making him spend on her and her handsome boyfriend. 'Chad really, really likes expensive wines!', she announced with a dramatic wave of her hand. 'The fruit of the vine's got to be at least ten or fifteen years old and aged in oak or cedar! He has to have an after dinner brandy or whiskey on ice too! Always very top shelf stuff! Something that runs about $160, $185 a bottle is his favorite. I forget the brand...'

About to be wallet-Slick-Willied, Agent Guy wagged his finger at her in defiance. 'Okay, don't go counting your bar tab before the waitress brings us the first drink, little girl! I'll grant that your Epsteining or assisted suicide or whatever of Hilly-girl and Billy-boy was pretty epic – but that's all just window dressing! The Clinton Foundation is a parasite and they deserve to kill each other like the dogs they are! But establishment types are all on the take – the Clintons are just the most obvious offenders!'

'I thought Monica's dress was the window dressing?', heckled Rosenstern.

'I don't want to even think about Slick Willie defiling that poor inno-cent little dress!', Agent Guy Guildencrantz roared in disgust. He held up his hands like a stop sign to get off that image before it could fester. 'But Billie-boy and Hilly-dyke are yesterday's news! They aren't the Camelot couple! They aren't the King Arthur and Guinevere of the Dims!'

Rosenstern's cheeks puffed out in defiance. 'No – that was JFK and Jackie, the fictional perfect couple of the sixties! The woke-believe dysfunc-tional poster family for wedded bliss who were not-so-secretly cheating on each other and in bed with gangsters and every possible criminal element in the United States – ', she declared stridently. 'And they're both long gone!'

'That's not who I'm talking about.', Guildencrantz answered with a shake of his head, making a slashing motion with his hand to dismiss JFK and Jackie from the conversation. He wasn't talking about dead democrats but clear and present danger ones. He held up his finger. 'You want to take down the Douche-party, you gotta take out Mr. Fabulous! You gotta rip a new one in Mr. Untouchable! You gotta do in the *Strutting Peacock!*'

Emily blanched. 'You mean – the Unholy Obamination?'

Guy brought his fist down for emphasis. 'Hell, yes! That's the real power couple in the Dimm party! Mr. and Mrs. "You dispute me on anything and you're a racist!" The shithead of shitheads! The Snake Oil salesman deluxe! Barrack "Third Person" Fucking-Obama!!!'

Knowing it had to happen but skeptical of Guy's ability to do it, Emily Rosenstern scoffed. '*You're* gonna take him down?', she bleated, convinced no one alive could do it. Obama was god to the demi-crats and the machine to keep his image untarnished was still working overtime years after he'd finally been banished from office. 'And just how are you gonna accomplish this miraculous feat, big guy?!'

'Oh, you watch! I got ways, little miss! I got ways!', Guy promised.

Certain her partner was about to fail epically and fall flat on his face, Em shook her head. 'Remember: we agreed no assassinations.', she warned, certain he couldn't take out the Untouchables without cheating. 'Rules are rules...'

Guy wagged his finger like the proverbial wag-the-dog. 'Oh, nothing so pedestrian as a bullet for Mister and Missus Douche Bag.', he insisted. 'No, no – only an ironic end to their political shenanigans will do.' An epic plot congealing in his head, the big agent smiled and rubbed his hands together mischievously. '"No Malarkey" as his former second-in-chief promised during the campaign.', he mocked.

Em grunted. 'Oh, now you're invoking "Grab Ass"?! That's dangerous turf, my friend.'

Dismissing Mail-In from the conversation Agent Guildencrantz cracked his knuckles. 'This one's gonna be so ironic you'll swear a magnet would stick to it! Prepare to be awed, little miss!! Prepare to......'

Fade to White

'This shit be ice cold...Michelle Pfeiffer that white gold. This one for them hood girls, them good girls, straight masterpieces. Stylin', high as fuck, livin' it up in the city. Blah, blah, blah, blah, gotta kiss myself I's so pretty...'

Mouthing his own private version of Bruno Mars' *Uptown Funk*, former President of the United States Barrack Hussein Obama posed to admire his profile in the mirror. 'Who did those white Euro-trash fucks give the Nobel Peace Prize to? Barrack Obama. Who got the Affordable Healthcare Act passed? Me, Mister Barrack Hussein Obama. Who is responsible for all Donald Trump's successes? Me, Mister Barrack "mutha-fuckin'" Hussein Obama. Thank you, President Obama.' Getting back into the song he momentarily stopped admiring himself in the mirror and started shaking his booty out of time to the music: 'I'm too hot! Hot damn! Say my name you know who I am: BAR-RACK! Hot damn! Am I bad 'bout that money? Obama break it down...'

Oblivious to her preening show bird husband's absurd gyrations former First Lady Michelle Obama lay on the bed engrossed in her latest copy of *Ebony*. The disinformation campaign to convince the sheep was going well. Nearly every major cultural outlet was promoting the false narrative that African-Americans were the victims of "Systemic Racism". Major studies proved that wasn't the case (and the obvious fact that her unqualified and economically inept husband had been elected president solely <u>because</u> he *was* **black** aside) it still seemed so easy to convince the less intelligent people in America to take to the streets to protest something that didn't exist. All you had to do to get them to buy woke-believe was to constantly shove it in their face and not allow anyone else to present the facts – as Hitler once said: "The bigger the lie the more people will believe it." Repetition hammered the message into the people's little brains like passages in a children's book. Got pulled over because you were speeding?

71

It's because you black. Didn't get the job you wanted? It's cause you black. Got questioned by the cops? It can't be because some thug committed a crime and you fit the description. No, it's because you the victim of "Systemic Racism". You a slave to the Man – even if you make millions of dollars playing some game in a fucking stadium and got models begging on they knees to suck your big black dick! You gots to hate on them privileged white folks who gots that great job workin' at the Walmart! It ain't racist cause they white! They bad peoples who done you wrong! It were American slave labor that built the Pyramids of Egypt! The world was perfect until America the Racist Whitey came along! And if Whitey ain't suckin' the liberal gender-neutral organ, he be a Nazi!

Reminded of how ignorant of world history her voting demographic was Michelle Obama chuckled. Hillary Clinton was right about one thing: the average Democratic voter really wasn't too bright. Rich White Bitch still fucked up in 2016, though. 'You got another speaking gig?', she inquired, turning her attention back to the ever-present matter of money. It was the only reason they went into politics in the first place – well, that and the fact that neither one of them was any good at anything else.

Barrack Hussein Obama paused his ridiculous anti-rhythmic gyrations. 'Got a charity speaking engagement booked for next Sunday.', he promised.

'How much does it pay?'

'Five thousand a plate.'

'Expensive dishes.', she noted appreciatively. 'What's the charity?'

Barrack shrugged that he didn't care. 'Oh, some bullshit climate change thing. Dumb asses are still protesting the weather. There weren't any seasons before cars came along, you know.', he noted wryly.

'What's our split?'

'Eighty-twenty. The twenty goes into the "Climate Defense Fund".'

It was a good haul and she had to begrudgingly approve the cut they were receiving. 'Clinton's wetting their beaks?', she queried, knowing the bastards had to be skimming something off the top from somewhere.

'Of course. Who do you think's on the board of the CDF?'

Feeling her profits getting pinched yet again Michelle Obama grimaced. In spite of being out of office, Bill and Hillary's well oiled pay-for-play kick-back machine was still working overtime. The Clintons had built a 200 million dollar fortune out of a job that paid less than a half million a year – and somehow their idiotic supporters still managed to delude themselves into dismissing their obvious corruption as a Republican political ploy.

Michelle was committed to learning all she could about how the Clintons did it so she could play the same confidence game after they were gone. Sooner or later the sheep would stop buying her husband's bullshit – he was old news and real history was a bitch that would come back to eventually bite the Obamas in the ass. Being America's first black president wasn't enough to bring in the big bucks anymore and even propaganda movies like *Southside With You* would eventually not be enough to boost Barrack's flagging popularity. Trump's successful administration had burst the bubble on their fiction. 'Still good money, though.'

'Hey, you give me a dollar, I'll give you change!', B.O. sassed, renewing his flailing gyrations.

Breaking a smile, Michelle Obama shook her head. Their private little joke never got old; Barrack had changed America all right – he'd made everything worse. But it was the obvious play on words: getting millions of dollars in donations, pocketing a huge chunk then giving the voter pennies of "change" in return – that made her laugh her ass off every time. If a hood rat did that to you you'd say you just got conned, but put a smooth-talking nigga in a fancy suit up on stage and stupid-ass white people ponied up the bucks like they just got passed the collections basket at church. Growing the size of the government so they would have a greater pool to skim off the top from was the way Democrats did business and always made things worse. Obamacare was a perfect example: adding government made things more expensive and took away citizens' ability to choose their own doctor.

Senator McCain (suffering from a brain tumor and mentally incompetent) had managed to keep President Trump from repealing it, but beginning in 2021 the hospital cost transparency he'd ordered was lowering healthcare costs by making hospitals compete for patients on the free market. Democratic policies and Obama's dumb ass former VP had already fucked that up, though; Democratic-induced inflation and supply-chain disruptions were killing every industry. Labor costs were up but company profits were down over 10% and employee wages weren't keeping pace with the cost of living. Democrats had turned America into a total shit show.

Ignoring the reality of his epic incompetence and still engrossed by his reflection in the mirror petty-boy Barrack paused and waved to himself. 'Stop! Wait a minute. Fill my cup put some liquor in it! Take a sip, sign a

check – Julio get the stretch! Ride to Harlem, Hollywood, Chicago City...
if I show up, you gotta show out...I's smoother than a fresh jar a Skippy!'

Ignoring her narcissistic husband's preening Michelle tossed the magazine aside and paged through the rest of her stack. The cover of one promised a small article on First Lady Melania's excellent charity work over the
past four years. 'Damn skinny little white ass ho.', she grumbled jealously.
'Bitch shouldn't be on no damned cover.'

In spite of the fact that it stuck in Michelle's craw it was undeniable
that President Trump's wife was obviously the most beautiful First Lady
ever. She'd been a professional model and in spite of the press dissing her
for her wise clothing choices Melania was clearly the first prize winner in
both style and beauty. Even Jacqueline Kennedy couldn't hold a candle
to her. The deposed First Lady wasn't just a world class beauty, however;
she was also kind, forthright and extremely intelligent – and spoke five
languages fluently. While the press treated Michelle's daughters with kid
gloves they'd gone after Melania's and Donald's teenaged son Barron Trump
with a vengeance – and in a truly despicable outrage his little four year old
grand daughter had actually received death threats. Even the worst liars of
the press core had difficulty going after Barron Trump, though; he was an
exceptionally tall and handsome young man all the young ladies swooned
over. More desirable and intelligent than JFK junior he'd no doubt have
his choice of women when it came time to decide who he wanted to settle
down with.

The offspring of a con man, Michelle's own daughters regrettably
wouldn't be in the running. 'Hey, what's this new product you're supposed
to be hocking?', she asked him to get her mind off it.

'Some tanning/massage lotion.'

'FDA approved?'

Unwilling to pause his "dancing" Barrack Hussein shook his empty
cranium like a bobble head. 'Not yet. Got some chemicals in it that are on
the iffy list. One of the ingredients is derived from the oil of some kind of
endangered snake that lives only in the Amazon. We get a 20% stake when
I get it pushed through, though.', he promised.

'You say it's a massage oil?'

The flailing fool reluctantly stopped his gyrations. 'Supposed to be, yeah.'

Michelle stacked her magazines and put them beside the bed. 'Well
then, get your skinny little brown ass over here and rub me down, bitch.'

Subservient to his queen's whims Barrack Hussein Obama lowered his eyes. 'Yes, ma'am.'

As was their nightly ritual the forty-fourth President of the United States knelt down in front of his boss and kissed his wife's toes one by one.

'That's a good little bitch.', Queen Michelle cooed, shoving his face away with her foot once he'd accomplished his task. 'Now strip and go get the lotion.'

'Yes, ma'am.'

While the Queen of the household took off her clothes Barrack rumpled his up and tossed them in the corner. Both of them naked now he retrieved the contraband massage oil from the closet. 'Come on dance, jump on it...if yo' sexy then flaunt it....if you freaky then own it...'

Unimpressed by his pathetic dancing display The First Queen grimaced. 'Quit acting the damned fool and get your dumb brown ass over here! You look like a goddamned faggot!'

Called out for his swishy tendencies Barrack dutifully knelt by the bed. Michelle turned over and pointed at her shoulders. Opening the bottle he squirted a sizable load on his palms and began smoothing it down her back. 'Anyway, we'll make a killing.', he promised, knowing wealth always tempted her. 'They figure with my connections I can ram it straight though.'

Ignoring his boasting, once her back was all wet Queen Michelle flipped over so he could do her front. Soon her skin was all shiny with snake oil.

Feeling exceptionally alive a very pleased Michelle Obama stretched her arms over her head. This lotion rocked – her skin was positively tingling. 'Your turn.', she declared.

She rose and Barrack happily took her place on the bed. With gusto she squirted the oil on his person and rubbed him down. Soon he too was glistening head to toe with lotion. 'Hmm. Seems like this stuff's got some unintended side effects.', she smirked, liking how he was responding to the magic snake oil. 'Could be very good for sales.'

'Mmm-hmmm...', he agreed.

In the mood now, Queen Michelle the First locked Barrack's knees together. Pinning them back against his chest she straddled his hips with her own. 'Seems appropriate we honor the source of this wonderful oil by doin' it in the Amazon position.', she declared.

'The Amazon?', he bleated.

Pressing his knees harder against his chest she nodded and replied sternly, 'Yes – that's what this is called. Now, lay there and take it, bitch!'

Dominated like always, forty-four nodded meekly. This was worse than when the camera mikes overheard him boasting to Iron-man Putin how flexible he could be after the election!

*   *   *

Following their reverse coitus the former Forty-Forth President and First Queen Lady of the United States slept peacefully. With no sycophants to part from their money today there was no pressing reason to get up and it was ten o'clock before either bothered to stir from their oil stained bed. Eventually the bathroom beckoned, however, and Michelle padded off to go wee-wee. Relieved of the reason she got up the dominant half of their partnership ambled back to bed. The soft morning light was shining beautifully through the bedroom window catching sight of the four-poster – but it was what she saw laying in it that drew her attention. In the place where her husband Barrack Hussein should be was someone else, a man she did not recognize. 'What the – ?'

Thinking she was seeing a mirage Michelle Obama rubbed her eyes and realized abruptly that the hands and arms against her face did not look like they should. Her skin was mottled, a mixture of the normal deep brown she was accustomed to and lighter discolored patches. 'What the fuck – !', she exclaimed in shock.

Heart pumping like she'd just seen a ghost she raced back to the bathroom and flipped on the light. In the mirror a hideous specter stared back at her. 'AHHHH!!! AHHH!!! WHAT THE FUCK!!!', she screamed at the top of her lungs.

'What? What is it?', forty-four exclaimed, bolting upright in bed.

From the bathroom the former first lady screamed again. 'WHAT-THE-FUCK!!!!!!'

'What?!!', sleepily repeated Barrack with annoyance. This was worse than the night of Benghazi! He just wanted to curl up and go back to sleep!

A flailing motion came from inside the spacious toilet chamber. 'Ahhh! Come here! Come here, quick! Get in here right now!!!'

Half-awake Barrack Hussein Obama drowsily stumbled out of bed towards the bathroom only to stop and stare stupidly at the woman standing in the doorway. Sounding just like his wife the creature he saw there bore absolutely no resemblance to her. Whoever she was she looked absolutely dreadful! Sweet Lucifer – what the fuck happened to his Queen Michelle?!!!

In horror Michelle Obama pointed at Barrack. 'Your skin!!! Your skin!!! Look at your skin!!!'

'What?!!!'

'Your skin!!!', she repeated. 'Look at your fucking skin, stupid!!!'

With rising trepidation Barrack Hussein Obama did as his queen commanded, looked down and beheld with unfathomable horror what had become of his beautiful person. His legs and knees and feet were no longer as they should be. They were no longer caramel brown. They were... they were....

'What the fuck was in that shit?!!!', Michelle screeched, bursting into tears.

'I don't fucking know!', blathered Barrack Hussein Obama. For the first time in his life the man with the gift of gab was at a complete loss for words. What the – !!!!!

At her wits end the former first lady grabbed at her curly hair only to have it come out in fist fulls. She looked at the matted mane in her hands in horror. 'Wh-wh-what the fuck did you d-do to us???!!!', she stammered.

Totally devoid of cool the finally awake fool of an ex-president backed away from the apparition that had somehow replaced his wife. 'Oh-my-God....oh-my-God...', Barrack Hussein murmured, on the verge of fainting to the floor like a schoolgirl.

'What the fuck...', breathed Michelle, ready to pass out herself. What could they do?! What could they do??!!! 'We need a doctor! We need to go to the doctor!!! Right away!!!'

*　　*　　*

Trying to hold it together, Dr. Isabel Merriweather looked back and forth between the patients in her office with trepidation. 'The test results have finally come in. I'm sorry to have to tell you this Mr. and Mrs. President....but I think we may be dealing with a permanent condition. Your skin seems to have been affected all the way down to the dermal layer. The cells that form new epidermis have apparently become.....permanently altered.'

Barrack Hussein Obama looked at his doctor in shock. 'What?', he gasped.

'Do-do you mean we'll always l-look this way?!!!', Michelle trembled.

Dr. Merriweather tilted her head sheepishly. The truth was she didn't know for sure. The chemicals they'd come into contact with were experimental and not FDA approved. 'Not exactly. The skin will most likely continue to lighten and even out and the mottling will disappear, but I'm afraid your skin tones won't ever return to normal.'

Nonplussed, Barrack and Michelle Obama stared at their personal physician with unconcealed horror. 'Can't you – can't you do a skin graft?!!!', forty-four finally exclaimed.

'No – ', Dr. Isabel declared, shaking her head adamantly to make sure her patients did not cling to that false hope. 'Not with this amount of skin. The scarring would be extensive and there's too great a risk of infection to even consider it. It's not an option.'

'But – but we can't look like this!', bleated Obama like a terrified ewe. 'My career! My speaking engagements!'

Merriweather shrugged impotently. 'I'm sorry, but there's absolutely nothing I can do. I'm still uncertain how the oil managed to do this to your skin.'

Rejecting absolutely what she'd just been told Michelle Obama grabbed her head in her hands and shook it vigorously. There had to be a way to fix this!!! There just had to be!!!! 'What – what about tanning treatments?!', she blurted, grasping at straws. 'Isn't the color of our skin determined by the amount of melanin in it?'

Dr. Merriweather tilted her chin to show that this was factually correct but again shook her head firmly in the negative. 'Normally, yes. But you have to remember that there has been extensive damage to your dermal layers. I'm afraid UV radiation – tanning – will almost certainly cause the rapid formation of metastatic skin cancers. You are both at extremely high risk for basal cell carcinoma. I strongly, strongly, *strongly* recommend you wear heavy sun screen and stay out of the sun! You'll be at great risk if you ignore this advice! Even getting a sunburn could be fatal! I'd also advise against make up of any kind. We simply don't know how your skin will react to it.'

Left with no recourse the distraught couple looked at each other, each ready to retch. No sun? No tanning?? No make up to cover their disfigurement???!!!!

'Isn't there some specialist you can send us to?', Michelle begged, nearly breaking into tears.

'I'll ask around to all of my contacts. Discreetly, of course.', Dr. Merriweather promised, acknowledging the sensitive nature of their particular situation. Given how many Americans' private information had become public due to the problems with Obamacare she'd have to be extraordinarily careful about how she worded her medical notes just to be sure in case it got hacked again and her notes got leaked. 'But for now the best thing you can do is stay inside and wear plenty of sunscreen. Maybe if we are lucky I'm wrong and this condition will resolve itself over time.'

Realizing there was nothing more she could do for her patients, Dr. Isabel Merriweather stood to signal an end to their visit. 'I realize this is a lot to process. Take some time. If you have any questions feel free to call. I'm always available to you, day or night.'

Former Queen First Lady Michelle Obama rubbed her face with her hands. She couldn't go on like this!!! She just couldn't!!!

'Thank you, doctor.', Barrack Hussein mumbled. He put his arms around his wife's shoulders and steered her out of the chair towards the door. 'Come on dear.'

Making sure their hats, Covid-masks and sunglasses were on to conceal their features he ushered Michelle out of Dr. Merriweather's office and made for the elevator. Once they were safely inside Barrack hit the button for the lobby.

'Damn you! Damn you and your snake oil! You stupid son-of-a-bitch!', Michelle screamed at him. 'Fucking asshole!!!'

She hit him several times in the shoulder then slugged Barrack in the head, knocking his hat, mask and shades off. As he reached down to pick up his disguise Barrack Hussein Obama caught sight of himself in the reflection of the shiny metal lining the inside of the elevator's walls. Straight grey-white hair, pale features....he was almost handsome....

For a white man.

*　　*　　*

'Ahhhh, fuuuuckkk!!!'

Staring at Guy in disbelief, a thoroughly demoralized, defeated and astonished Emily Rosenstern shook her head. She was sure she had him!

79

After whacking the crap out of her buddy by Epsteining the Clintons she was confident there was no way he could ever recover! But turning _Barrack Hussein Obama_ into a **white** guy?! How could she compete with that???

Grinning victoriously like Johnny in the famous Charlie Daniel's song _Devil Went Down to Georgia_ Guildencrantz crossed his legs. 'Game, set and match – Guildencrantz.', the big agent breezed.

Knowing the game had just flipped and she'd just gotten seriously one-upped, Emily rubbed her face with her hands. Turned 100% Caucasian instead of being only half white – for race-card playing Barrack Obama that was the ultimate political kiss of death! He accomplished _nothing_ as a senator – his career would have been over before it began if the smooth talking con man hadn't been able to shield himself behind the notoriety of becoming the nation's first black President! African-Americans voted for him at a rate of 98% in 2008 just because of the color of his skin! And he left office having increased the economic divide between every ethnic demographic! For Heaven's sake, he actually wanted _quotas_ based on a person's ethnic background to decide who got to work where, not how good the person was at his or her job! Barrack Obama was the poster-child for outright discrimination – the ultimate racist!!!

Faced with such a devastatingly perfect comeuppance for the most popular demigod in the deviously corrupt Democratic party, Emily was at a loss. She didn't have a clue how to reverse her fortunes in this little game of theirs! She was going to have to pick up the tab for an extravagantly expensive dinner if she didn't come up with some fantastic story – and quick!

She was only just beginning to formulate the very roughest of drafts for her desperate counter attack when a sudden commotion came from the room adjacent. Her training kicking in reflexively Agent Rosenstern immediately reached for her weapon. The move proved prescient but ultimately unnecessary when the door suddenly opened – and the sleepy-eyed imposter Mr. Grab Ass himself strode forth. Looking like an old rumpled suit tossed carelessly on the floor Joey B rubbed his bleary eyes. After a typical moment of disorientation the leader of the free world took in the Secret Service agents ordered to protect his person. 'Where's my wife?!', he demanded rudely.

'Your wife?', Guy replied. 'I'm afraid I don't know, sir.'

'I want my wife! My goddamned wife!', Sleepy Joe barked a second time.

Hoping to avoid getting pawed, Emily Rosenstern kept her behind planted firmly in her seat and pointed towards the door on the opposite side of the room far away. 'I think the First Lady is in the residence, sir.'

'Not that one!', stammered Creepy Joe, looking all out of sorts. 'My wife! My wife! I mean – I mean – my sister! No, not her! Not my sister – ', he blathered, trying desperately to make sense of the fleeting thoughts bouncing around inside his senile scatterbrained, white-haired old head. 'My wife! My wife!', he repeated.

'Like my partner said we believe she's in the residence, sir.', answered Guy patiently.

Biden looked left then right, then dug into his pants pockets like he was looking for his keys. Completely befuddled, after a moment he stopped and remembered why he'd left the safe confines of his jerk off room. He was looking for someone – who was it again?

Seeing his obvious mental confusion Agent Guildencrantz spoke up. 'Do you need help, sir?'

'No, I don't need no damned help, you dog-faced, monkey-butted pony show!', Sleepy Joe cursed at him. 'Goddammit, I told you – I'm looking for my wife!'

Mustering as much patience as he could Guildencranz glanced at Rosenstern knowingly. Swallowing his anger he reached for his wrist. 'Central: Current location, Caregiver?'

After a momentary pause his comm sprang to life. 'Caregiver location – section 47, residence.'

'Your wife is in residence, sir.', Agent Guildencrantz relayed to Obama's former understudy.

The Vice President from 2008 to 2016 shook his head in confusion then angrily stamped his feet like a preschooler throwing a temper tantrum. 'Not my wife-wife!', he roared, his face turning fire engine red. 'My wife! The other one! The nigger! The nigger-wife!! The fucking nigger wife!!'

Realizing Uncle Joe wasn't looking for Aunt Jill – his primary caregiver, hence her code name – Agent Rosenstern's brows knitted. She wanted to get the dotard away from here and out of their hair as quickly as possible. Who in the hell was the old buffoon wanting them to find for him??? 'Do you mean...Mrs. Obama...sir?', she suggested, trying to placate the racist old fool who occupied President Trump's office.

The blustering former Vice-President shook his head so forcefully it almost seemed like it might fly right off his shoulders. 'No! No! No! No! No!! Not the [racial slur]'s [racial slur]-wife – *my* [racial slur]-wife! The black bitch who was saying I was a racist! The one who said – who said – the thing! When we were on stage! During – during – the – the debates! The black one! The [racial slur]!! The one from that state! You know! The one who – who – who – the funny one! Yeah, the funny one! The one who always laughs! The laughing [racial slur]! The one who's family owned all them slaves! The [racial slur] slaver!'

Subjected to his offensively racist rant Emily Rosenstern's face turned pale. Eying Biden like he'd taken more leave of his senses than usual she slowly and carefully inquired: 'Do you mean "the Vice-President", sir? Is that who you are talking about?'

'Yes, goddammit!', he retorted angrily. 'Don't you know who the fucking Vice-president is?!'

Seriously doubting the imbecile she'd been assigned to protect knew, Agent Rosenstern tapped her wrist communicator and put in a query as to the VP's current location. Knowing that the only places she knew for certain Central *wouldn't* find Harris was at the southern border (or in front of a hostile press) Emily waited impatiently for an answer. The longer Sleepy Creepy was around her the more likely she was to get her butt patted or her shoulders rubbed.

At last her radio crackled to life. 'Hyena is at "The Spa".'

'Sir? She's at the Spa.', Rosenstern parroted.

'The Spa! The Spa! Why isn't that black bitch taking care of the thing! That thing I sent her to fix! Why in the hell...?! Why is she...in Arizona...? No Afghanistan....? Oh, shit....where in hell's the goddamned Spa again?!'

The big Guy cleared his throat. 'She is in California, sir.', he supplied.

'Well, why the fuck didn't you just say so?! What the hell's the matter with the people around here! Can't get a straight answer from anybody! It's all fucked up! Fucked up and stupid! And nobody can get a damned thing done right! They can't even make the fucking teleprompter work so – so – so the speeches are good! I don't know what the hell's the matter with people! I'm surrounded by idiots!', he ranted. 'Things weren't like this when – when – the goddamned black guy was here! And fuckin' Trump had a smooth runnin' engine! We tried to throw a monkey wrench in the gears but it just kept on hummin'! I swear it's ol' Anonymous that's doin' me in! It's that fucker Anonymous! That fucker is a goddamned traitor! He's a goddamned fuckin' traitor! A goddamned fuckin' shit-toter!!!'

Little Sleepy Joe stamped his feet like a three year old then just as suddenly became ramrod stiff. Feeling something happening he reached around and felt the back of his pants. His flushed skin turned a deeper shade. 'Ungh. Oh, dammit. Shit. I – I...'

Knowing all too well what had just happened, Guildencrantz thumbed his mike. 'Mail-In, Code Brown.', he said, trying to keep his voice down so he didn't announce it to the whole west wing. 'I say again Central: Mail-In, Code Brown, section 40.'

The voice across the receiver sounded tired. 'Please repeat Forty. I didn't catch all of that – did you say: Mail In, Code Brown?'

'That's affirm, Central. Mail-In, Code Brown, section 40.'

'Again?', dispatch repeated incredulously.

Though control couldn't see, Agent Guildencrantz nodded. 'Yes, Central. Again.'

The voice on the comm paused. Biden was tedious most days, but now... 'Dispatching the nurse. Request you remain on site.'

'Copy that central. Will remain at present location.'

Guy thumbed the channel closed. He pitied the poor changing nurse. This was the third time Joey B had had an accident this week!

Though she didn't want to get anywhere near him – especially now that he had a smelly load in his shorts – Emily rose and ushered the old dotard towards the corner of the room. She hoped the nurse arrived soon. Officer Grab Ass tended to try to run away when he shit his drawers. He'd even been known to leave a trail of "breadcrumbs", so to speak. 'You just wait here, sir.', she placated. 'The nurse will get you all fixed up very soon.'

Biden nodded sheepishly and for a moment Agent Rosenstern felt a twinge of pity for the incontinent old man. That sympathy disappeared as soon as he leaned into her side and snaked his arm around her waist. Wanting to get his paws off her person Em looked helplessly to her partner. 'Can we get her here soon, please?', she pleaded.

Aware of Emily's predicament instead of calling to hurry the unfortunate nurse along Guildencrantz came over and gallantly relieved her of her burden. 'Here, sir, allow me.', he said, disentangling Creepy Joe's hand from his partner's ass. 'Miss Emily here is nursing a bad heel. Nothing to be concerned about but we don't want it to become an issue.'

'Don't want anything bad to happen to that athletic body.', mumbled the lecherous old fart, reluctantly releasing his hold on Agent Rosenstern's person.

The burly agent took hold of the elderly dotard he'd been assigned to watch over and steered him away from his partner. 'Agent Rosenstern – ', Guy announced loudly to make sure half-deaf Joey B heard clearly. 'Will you go out into the hall and make sure the nurse knows exactly where to find us, please?'

'Of course.', Emily replied with relief. Mouthing a silent "thank you" to her friend she slipped with alacrity out the door.

With nothing to do and no one left to grope Biden stood sullenly in the corner and waited for the nurse to usher him off to the diaper changing station. Forced to endure the smell of his charge Agent Guildencrantz held his head as high as he could to reduce his exposure. The wait was long and Guy's nose was almost accustomed to the horrific stench when the knob on the door finally turned. Emily held the portal open and a twenty-some-thing nurse walked in. Dressed in scrubs the girl was pretty but held herself with that vague air of disillusionment all young people had when they transitioned from the realm of empty campaign promises to actually working in a real-life Democratic administration. Her official government job was health care nurse but in reality she was just another janitor; she got to wipe Joseph Robinette Biden's ass for him and then help him redress. 'Ready, Mr. President?', she inquired, trying to mask her growing disdain for the old coot.

'Sure! Sure, young lady!', he answered with glee. Not bothering to hide his appraisal of her nubile form he said, 'Looks like I had myself another accident! I gotta lay off those enchiladas from now on! Spicy food seems to run right through me!'

'Of course, Mr. President.', she replied, accepting his fictions like she always did.

She came closer and he snaked his hand around her like he needed her help to walk. A trained nurse she pulled his arm up around her shoulder to bear the weight. In seconds Creepy Joe had it around her waist again. 'Let's get going, Samantha.', he ordered.

'It's Sarah, sir.'

'Of course, of course! I knew that! I was just testing you to see if you remembered.', he replied absurdly.

The changing area was in another room and the young nurse steered him out the door while doing her best to restrain the old coot's roving hands. Even so Biden's palm "accidentally" found her derriere several times along the way.

Feeling intense empathy for the poor girl Rosenstern frowned sadly as they disappeared down the hall. 'Is it really true he shit his pants when he met the Pope?', she whispered to Guildencrantz.

Her partner's lips pursed. It was true but it wasn't something they or any of the other agents talked about. After the way Biden had just mistreated his partner and the young nurse, though, the big man couldn't resist poking a little fun at the lecherous creep. '*Depends.*', he answered.

Depends? Depends on what? Suddenly getting the thrust of Guy's joke, Emily's eyes lit up. Biden was wearing adult undergarments! As often as he was incontinent it made perfect sense – but damn!!! Once was enough but the old fart was shitting himself so regularly they had him in diapers!

She exhaled sadly. Not that he'd actually been legally elected, but how could anybody – even in the swamp – voluntarily install a racist, mentally-deficient, never-having achieved-a-damn-thing in over forty years in government buffoon into the highest office in the world?! Someone who was so old and decrepit he regularly dropped a load in his pants? What were they thinking??? What was the upside here??? After the news of the huge bribe Creepy-Joe Grab Ass accepted from Ukraine when he was Vice-President broke why didn't they just admit they'd made a huge mistake and Impeach him?! How could any Democrat actually think their political career would survive *not* voting to remove Joe Biden from office?! How could they possibly –

The Secret Service Agent's face suddenly went pale. Removing Mail-In would put "The Toe" in charge. Oh-my-merciful-God!!! That bitch was so over the top crazy she might actually start World War III!!!

Compelled to talk about the former crazy prosecutor/crazy senator who'd illegally been appointed understudy for the highest office in the land, Agent Rosenstern cleared her throat. With Mail-In off in the changing room having his diapers changed she knew who all of America needed to see skewered next: VP twenty-eight percent and falling herself: Kamala Harris – aka the Hyena.

The Hyena: Excerpts From The Case Files of Dr. Miriam Maximueller-Ford, MD, PhD

Seated in the dank room that served as her office Dr. Miriam Maximueller-Ford paused the video recording she had just begun to stream. A diet Pepsi was fizzing in the cozy just to the right of her mouse pad and she paused to take a drink before continuing. In the twelve years since she'd earned her post-medical school PhD in clinical psychopathology this was the first time she'd been presented with a case like this. The patient was *famous* – and extremely well connected. It was almost inconceivable to think that a person who had been elevated to such a high office – even illegally – was truly mentally ill. Yes, all leaders (with the notable exception of Jesus Christ) suffered from a least a touch of narcissism and megalomania, but this was different. The last example she could remember of a world leader being truly insane was Adolph Hitler – and the whole world paid the price for that horrible mistake. Thank God that in 2024 President Donald Trump had been re-elected (for the second time) by a sizable margin and the world had averted another global war.

Striving for objectivity, Maximueller-Ford put such idle thoughts out of her mind. She was a scientist and physician – she would perform her initial examination without bias before arriving at her own independent diagnosis. According to all the previous doctors who'd been involved with the case this patient had a long history of unusual behavior and to obtain context she needed to view the public video case file material to see for herself if (in her professional opinion) their opinions had merit.

She looked over at her Alexa. She knew that thanks to the Freedom and Privacy Oversight Act of 2026 the little contraption could no longer spy on her but she still didn't trust it. How many times had the US government assured citizens that their privacy rights were being protected while at the same time some secret star chamber in a long forgotten wing of an unlisted black building was unmasking them and had them under illegal surveillance? History was a song put on repeat – and absolute power corrupted absolutely. 'Begin playback.', she ordered uneasily.

The voice-activated spying machine did as she commanded and the montage began rolling. 'So Senator Harris – ', former CBS reporter Noral O'Donnell began. 'You've been called "The Most Liberal Senator" by the non-partisan independent Congressional Vote Tracker, GovTrack.us. Do you dispute this label? If elected do you plan on strongly pushing forward the progressive agenda?'

Sitting across from O'Donnell Senator Kamala Harris burst into laughter. When after several seconds she still hadn't stopped laughing, the woman opposite her asked more specifically, 'You've publicly supported the Green New Deal, Medicare-for-all and legalization of marijuana. Is that a Socialist perspective?'

The video capture of the campaigning Kamala Harris of 2019 stopped chuckling immediately. Trying to project a sympathetic persona the presidential hopeful's expression turned suddenly emotional. 'It is the perspective of a woman who grew up a black child in America, who was also a prosecutor, who also has a mother who arrived here at the age of 19 from India, who also likes hip hop.'

Confused by the complete irrelevancy of her interviewee's response O'Donnell's brow furrowed. Harris began to laugh again nervously.

'You plan to push for the legalization of marijuana.', the former CBS reporter continued, shifting to another topic. 'But as prosecutor you rigorously prosecuted marijuana drug offenders, pushing for sentences much harsher than your opponents. In fact, you disproportionately pushed for the harshest sentences against other people of color...'

Harris' incessant laughter increased in volume and pitch, drowning out the rest of what O'Donnell had to say. Getting no further response the CBS hostess changed the subject to something completely banal.

Dr. Maximueller-Ford expected more content but the screen suddenly went dim. Her cubicle suddenly feeling too dark for comfort she was about to order Alexa to pause the vid so she could turn on a light when the screen lit up again and another video started. This one was a clip from the Late Show with Stephen Colbert recorded the year following the O'Donnell interview. Maximueller-Ford remembered Colbert. Promoted by the establishment as a "Conservative Talk Show Host" Colbert's body of work had proved him to be exactly the opposite. Before the Honesty in Media Act – the act which prohibited media platforms from acting as unregistered campaign donors – he had been particularly adversarial towards President Donald Trump and anyone else who promoted American interests over globalism. Eventually Colbert was dumped (like the rest of the liberal talk show programs) when ownership of the networks changed and anti-American interests were no longer allowed to dominate American streaming services. 'Now that you've been anointed the Vice-Presidential candidate for Joe Biden you've just been endorsed on Twitter by Alexander Soros, son of multi-billionaire George Soros.', Colbert began, highlighting the fact that a foreign interest was promoting Harris on social media like it was a good thing. 'Is that right?'

Giggling, Harris nodded.

'But when you dropped out of the Presidential race you were only polling at 3%. How do you think that helps Joe Biden?'

Kamala guffawed and then smiled broadly. 'Well, four would be better, but three is all it will take against Donald Trump.', she assured the audience.

Despite his professional allegiances Colbert couldn't resist taking a dig at her. 'But you openly accused Joe Biden of being a racist during the primary. Now that you're on his ticket how do you think that will affect his candidacy?'

Senator Harris responded with a blithe chuckle. Once her laughter died down her face turned cold as a stone. Lips in a thin line she stared at the host seated across from her like a zoom chat screen that had just frozen up.

Faced with the task of promoting a staggeringly inept candidate, Colbert blinked. 'So...I take it you don't think Joe Biden is a racist anymore?', he suggested, teeing up the ball for her.

Harris abruptly shook her head and giggled like someone had just rebooted her system. 'No, no. Just during the primary, just during the primary...politicians say a lot of things during the primaries.'

'Is that right?', said Colbert with a frown. 'Makes you wonder what to believe.'

'Oh – ', she began to chuckle once again.

Her laughter went on and on until the screen once again faded to black. This time Dr. Miriam was ready for it, though, and as expected the monitor again lightened. The date on the vid said 2021. Kamala was outside in the open air surrounded by reporters.

'Ms. Vice-President – ', a female reporter began, making no mention of the clear and very recent election fraud which illegally installed Harris into power. 'With Covid-19 keeping so many people at home many working mothers are worried about the state of their children's education and well being. Depression, suicide and drug abuse among school aged children and especially teenagers are at all time highs. How you do answer work-- '

Kamala Harris burst out in hysterical laughter drowning out the rest of what the reporter was trying to say. When her giggles momentarily stopped another journalist, this time male, cut in: 'Some have argued that teacher's unions are to blame for our kids falling behind in school. How do you answer critics who claim that remote learning is a failure? Wouldn't making teacher's salaries merit based be a more effective solution to improving classroom outcomes? And how do you respond to those two million women driven out of the workforce by Covid-19 lock downs? People suffering from the massive economic disruption Democrats have pushed for – despite the facts that students are seven times more likely to be hospitalized from the ordinary flue than Covid-19 and there has been no massive increase in mortality among teachers who have returned to "in person" classroom teaching?'

Harris face twisted into a grotesque mixture of surprise, smiles and finally a stone cold blank poker face. Fembot-Harris' Central Processing Unit seemed to have failed completely. 'Unfortunate....people....women people.'

That was all the newly minted "Vice President" had to say to the reporters' questions. Her responses to further inquiries devolved once again into a mixture of babbling punctuated by inane giggles.

The out door scene became engulfed by darkness only to be replaced by tape from sunny Jacksonville, Florida. Taken the same year as the previous vid this time Harris was at a podium reading from a teleprompter. She announced that she would only be talking about the American Rescue Plan. As the ARP bill had already passed it was old news and the press was far more interested in discussing the crisis currently ravaging the southern border. Undocumented illegal aliens were pouring into the United States at will, bringing Covid-19, other rare diseases, crime and terrorism with them.

With a magical wave of her hand Kamala dismissed the issue like a cloud of smoke. Unprepared for what should have been an obvious question from the press she stuck doggedly to her prepared script.

Later on during an interview with Democratically-aligned NBC's Lester Holt, however, the subject again turned to the ongoing crisis. 'Do you plan to visit the border, Ms. Vice-President?', he asked.

'We are going to the border.', Harris insisted. 'We've been to the border.'

'But you personally have not gone to the border as Vice-President, is that correct?', Holt noted.

'I haven't been to Europe either.', she blurted irritably. After the ill-advised quip passed her lips Harris seemed to realize she'd just stuck her foot in her mouth and was barking like a bitch on camera at one of her closest media allies. Her mood abruptly changed, her face lightened and she chuckled blithely. 'I don't understand the point of your question.', she declared nonsensically, attempting to deflect attention from the gigantic and very obvious bright blue elephant sitting right there beside her. 'I'm not discounting the importance of the border. Donald Trump put children in cages there and he is the source of the ongoing difficulties.'

A primary staple in Democratic campaigns (before the Honesty in Media Act ended his career), Holt tried to give the brand new illegally-anointed VP an opportunity to correct her blunder. 'On the border, there's obviously a lot of political pressure from Republicans in particular on this administration. What can the administration do, at least in the short term, to assure people that it's really taking steps to make sure that the people, children in particular, are being treated humanely?', he said, teeing up the question so the freshman VP could save face by offering his viewing public some benign, non-specific reassurances and place all the blame for the crisis on her Republican counterparts' shoulders.

Still missing the ball Harris meandered around for several minutes but her answers remained as incoherent as the rest of her interview. She couldn't seem to grasp that she was speaking to the voters and that the show was being taped for posterity.

While she half-listened to her new patient's continuing incoherent babbles Maximueller-Ford took a moment to look over a historical report provided by the archives so she could better understand the situation Harris and Holt were discussing. The background report was troubling. It seemed that back in the year 2021 the cages being referred to were not built by President Trump – as Harris was falsely claiming – but directly by his predecessor, Barrack Obama. By the numbers, the Biden administration separated illegal border-trespassers from the children traveling with them (many of whom were proven not to actually <u>be</u> their children but victims of sex-trafficking) at a much greater rate than the prior administration and the offending cages in question were now being crammed full to ten-times their previous capacity. While the border from 2017 to 2020 had been very secure, within a few months of Biden and Harris taking over it was in complete shambles, with only an estimated 1-in-10 illegal border crossings being interdicted by ICE.

Kamala Harris was barking stridently now and the good doctor turned her attention from the dossier back to the screen. 'I haven't gone to the border as Vice-President.', Harris said aggressively. 'But I have before and I'm sure I will again.'

So....Harris had been sent to inspect the cages but hadn't really gone to do so, mused Maximueller-Ford. Interesting. Why didn't she go to the border?

Her idle pondering was interrupted by a video taken less than one month later. The former Senator installed as VP was discussing some hackneyed piece of governmental trivium when a reporter interrupted and asked her the tremendously important, terribly obvious question on everyone's mind: What was the current administration's plan to save the unprotected American citizens who found themselves abandoned in Afghanistan following Biden's abrupt and completely unannounced withdrawal of the American forces President Trump had stationed there to protect them?!!! Americans and American allies were being harassed, physically assaulted and taken into custody to be tortured and murdered by the Taliban terrorists responsible for 9/11! Prior to the coupe d'etat that removed President Trump from office the Taliban had been virtually wiped out and the few that remained confined to the tiniest out-of-the-way sectors of Afghanistan. Now the murderers responsible for the worst terrorist attack on American soil were in complete control of the whole Middle Eastern country!

Kamala Harris burst out in laughter like it was somehow absurd for the Vice-President of the United States to be asked to discuss any plans being made to save the helpless American citizens who found themselves trapped without warning by her administration's inept and precipitous withdrawal.

'Hold on, hold on, hold everybody.', she said, continuing to laugh. Just as abruptly her laughter switched off like water from a faucet. Harris' face turned deadly serious. 'I want to talk about two things, first Afghanistan. We couldn't have a higher priority right now and in particular our priority is making sure that we safely evacuate American citizens. Afghans who work with us, Afghans at risk, including women and children and that is one of our highest, if not the highest priority right now.', she double-talked.

Sitting in her dark office, Dr. Maximueller-Ford's brows knitted. Was it the highest or one of the highest priorities? If it truly _was_ important why didn't Harris talk about it as soon as she began speaking? Why wasn't she giving the press any details? Why these vague off-hand assurances about a critical situation where time was of the essence and American lives were at stake – lives she was duty bound by her oath of office to protect at all costs?

Troubled by these glaring omissions the physician-psychologist scratched her head. Should she consider Antisocial Personality Disorder as a possible diagnosis? Was Harris what is commonly known as a "Sociopath"?

The good doctor was just considering that very real possibility when the view changed to one of former "View" co-host Meghan McCain. Daughter of Donald Trump's late outspoken political enemy, Senator John McCain, the woman seemed to be seconding that line of thinking: 'Laughing at the crisis this administration has created out of thin air, craven Vice President Kamala Harris looks just like Joaquin Phoenix in the 2019 film "Joker". What is _wrong_ with this person?'

The television screen went dark and remained that way. Dr. Maximueller-Ford waited for more but the vids of Harris' public appearances had ended. After all the newly anointed VP's debacles the Democrats had decided the wisest course of action was to keep her away from the cameras and hope the public forgot about her.

Troubled by what she had seen – and by the historical fact that a year later in 2022 (many months removed from Democratically induced disaster that was Afghanistan) Americans remained trapped there at the mercy of terrorists – Dr. Miriam Maximueller-Ford MD, PhD sat back in her chair and thrummed her fingers on the desk in front of her pensively. Based on the public video evidence, even in 2021 it was impossible to deny that something was deeply, deeply wrong with the mental state of Kamala Harris. The recordings showed clear behavioral abnormalities – inappropriate laughter, sudden mood swings, rambling in public. Though she hadn't yet examined her personally it was obvious even to a lay person that Kamala Harris was not right in the head. The most obvious diagnosis in the differential was Pseudobulbar Affect; an independent examination would need to be performed before she could confirm that.

Maximueller-Ford sighed. Harris, like Joe Biden, had been very careful to avoid medical examinations during her tenure in office. She obviously knew she was sick and because of her mental illness refused to be examined and get medical treatment. The lure of power was too great and Harris just didn't want to give it up. The secret shadow puppeteers of 2020 – the cabal who thrust her illegally into power – must have known she was ill, but obviously believed that because of her mental deficiencies they could control her. So they didn't lose their influence Soros and his buddies protected Harris and Biden at all costs and kept the facts from the public. They were a conspiracy of traitors intent on enslaving and depopulating the world. Only Take Back America had stopped them.

Thanking God World War Three had been averted Dr. Miriam Maximueller-Ford took in a deep breath and exhaled it slowly. Kamala Harris had earned several nicknames during her brief tenure in government, including "Kamalatoe" for her cunt-like behavior to the staff and "Joe's Joker" for her clear resemblance to the titular Batman villain of the same name. But because of her consistently inappropriate laughter at clearly unfunny things and predatory conduct in her former role as prosecutor the one that suited her most was the code name used by the clandestine protection services: "The Hyena". Known for its vicious bone crunching bite hyenas of the wild were either dirty scavengers or pack hunters, and one type, the spotted-variety, matriarchal in the extreme.

The good doctor looked with trepidation at the remaining files she had teed up in queue. When Kamala Harris went completely off the rails and turned to a life of crime "The Hyena" was the name she chose for herself. Thus far Maximueller-Ford had only viewed the public archives the average lay person could view on YouTube; the rest of the former Vice President's files weren't assessable to the general public. These were the ones that had given her previous physicians nightmares. These were the ones that got Kamala Harris committed for life to the Arkam Asylum for the Criminally Insane.

Dr. Miriam Maximueller-Ford was about to learn precisely why. 'Play the video labeled People's Exhibit One.', she said, steeling herself.

* * *

Guildencrantz groaned plaintively. 'Girl, you're bummin' me out!'

Standing dutifully on the opposite side of the door like a good secret service agent while her "boss" got his diapers changed, Emily Rosenstern gave him a put upon look. 'Hey, it was an *American Horror Story*! I thought it was good!'

Guy shook his head. 'Too close to home, man.'

Disappointed he hadn't liked her tale his female partner shook her head. Harris was a hydrogen bomb waiting to go off! If Biden wasn't such a disaster (and it wouldn't kill their already hopeless 2022 election chances dead) the Dems would have found a way to replace her dumb ass already rather than just keep her on "house arrest".

Still it wasn't fair for Guy to fault her story just because the lead character was off her nut – pretty much every Democrap was a disaster these days! 'You didn't like me committing Hairy-ass to the "Arkam Asylum for the Criminally Insane"?', she pressed, thinking it was a perfectly poetic coupe d' grace for someone who went by the code name "The Hyena". 'You know, like in Batman?'

Guildencrantz scoffed. 'Batman should be campy – if you're gonna go "Batman bat-shit crazy", you gotta be campy.', he asserted.

Leaning against the door hinges, Agent Rosenstern gritted her teeth so she didn't slug her burly co-worker in the arm. There was just no pleasing some people! 'You're just pissed because it was a good story! I put her in the crazy house where she belongs!'

'You're makin' me crazy.', he needled.

Em was about to give him what-for when the portal to the infirmary suddenly creaked open. In danger of getting flattened she quickly leaped out of the way.

'Your security detail is here to take you back to your office, sir.', the young nurse announced loudly as she ushered Joseph Biden through the door. Looking disheveled the pretty girl wore an expression on her face that practically screamed: "Please save me from this dirty old man! He keeps touching me!"

Coming to the molested nurse's rescue Guildencrantz took Biden by the arm and lead him away so the girl he kept trying to fondle was safely out of reach. Released from his evil clutches and rethinking her political allegiances she whispered "Thank God" under her breath and hurriedly closed the door after them.

'Where to? The Oval Office?', queried Guy.

Sympathizing with the wavering Democratic nurse but cringing at the thought of Biden behind the President's desk, Rosenstern's eyes flashed at her partner in alarm. The damage the infirm old fart did daily to the country with just a piece of paper and a pen! You absolutely _never ever_, _ever_ encouraged Joey B to go anywhere where he might exercise the illegally-usurped mighty powers of President of the United States! 'It's just past lunch time – I don't know about anyone else but I'm starving!', she redirected cheerfully, appealing to the old coot's newly emptied digestive tract. 'Why don't you go back to that nice room you spent the morning in, sir? What would you like to eat? I'll send word to the kitchen – we can have them whip up whatever you'd like!'

Charmed by the pretty agent and feeling his empty stomach now that he'd loosed the Kraken from his bowels, decrepit old Mr. Biden's head bounced up and down excitedly. 'Sounds good! I'll – I'll have me a ham sandwich! Would you folks like somethin'? They make me whatever I want! I'll have them fry us up some hamburgers and fries! Do you want cheese on your ham sandwich? I like tomatoes on my ham sandwiches – fresh off the grill with onions and cheese! Yup, ya gotta love hamburgers!'

Rambling like the dotard he was Joey B happily grabbed Agent Rosenstern by the waist as soon as she got within reach. Literally taking one on the booty for her country, Emily suffered being pawed the whole way as she led the former Vice-President down the hall far away from the Oval office.

'Oh, I think there's something wrong with my shoe!', she exclaimed once they reached the antechamber to the secret Square room Obama's chosen understudy spent his mornings masturbating in. Bending down she pretended to fiddle with the laces.

Knowing his pretty partner was just trying to get the lecherous politician's hands off her ass Guildencrantz immediately picked up the baton.

'Sir? What would you like to eat again?', he asked, waving his big hand in front of the old coot's nose to make sure he had his attention. 'Was it hamburgers or a ham sandwich? Do you still want fries with that?'

Easily distracted, the moron-in-chief shook his head. 'No, no, no young man. We were having chicken, right? I thought it was chicken – didn't I hear you call in for chicken? Or was it tuna?'

'I'll do it right away, sir.'

While Emily stayed safely out of Mr. Creepy's reach and pretended to adjust her shoelaces the big man called in their order. Not knowing what the fuck the demented old fart actually wanted Agent Guildencrantz asked for a selection of finger sandwiches. After he placed the order to keep Joey B occupied while they waited for it to arrive Guy kept "confirming" the details with him. Fortunately cold cut sandwiches don't take much time to prepare and after four purposefully jumbled up recitations of the lunch menu their food finally appeared: a processed meat chicken club on white bread lathered with mayo and topped with lettuce and tomato, a tuna sandwich on rye, and roast beef on wheat with a plate of baked kettle chips. True to form, Biden took the chicken sandwich. Still adhering to her keto-diet, Rosenstern nabbed the roast beef so she could easily discard the bun and left Guildencrantz the tuna. Served her foolish partner right for mentioning the Oval office to Joey Bird-brain!

Stuck eating with the career politician who'd traitorously usurped Trump's second term the agents ate in silence to minimize their interactions with him. With any luck they'd be able to talk little Joey B into laying down for another nap following lunch. Both agents shuddered to think what might happen if he took it in his feeble mind to actually try and "help" the country again. God only knew which country Russia would decide to invade next now that the whole world was sure the steaming flagship *U.S.S. America* had no one at the helm!

'You know, young lady, I never wanted to be President.', Creepy Uncle Joe blurted suddenly between bites. Now that he was stuffing his face he'd completely forgotten all about groping her ass a few moments earlier. 'My people kind of talked me into it. Told me there was no way I could lose, that they wouldn't let it happen. I was worried there for a while on election night, though. Wasn't looking too good. Polls didn't look too good after the debates, either. Nobody showed up to my rallies! I don't know how Donald does it, getting all those people to show up! All them crowds coming to see him in all kinds of weather! We had a good private phone call there a while back, me and Donnie. This was back in 2008, back when he and President Blackie were still here, a few months before the election that made me President. It's not like it used to be – it's hard to get public support when you're a Democrat! Nowadays we have to pay people to troll the internet to promote our stuff! Why does there have to be tape of everything?! Back when I had my first stroke – oh, when was that? Back in the 1920s, I think – we didn't have to worry about people looking stuff up on the internet. You had to turn on your phonograph player to get the news. It's not like it is nowadays – too much malarkey! That's all you hear on the internet! Malarkey! Anyway, thank God those ballots showed up a week before election night! For a while there we didn't know where we put 'em – some fool stashed them away somewhere and couldn't remember where she left 'em! I'm like that with birthday gifts for Jill – put a set of pearl earrings in the attic and couldn't find 'em for three years! Anyway, my people had those ballots ready and waiting eight months before the election. Think of what might've happened if we hadn't prepared?! Might have lost the whole damned thing!' Biden swallowed a load of chips then belched. 'People think I'm not prepared for stuff, but me and my people, we're prepared! My people had the wheels greased and we were ready to burn rubber! You gotta always have some emergency stuff stashed away somewhere just in case LOL.'

Wishing to God he'd been taping "President Biden" as he confessed Agent Guy swallowed the last bite of his sandwich and sat there in sullen stunned silence. For his deathly-pale partner opposite him it was all Rosenstern could do not to spit hers out and then puke what she'd already eaten all over the moronic bastard. This son-of-a-bitch – this illegitimate "president" – had just admitted, plainly and clearly, that the Democrats used fake ballots to steal the 2020 election! They knew it!!! Every sane person in America knew the election was a fraud!!! And the audits since then had confirmed it!!!

Finishing his meal like he didn't have a care in the world, Sleepy Joe yawned. Even for his advanced years he was old and frail and the food was making him drowsy. Making his best "command" decision of the month he announced to his reluctant lunch mates that he could use another nap. In no mood to argue (and wanting to smother him in his sleep for all the innocent Ukrainian men, women and children and pro-American Afghan allies his ineptitude had so far killed), Guy Guildencrantz escorted "The POTUS" back to his little square self-gratification cell. Secreted away from the public eye Joseph Robinette Biden Jr. was soon laying comfortably on the plush presidential couch counting sheep.

'Wow.', Guy hissed angrily, closing the door behind him. He felt like he had just tucked a mafia boss in bed for the night! Yes, Sleepy Joe had dementia...but Christ Jesus! The public rape of Lady Liberty!!! How could anyone do this???!!! How could the patriots in the Deep State allow this???!!!

Squirming in her seat Rosenstern wanted to rip her hair out. 'I can't believe how calm he is about it! Like it was no big deal!', she blanched.

The only response her partner could think of was to shake his head ruefully.

Hurting, Emily looked up at her big friend with big sad eyes. 'Still think my story about Kamalatoe Hairy-Ass was too dark?', she asked quietly.

'No.', he said morosely.

Searching anywhere she could for solace Emily rubbed her face. The United States of America, the country she loved and served with every fiber of her being, was in the hands of a non-elected imbecile – one totally beholden to foreign interests! Biden openly accepted bribes and didn't know where he was! He shit his pants! For fucking-Christ's-sake!!!!

Feeling lost Em whimpered under her breath. The bad guys were in control!! For the first time in American history democracy had failed!! 'How did we come to this?', she pleaded to the ether.

'The Swamp.', Guy answered, his face deathly pale. 'It's really deep.'

Emily nodded sullenly. 'We need to drain it. Bad.'

'Yeah. Bad.'

For several moments the patriots sat in somber silence. They felt like they were at a wake. Something terribly precious had just died. What about the children?! What about the next generation's right to vote??!! Democrat, Republican, Libertarian or Independent – every American depended on free and fair elections to protect their rights!!! The United States of America was a Republic!!!

To break the awful quiet Agent Rosenstern sighed despondently. 'We need heroes. People wiling to stand up to it, to stand up for America.'

Guildencrantz nodded. 'That's what the President was *doing*.', he said after a moment of reflection, referring to the last President actually elected by the American people. 'He was working for *us* and not *them*. It's why they kicked him out of here.'

Emily sniffled. 'You think maybe we can get him back?', she asked.

Guy paused to consider their prospects for restoring democracy. It seemed like the whole world was against them. 'He'd have to be a superhero to overcome these odds.', he replied soberly. 'Sleepy Creepy here just admitted the fix was in.'

It was true. The Deep State was a monster intent on devouring the world whole. They didn't seem to care who they hurt, or even if ultimately it hurt their own interests. It was all about power and dominance.

But Rosenstern wasn't ready to give up the fight – not until the last shot was fired and she was completely out of ammunition. There was too much at stake! 'There's a lot of us that feel this way.', she declared breathlessly. 'A lot of us! We read the bullshit they put on the internet and don't believe the lies they're peddling! That thing with Rittenhouse showed a lot of people just how misinformed they've been! The lies they told about hydroxychloroquine, about wearing masks! They killed so, so many people with their bullshit! Those weren't just numbers on the TV, but real people! And the more you learn the more you see how blown out of proportion the threat of coronavirus has always been, that it was never about public safety but about abridging civil liberties and forcing unsecured mail-in voting! It's too easy to steal ballots that come in the mail when everyone gets one! Drop off ballot boxes are totally unsecured! They've been declared illegal even!'

'Yes. It's true.', Guy replied soberly. 'And audits showed that 97% of the "votes" dropped in those boxes went Democrat – that's just not realistic.'

Knowing her friend and partner agreed with her but was just as helpless as she was to make things right, Emily raised her hands helplessly. Short of another actual shooting Revolutionary War what could they do? Wait until two days before the election then burn all the places warehousing the fake ballots to the ground??! 'You got any bright ideas?', she asked.

Sensing an important moment was upon him Guy paused gravely. Feeling like a teenager who's prom date had suddenly canceled out on him at the very last minute he realized he was out of his depth and wilted into his chair like a plant on a scorching July day.

At the last second, though, he suddenly brightened. When you're faced with the impossible, do the impossible!! Americans *never* say die!! 'We need

Batman and Superman!', he declared to Emily Eleanor Rosenstern with wild enthusiasm. 'We need the Avengers! We need the X-Men! We need super heroes!' Choosing hope over despair, Guy Guildencrantz faux-tagged his broken-hearted partner gently on the chin. It was time for larger than life! It was time to get silly! It was time for a story about heroes *everyone* could look up to! 'I'll show you how to channel your inner Batman – I mean your inner B.M.!', he joked. 'It's time for a story with a happy ending! No more of this doom and gloom and Sleepy Creepy Joe taking a giant dump in his Fruit of the Looms! It's time to laugh! It's time for fun! It's time for people to be Americans again instead of Democrats and Republicans! It's time to stop hating on President Donald J. Trump for being successful and for being such a great President! It's time to stop believing the lies the media outlets and the internet are peddling! It's time to come together and Take Back America! It's time for....MAGA MAN and THE TRUTH!'

Maga Man And The Truth
Vs.
Lie-Guy And The Fibber!

We follow the scene to where our intrepid duo of heroes – MAGA MAN and THE TRUTH – are pursuing dastardly villains LIE-GUY and THE FIBBER through THE SWAMP. Lie-Guy and the Fibber lie, cheat and steal from the American People and are secretly working for the insidious totalitarian nation of CHINA. Enemy of the Free Peoples of Earth, China seeks to overthrow goodness, upset the balance of world peace and destroy the UNITED STATES' economy by releasing the deadly CORONAVIRUS into America's civilian population...

'Which way do you think they've gone, TRUTH?', asked MAGA MAN.

America Liberty stopped and examined the scene closely for clues. A super model by day, MAGA MAN'S loyal African/Hispanic-American partner in fighting crime was not prissy and knelt to examine the city street for any signs of their insidious quarry. 'I think they may have gone deeper into the Swamp, MAGA MAN! It looks like they are going to see the wicked Dr. Fauci in the Deep State!'

MAGA MAN shook his head. Ever since America's French allies had discovered that Hydroxychloroquine was an effective treatment against the deadly Coronavirus the Deep State had been trying to misinform the public regarding HCQ's usefulness and discredit the science. If the truth didn't get out hundreds of thousands of America's citizens could die – and LIE-GUY and THE FIBBER would be guilty of murder! 'We have to find them – and soon!'

'I'm on it, MAGA MAN!'

In the lead the sultry patriot dashed on through the muck. Hot on her heels MAGA MAN turned the corner only to find TRUTH had just been ambushed by the very villains they were pursuing! She was stuck like a butterfly in a spider's web!!

'MAGA MAN! Help!', screamed America Liberty. 'LIE-GUY's got me trapped in his CYCLIC VERIFICATION WEBS!'

Lie-Guy's most insidious weapon the Cyclic Verification Web linked multiple false claims together creating a string of interwebs that created the *illusion* of independent verification while still only coming from one source. Aided by China's allies – Google, Facebook and Twitter – it was a potent and deadly combination that could keep TRUTH mired in the muck forever!

'Don't worry! I'll use my SWORD OF REAL SCIENCE on it!', exclaimed MAGA MAN.

The Hero of America unsheathed his mighty blade and sliced straight through Lie-Guy's insidious Webs. Dismantled by c19hcq.com and nearly a thousand real time medical studies regarding the effective use of HCQ against the deadly and dangerous Coronavirus MAGA MAN made short work of TRUTH's restraints. LIE-GUY'S webs were no match for Real Science!!!

Freed from her chains America Liberty cheered and stretched her arms. 'Free at last! Their lies can never stop THE TRUTH!'

The villainous disfigured penguin-man thrust his fist in the air. 'Blast you, MAGA MAN! You and your cursed Science!'

'We're not defeated yet, LIE-GUY!', growled THE FIBBER. 'Not while I've got my BASELESS PROBES to throw at them!' The masked villain pulled stacks of paper and red tape from his pocket. He quickly fashioned them into paper airplanes and hurled them at the unlucky patriots. Soon multiple deadly projectiles were hurtling towards our intrepid pair of HEROES.

'Quick, TRUTH! Use your SHIELD OF EVIDENCE to deflect them!', cried MAGA MAN.

Beautiful America Liberty expanded her Star-Spangled Banner into a fact wall and the deadly Probes bounced off and exploded. Most clattered harmlessly to the ground, however, some ricocheted back and struck THE FIBBER and LIE-GUY in the foot. Pierced by proof that the DNC purchased lies directly from Russian spies to attack honest Presidential candidate Donald Trump and by evidence that former Vice President Joe Biden had accepted a $900,000 bribe from the nation of Ukraine in exchange for US aid and the Biden Foundation had taken another $50 million from China both villains fell to their knees screaming in pain.

'Curses! Our own weapons have been turned against us!', exclaimed the ugly penguin-man.

Crying like a little girl THE FIBBER grabbed his foot in agony. 'Arggh! Quick, LIE-GUY – Use the SPIN-DOCTOR! Quick, before the FACTS kill us and the Democratic Party is destroyed!'

With a twist of the dial on LIE-GUY'S wrist the projectiles wounding them were turned inside out saving the villains from certain doom. They clattered harmless to the ground, buried and forgotten, with the terrible twosome suffering mere flesh wounds.

'See, MAGA MAN!', roared LIE-GUY. 'You can not defeat us! We can spin truth into lies and lies into the truth! Our allies in BIG TECH can make REAL NEWS disappear like a Fart in the Wind! You are no match for us! Fascism and FAKE NEWS will rule the world – now and forever!'

MAGA MAN held up his hand in calm, confident defiance. 'Not so fast, LIE-GUY! Even you can not escape my...RAP OF REALITY! Play those **FORTY-FIVE RECORDS**, TRUTH!'

The lovely superhero stood on top of a trash can and like her name-sake crowed the TRUTH for all the world to hear. 'HISTORIC TRADE DEALS!'

'To benefit everyone!', quipped MAGA MAN.

'LOWEST UNEMPLOYMENT, EVER!'

'To empower Americans!'

'FOUR NOBEL PEACE PRIZE NOMINATIONS!'

'Peace in the Middle East!', MAGA MAN boogied.

'LOWEST PEOPLE'S CONFIDENCE IN YOUR CORRUPT MEDIA!'

'In history! You're weak and powerless without your lies, villains!'

'DEFEATED MUELLER WITCHHUNT!'

'That's right! It was proven to be total bullshit! The only evidence Democrats found was evidence of their _own_ corruption! BLEACH-BIT HILLARY!! And THE DURHAM PROBE is just beginning to issue Indictments!'

'DEFEATED _TWO_ PARTISAN-SWAMP IMPEACHMENTS – MPEACHMENTS STARTED OVER NOTHING!'

'America sees you for the useless Swamp Creatures you are!'

'DOUBLED THE VALUE OF THE STOCK MARKET!'

'That's real money! Real money in the People's pockets! In Citizen's retirement funds!'

'MOST VERIFIED VOTES, EVER!'

'In history! Most popular President – OF ALL TIME!'

'WARP SPEED VACCINES!!!'

'You Progressives love to order everyone to get the vaccines – but you don't want to give credit for their creation to President Trump!', crowed MAGA MAN.

America Liberty's voice morphed into that of the heroic otherworldly Saturday morning cartoon character *Space Ghost*. 'SPACE FORCE!!!', the athletic super-model sang.

With each successive blow THE FIBBER and LIE-GUY doubled over in pain. The HONESTY of TRUTH and MAGA MAN's epic RAP OF REALITY was too much for the villains to take. Beaten to a pulp by the *Forty-Fifth President of the United States'* accomplishments the two dastardly criminals collapsed to the ground writhing in agony.

'Argggh!', screamed LIE-GUY.

'Ahhhh!!! No!!! Please! No more!', begged THE FIBBER.

MAGA MAN puffed out his mighty chest. 'Oh, I think you'll be getting four more years, SWAMP-CREATURES! You may have FIXED – that is <u>BROKEN</u> – the 2020 ELECTION but the tide has turned now. Twenty-twenty is hindsight and America has had more than enough of your SHENANIGANS! No more MALARKY! You're finally about to get your COMEUPPANCE!'

'Let's see who these villains really are behind their masks!', exclaimed America Liberty. The model with the African-American mother and legally immigrated Brazilian biochemist father ripped off THE FIBBER'S mask. To her horror she gazed down at the disfigured mutant who's features it concealed. The hideous creature looking back at her with hate in his eyes had two distinct faces on each side of his head! 'Heavens! It's – it's CONGRESSMAN ADAM SCHIFF! He's even uglier without his mask on! Good heavens!! He's truly hideous!!'

'SWEET VOTER INTEGRITY!!!', gasped MAGA-MAN. 'Then this one must be – '

MAGA MAN yanked off LIE-GUY'S shroud. Looking like a stand in for recurring Batman foe The Penguin, villainous CHUCK SCHUMER stared back at him. His nose was nearly a foot long! 'Wah-wah-wah, MAGA

MAN! You never had a clue it was us, did you? All these years we've been working with America's enemies to bring about your downfall and no one EVER suspected us! China will one day rule the world, you peasants! And *we* will be rich!'

'Not if the law has anything to say about it you won't, you viper!', retorted THE TRUTH.

Schumer cackled. 'Ha! We own the law! Next to Washington D.C., New York is lowest and deepest part of the SWAMP! You'll never get us out of office! Our party will never vote to IMPEACH us! We will rule over you forever!'

'Well – let's see if you can dodge this im-peach-ment, villain!', America Liberty retorted. Taking the ripe Georgia peach from her lunch sack she stuffed the succulent fruit from the great sovereign state the swamp-dwellers had violated in 2020 into the fat troll's mouth, then did the same to THE FIBBER. 'That should shut these traitors up – for now.', she declared.

'Excellent work, TRUTH!', MAGA MAN cheered. 'Now we've got to get the message out to the good citizens as quick as we can! Lives are at stake! We must hurry! WARP SPEED to the cure!'

'We can do it! Americans can do anything we put our minds to!', America Liberty exclaimed. The dark-haired beauty gestured to the miscreants. 'What should we do with these two? It's pretty obvious they've been fixing the votes in their own states to stay in power all this time. If they can do it to the 2020 Presidential election it's a good bet they've been doing it in the smaller races for years! They certainly did it in Georgia – and the audit definitively proved they did it in Arizona too! There really are no "blue" states anymore – only red states and swing states!'

MAGA MAN set his jaw defiantly. 'There's only one thing we can do: set the BEACON OF TRUTH next to them and light it up! With enough light on the subject AMERICA will take action to protect the VOTE! The VOTE is what keeps us all free!'

'N-No! C-curse you, M-MAGA MAN!', shrieked Schumer through his fruity gag.

Ignoring his protests the CHAMPIONS OF AMERICA set up the fabled BEACON OF TRUTH and let its light shine forth bright and true for all to see. The triumphant emblem of Truth, Justice and the American Way flashed red, white and blue sparks of lightning into the air like fireworks on the Fourth of July. 'That's it, MAGA MAN! The HONEST-TO-GOD TRUTH should finally take care of these villains!'

'Yes, my friend!', the Hero of America replied. 'And with any luck the other CREATURES OF THE SWAMP will devour THE FIBBER and LIE-GUY where they lay! SWAMP CREATURES eat their own!'

'Sick creatures! They are Cannibals!'

Paying the traitors no more mind MAGA MAN swung his cape behind him heroically. 'Now we must hurry, TRUTH! Our America – THE **REAL** AMERICA based on TRUTH, JUSTICE and FREE SPEECH – is under attack!'

'Lead on, MAGA MAN!! **All** of **AMERICA** is with you!!'

With that our two intrepid duo of heroes dashed away into the darkness of the SWAMP. The nation they LOVE was under attack by ENEMIES FOREIGN and TRAITORS DOMESTIC intent on TERRORIZING and ENSLAVING the innocent peoples of the world.

But the heroic patriots had the cure and they did not fight alone! They had two powerful allies: THE AMERICAN PEOPLE and THE AMERICAN SPIRIT. The TRUTH would set them free! They knew GOOD would find a way to defeat EVIL! LIES were passing – THE TRUTH was FOREVER!

*　　*　　*

'The End.', Guy breathed with a smile.

'No – no!', gushed Emily with tears running down her pretty cheeks. 'It's the beginning! The beginning of something wonderful!' Clapping with enthusiasm and real hope she wiped her eyes, reached over and gave her big burly partner a warm hug. 'God! I needed that! I needed that so bad!', she laughed effusively. 'Thank you! Thank you so much!!'

Glad to have cheered both of them up Guy smiled modestly. 'I think it all started back in 2016 – no, back in 2014! America had finally had enough! After six years of Obama's lies and screw-America business-as-usual Swamp corruption – six years of economic stagnation – America wanted change!'

'No – not just change!', Emily roared like the little tigress she was. 'Not the empty promises of change stupid Obama was peddling! Not more lies and inept leadership! America wanted positive change! Real change! Change for the good!'

Grinning back at her Guy nodded. 'Exactly! We all need superheroes! Good examples we can look up to! Role-models, people we can trust to do the right thing! Leaders we can follow!'

Barely restraining her ebullience Emily beamed. 'Yeah! No more doom and gloom! No more shit-head Obama or his illegitimate successor! No more election fraud! It's time for the good times to roll again! America first!'

'Amen to that!', Guy seconded feeling in his heart that the light would eventually return and banish the darkness. This entire country – America – was built on hope, not despair!

Feeling the same as he did, Em shook her head. 'How can the Left even peddle the *shit* they are peddling?', she mused. 'Peddle all this doom and gloom? Why does anybody *buy* into it? It seems so stupid! What does it even offer? I mean, Obama was doing the whole "Hope and Change" bit. That I get at least – selling the promise of something better, even if everything he did was the opposite of what he promised. But what's this "America is the bad guy" bullshit all about?'

Guy shrugged that he didn't really get it either. 'It must fill some strange, twisted need for self-loathing. It seems like a religious thing to me – a replacement for religion. They seem to think everybody must be guilty of something, so they invent some great evil to rail against.'

Emily nodded, beginning to understand the cycle these self-flagellators were trapped in. 'And of course *they* are virtuous because *they* are pointing out how wrong the "whatever" they are bitching about is! They are never the bad guys – everyone else is!'

Guy's head bobbed up and down. 'The holier-than-thou cult of virtue-signaling. Thing is they keep rewriting history to fit their bullshit narrative. They pick out a crime, then pretend like that is the norm rather than the exception. It's like racism: they keep trying to make-believe that racism is what America is all about, which it's not and never was. The *whole world* used to be racist and thought *their* ethnicity was the best and all others were inferior but *this* country was the one that finally said: "Hey! Everybody is equal! We accept anybody of any color, creed or nationality! Be a law abiding citizen and you are welcome here!" For a while a few people didn't accept that and clung to the old prejudices that they brought with them from their old country – but the truth always wins out in the end and the system's been fixed for a long time. As Martin Luther King, Jr. said "I have a dream"...and white kids and black kids have been happily playing together on the playground for years now! Funny thing is the people who opposed MLK – the segregationists and racists – were all Democrats!' He smirked and shook his head. 'Now these woke-ass, broke-ass Democratic bozos come along and try to pretend *they* invented equality! Like it's some glorious epiphany *they* came up with one day while they were out tripping on acid!'

'The thing that gets me is how at the same time they are anti-religious!', Emily Rosenstern scoffed. 'Don't they know that every major faith – Islam, Buddhism, Hinduism, Christianity – all of them literally preach from the cradle that all human beings are <u>one race</u>?! How can they be against ***that***?! <u>Why</u> are they against it?!'

Guildencrantz gritted his teeth. 'It's gotta be a power thing. Control hearts and minds – brainwash the young and the stupid into your cult, then tell your followers everything else is bad.'

'"No established religion" does not mean no religion at all! The Left is a cult of hate! They should apply for non-profit tax status!', she ridiculed, mocking the traitor party.

'If they thought they could get away with it, I'm sure they would.', Guy snarked knowingly.

'The only reason they don't is because then they'd have to admit they are actually a religion – ', Emily replied, agreeing with him 100%. 'And a make believe one at that!'

'Exactly – it's why they censor everything on social media. Don't let anybody oppose your false catechism and keep pounding the propaganda. You can't even post a video on YouTube that discusses Election Fraud!'

Rosenstern's face took on a dark, angry cast. 'Big Tech really pisses me off! This country is *supposed* to be all about 1ST AMENDMENT FREE SPEECH!'

'They don't believe in free speech.', Guildencrantz declared stridently. 'Virtue-signaling, my ass! Bunch of damned hypocrites if you ask me!'

'Do as I say, not as I do – or else!' Em folded her hands on her lap. 'Gotta change that tune.'

Guildencrantz cleared his throat. 'I hear – ', he cooed with a smile. 'Trump has got a media company now. "Truth Speaks" or "Truth Social" or something.'

Deeply interested, Emily leaned forward. 'Like Parler.com?'

Guy shook his head. 'No, no – much bigger. Something big enough to swallow Twitter whole and shit out the bones. It's partnered with Rumble so it even has video streaming!'

Enlightened by the news, Em's spirits brightened like the sun. Because its technology was cutting edge and more sophisticated Trump's new social media company was better and had more features than boring old Twitter! And swallowing the Woke echo-chamber whole?! Restoring freedom and debate?! That would be like bringing America back from the dead!!! 'That's....that's great news! I hope He totally squashes those turd-blossoms out of business! Beat Big Tech at their own game!' She sighed with exasperation, put out by all the propaganda she was forced to endure every day. 'I'm tired of every time I sign on to the internet to check my mail getting a bunch of "suggested" articles in my "feed" from MSN! The internet is a basic utility! I don't have to endure a bunch of brainwashing every time I switch the lights on in my apartment or my furnace kicks on!'

'Or when the garbage guy picks up the trash.', noted Guy.

'Exactly!', Emily replied, expostulating. 'And their suggestions are trash! "Anonymous this, if true that"! It's all bullshit! They don't report real news they don't like, either! Oh, the things I want to do to Google and the rest of those Techie douche bags! It makes me want to...!'

'Makes you want to what?'

Tigress Emily slammed her fist into her palm. A highly trained Secret Service agent it collided with her hand with a snap. 'Seriously fuck them up! Send some monster to devour them and everything they touch! Bankrupt those fuckers down to the last penny!'

Laughing merrily, Guy rubbed his big hands together. 'Oh, that sounds like a story I want to hear! Now you're getting into the spirit! Lay it on me, hon!'

Feeling divine inspiration descending upon her Emily Rosenstern sat up straighter in her chair. Seeing one of the trashy pop culture magazines the Left uses to stealthily spread their propaganda laying on a nearby table she opened it up and laid it across her lap. Licking her finger she pretended to turn the glossy pages. 'Once upon a time, in the magical land of America...'

That Big, Bad Internet Monster

Encapsulated deep in the bowels of his bloated internet company Merc Suckerborg twiddled his thumbs across his series 15 Supertouch Awesomeness Notepad. His company's latest creation was still in the experimental stage and as CEP (Chief Executive Prick) he prided himself on working out at least a few of the bugs personally. Having first hand experience playing with his latest toy allowed him to better critique his engineers' progress; the subservient worker bees who slaved underneath him could always benefit from someone of his great genius – and it was good to occasionally remind the peons that he was the one in charge because he was much better and smarter than they were.

Bored after fifteen seconds of "work" Merc set his latest creation down (well, the latest thing that had popped into his head and that he'd demanded his staff hammer into existence for him) and grabbed his Super-Duper Tesla-Zephram WiFi Laptop. Calling up several screens at once he began streaming the latest episodes of *Real Housewives* while simultaneously playing Minesweeper and Checkers. Hyperactive from birth the constant stimulation kept Suckerborg's mind occupied and further dulled his already dull imagination. Painfully skinny and muscle-free because his diet consisted almost entirely of coffee and Twizzlers, Merc's constant craving for sugar and stimulants was something his doctor attributed to all the drugs his free-spirited hippie mother took while she was carrying him in utero. Because of his unusual back story Suckerborg preferred to think of himself as a high-tech superhero rather than just another young man with ADHD: he'd developed lightening-quick intellectual super powers via exposure to all the mysterious exotic chemicals his mother had introduced into his system before he was born and became a "real person". In reality, his mother's irresponsible partying had left him with permanent Attention-Deficit-Hyperactivity-Disorder – and he'd simply been extraordinarily lucky in his business ventures. His target audience was so ignorant of what came before and had been so dumbed down by constant exposure to what passed for media entertainment these days that they didn't realize his first app creation "Mindboggler" was really just a ripoff of two classic Atari 2600 games that (while playing them simultaneously) he decided to smash together.

But like most derivative retread crap "Mindboggler" made Suckerborg money so he cashed in and used his new wealth to hire a team of actual genius engineers to create *Behemoth*, the giant social media platform that over the last three years had carved out such a huge niche in the tech marketplace. Fully compatible with Facebook, Twitter, Snapchat and Tiktok, *Behemoth* existed simultaneously with all other media platforms in real time, allowing the user to log in to only one site while still remaining active in *all* of the others. With this inter-connectivity *Behemoth* had become *the* central hub for the whole social media experience – and by piggybacking his company on top of everyone else's work Suckerborg had become hideously rich.

An intern barely out of college rapped on the sill of his office door, breaking Suckerborg's fleeting reverie about how awesome he was. 'Yeah?', Merc replied as he posted yet another narcissistic Tweet proudly announcing to his adoring audience in cyber-world that he was playing Checkers and Minesweeper while simultaneously streaming *Real Housewives* in real time as he ate Twizzlers and drank his non-fat double-sweet mocha espresso from Starbucks with organic soy and almond milk.

'Um, Mr. Suckerborg...we've got a serious problem out here.'

The hyperactive juvenile junior grade lieutenant of industry reluctantly took his sandals off his desk. 'What is it?', he whined nasally.

'Well, um...'

'Shit, I don't have all day – ', Merc lied, secretly pleased to have another task to divert his limited attention span. The self-important, ego-inflated internet mogul found it wonderfully satisfying when the peons had to admit they required help from his genius super-brain. 'Spit it out, dammit!'

'Sir....well.....everything is being fact-checked.'

Suckerborg set his mocha non-fat, organic soy-almond latte down on the desk on the spot his feet had recently vacated. 'So? That's what we pay our people to create algorithms for. Can't have the wrong messages being posted where everyone can see them.'

The anxious boy in the doorway shook his head. 'No, you don't understand – whatever's doing this is doing REAL fact-checking! It's correcting whatever the censor team puts up!'

Suckerborg blinked for a moment. Perpetually distracted it took a moment for his brain to catch up to what the intern was saying to him. 'Huh?', he replied quizzically.

'The *censor team* is being corrected – it's changing whatever they put up!'

Realizing something was truly amiss Merc lurched forward in his chair. 'What do you mean, "Corrected"?', he bleated in alarm.

Put on the spot the intern's brow started to bead a droplet of sweat. 'Whole sections of the internet – the stuff that our team wrote – it's missing! Wikipedia is being rewritten as we speak! All the things we posted but were unsubstantiated or flat out untrue are gone!'

'You're shittin' me!', Merc breathed smartly, his eyes going wide.

The slightly younger boy turned a pale shade of green. 'And it gets worse! Things we tried to keep quiet are being filled in! Feinstein, Schiff, Schumer, Pelosi – all their scandals and doublespeak are being posted in their wikis! All the things we've been removing from their pages every time a user tries to update their information with true facts is there now – and we can't get rid of it!!! Even Elizabeth Warren's Native American gaffe is back! It's all there!!! Mr. Suckerborg – *someone is filling in the blanks!!*'

Caught completely flat-footed the CEP of Behemoth turned white as a sheet. 'What? How in the hell can this happen?!'

'We don't know, sir!', the child-intern bleated. 'The *New York Times* entire opinion section for the last fifteen years has already been deleted – and from their back up servers too! And 98.6% of CNN's database has been changed! It's like a systemic core rewrite! Like someone is using the Find-and-Replace button to change the content across the board! Every time we try to write the story we're pushing it gets automatically reworded back to the actual truth!!'

In a panic now, Suckerborg leaped to his feet. On a quest to find out what in the hell in his world of wake-believe was happening the obscenely rich bastard dashed past the hapless intern into the cubicle maze.

He threaded his way past his worker bees through the honeycomb until he reached the Director of Disinformation's desk. The woman with the double hyphenated last name squinting at the little machine in front of her was named Alicia Mary-Moe Alphonslade-DeWittbuchater-Shlop.

A forty-something who's professed "high standards" would have been unrealistic in her prime Suckerborg's Director of Disinformation was dressed head-to-toe in rainbow colors and studded with enough metal to set off an airport security alarm.

Sensing the approach of one of those "white-privileged heterosexual Caucasian males" she hated so much AMMADS tossed her hair aside snootily to reveal the recently polished vintage 2016 "I'm With Her" Hillary Clinton pin she sported atop her "Pro-Democrat Means Pro-Vaccine" tee shirt. 'This is bullshit.', the bitchy cunt groused, not bothering to glance in her boss' direction to acknowledge the CEP's presence.

'What's bullshit?', demanded Suckerborg.

Alicia Mary-Moe Alphonslade-DeWittbuchater-Shlop quickly rattled some keystrokes across her keyboard. On the monitor the words: "The vaccines have nothing to do with Trump. Trump taking any credit for their creation is fucking ridiculous." appeared. When the sexually frustrated forty-something pressed enter, however, her words disappeared like magical text in a *Harry Potter* movie. But the words didn't just fade; they were replaced with blasphemies so incredibly heinous and offensive they were enough to make the pseudo-lesbian's blood boil: "Claiming Trump and Warp Speed had nothing to do with making the Covid-19 vaccines is like claiming the Manhattan Project had nothing to do with the creation of the A-bomb and Oppenheimer made the whole thing up in his garage by himself."

'See!', Alicia Mary-Moe Alphonslade-DeWittbuchater-Shlop bitched, objurgating Suckerborg like whatever was happening was his fault.

At a loss Merc stared at the screen in wonder. 'What the shit is going on here?', he gasped.

'How the fuck would I know?!', AMMADS screeched like a PMS-ing harpy. The man-hating twat thrust her metal-spiked chin out at him. 'It just started doing this unholy shit all the sudden!'

Rubbing his Twizzler/coffee-addled head, Suckerborg frowned. Sure his genius super-brain could eventually figure out the problem he gestured for Alicia Mary-Moe Alphonslade-DeWittbuchater-Shlop to rise up and vacate her seat. Wanting him to fix the issue (but not wanting to admit she needed a man's help) AMMADS did so with a frown and the junior grade lieutenant of tech slid into her chair.

'Try typing in "former President Donald Trump".', demanded the controlling bitch.

Merc did exactly as she directed. Though he tried time and again the browser kept omitting "former" and the text read "President Donald Trump" instead. He tried copy-pasting the adjective into the sentence but as soon as he moved the cursor away it disappeared. 'What the fuck!', the lucky-but-not-so-bright tech mogul decried, gesturing plaintively at the vid screen like a frustrated child.

'See?!', his Director of Disinformation exclaimed, pointing at the offensive text like she would if she saw a father rocking his sleepy child on his chest without a face mask on.

'What-the-fuck!?', the Chief Executive Prick repeated. The self-professed super genius sat back and stared at the monitor like it would magically fix itself if he wished at it long and hard enough.

'It's even worse than that! Look at this shit!', AMMADS growled, practically shoving Suckerborg's boyishly effeminate body aside to get at the computer. Viciously stabbing the keyboard with her sharp fingernails she typed: "Supporters of the former President have tried repeatedly to deny President Joe Biden's victory in November."

As soon as she hit the return key the screen rewrote what she'd typed to instead read: "The Biden camp continues to find no way to refute the numerous substantiated allegations of voter fraud and ballot tampering in the 2020 election, preferring instead to repeatedly make the claim that no evidence of voter fraud exists while at the same time ignoring the copious and well-documented examples of widespread corruption the audits have revealed. Eight-thousand pages of testimony, video tape of hundreds of thousands of secret votes being run through voting machines when the vote counting office was officially closed, affidavits from poll watchers of every political affiliation ejected without cause or prevented from insuring the election counts had any integrity and overwhelming physical evidence of vote-switching and the disappearance (and sudden appearance) of votes post-election leads even the most die-hard Democratically-aligned observer to conclude, with certainty, that Trump – and not Biden – was the true winner of the November 2020 Presidential election.'

The coffee/sugar addled internet media sensation's jaw hit the floor. 'What-the-actual-fuck???!!!', Suckerborg exclaimed.

'I know!!!', Misinformation Director Alicia Mary-Moe Alphonslade-DeWittbuchater-Shlop mewed in horror, for once agreeing with her privileged white heterosexual male boss without openly (and prejudicially) holding his race and gender against him.

An aide suddenly appeared from out of the wings. 'Mr. Suckerborg! Mr. Suckerborg! The Durham probe results are in and just trended on **Truth Social**! Half the people in the Democratic party are being indicted! Strzok! Paige! McCabe! – they've all flipped to save their own skins! They're turning over the goods!! Everyone is totally fucked!'

Faced with a calamity of such monumental proportions Suckerborg teetered in his seat. His dangerously high blood sugar plummeting he was close to fainting to the floor like the ingenue in a cheesy nineteenth century romance novel. The Dimms could never hope to spin all this damage! Everything they'd worked for all these years was going straight to Hawley-in-a-hand-basket! 'Well, shut it down, dammit!!', he bleated. 'Shut the whole fucking thing down!!!'

'We can't! We've been trying! Nothing we do seems to work!'

Feeling like a child who suddenly found himself lost in a gigantic department store, "super-genius" Merc Suckerborg glanced one by one at his worker bees looking desperately for answers. All the drone-master saw staring back at him were blank faces. Nobody seemed to know what the hell was happening! They had to solve this problem and figure out a solution fast!! They just had to!!! If they didn't *Behemoth* would lose control of the masses!! All the Dems had going for them was their publicity disinformation campaign – the Truth would kill them!! 'What the shit!!! We're the tech people!!!', he screamed, tears welling up in his eyes. 'We own the whole damned fucking Internet! How in the Fucking Hell is this happening?!?!?!'

'It must be some kind of virus, sir.', the nameless child-intern who'd followed him out of his office replied meekly. 'That's the only thing I can think of...'

'Well, fix it, dammit!!! Fix it!!!', screeched the CEP of the company.

The under-paid peons Suckerborg made do all the dirty work for him scurried back to their stations like ants afraid of being squished under the boot of a demented child. Diligently attending to their computer stations they tapped their fingers across their keyboards and kept their heads down. Nobody had the faintest idea what they could do to fix this disaster but it was important to look busy – their clueless leader had lost it completely.

Amid the chaos, the experimental new phone in Suckerborg's pants pocket abruptly beeped. Faced with an impending catastrophe of monumental proportions he pulled it out and thrust it into his Director of Disinformation's hands. 'You take it.', he commanded.

Given orders by a man, Alicia Mary-Moe Alphonslade-DeWittbuchater-Shlop bristled and bared her teeth at him. There wasn't anything in her obnoxious boss' statement she could potentially twist into a charge of sexual harassment, though, so she gritted her teeth and did as her white privileged heterosexual male employer directed.

'What is causing this...?', CEP Suckerborg murmured to the abyss as his reluctant and resentful underling answered his phone. It had to be some kind of super-virus! Their code had been corrupted! Could they do a reboot and wipe it clean??! No, they would lose all their consumer product information if they did that – he'd lose tens of billions! They had to find some way of staying operational while they purged this infection from the system!!

Trying to puzzle it out he was suddenly distracted by Alicia Mary-Moe Alphonslade-DeWittbuchater-Shlop abruptly pulling the phone away from her ear. Even from five feet away Suckerborg could hear a woman screaming at the top of her lungs from the tiny speaker. 'It's the national director of Planned Parenthood on the line.', his Director of Disinformation explained with a pained wince. 'Every time someone calls up their website the scene from the movie *Unplanned* depicting an actual real life abortion pops up. The clinic director is screaming bloody murder for you to drop everything, come there and fix it immediately. If you don't, she swears she's gonna come down here and "personally abort your penis". That's a direct quote.'

Faced with horrible calamities on every side and now threatened bodily by a woman more aggressive and masculine than he was, Suckerborg tore at his hair. The virus – it was in more than just their system!!! If it had got into Planned Parenthood's server it was probably being disseminated by *Behemoth* throughout the whole internet!!! The centralized nature of their propaganda disinformation apparatus was destroying everything! 'There's got to be some way to stop this! Hey – where are you guys going?'

Two of his employees had just risen from their chairs and were gathering up their things. 'We're getting the hell out of here.', the male half of the couple answered.

'Wh-What?', stammered Suckerborg. 'No – no one's leaving! We're in full crisis mode here, dude! Everyone get back to their workstations! Get back to work!!'

Debating with himself whether or not to bother to reply, the bearded man finally paused. 'I just watched that video, "dude".', he said to *Behemoth's* Chief Executive Prick. 'The scene came directly from a woman who used to run one of Planned Parenthood's clinics. Sickest thing I ever saw.' The husky man shivered, utterly horrified. 'I'm leaving this dump. I'm going to go join the protesters outside of one of those death camps.'

'Have you lost your fucking mind?!!!', Suckerborg bleated, flabbergasted. An employee of *his* was leaving to be a Pro-Life nut job?!!! 'Get back to work, dammit! Get back to work or you're fired!', he demanded.

'Have I lost my fucking mind?!', the beefy programmer replied, staring at the effeminate shithead he used to work for with thinly veiled contempt. 'Have you ever watched an *actual* abortion? Seen a peaceful kid laying there sucking its thumb, then watch it squirm when the probe goes through the amniotic sack? Hear the "doc" say: "They all do that." Watch the poor little kid wriggling around like a two year old to get away, see it's mouth go open to scream and see it's arms flailing around frantically when the suction starts?' The stout bearded man blanched white as a sheet like he was going to puke. 'I just watched a little screaming child get its fucking legs ripped off!! The poor thing lay there afterward, perfectly still, like a five year old on the side of the road that just clipped by a drunk driver!! This wasn't some grainy video from the 1970s – it was high-definition, so clear you could actually see the eyelashes on the baby's face!!! It was the most horrifying thing I've ever seen!!!! Then – then the suction tore the rest of the kid's body apart like fruit in a goddamned blender!!!' Knowing his ex-bosses where both major Planned Parenthood donors the bearded man stared at Suckerborg and AMMADS with open, repellent disgust. 'Any pro-choice *fuck* who says that ain't a baby is *fucking bat-shit crazy*!!! I just watched a goddamned snuff film!! A real life snuff film!!!'

Alicia Mary-Moe Alphonslade-DeWittbuchater-Shlop rolled her eyes. 'Oh, get a grip, you Right-wing wing-nut! It's just cells! It's no different than dandruff!'

Knowing they would never actually look at the film and see the horrible truth for themselves, the bearded man nodded to his fiance to leave. They did one last sweep of their respective cubicles and headed for the exit.

'Hey! Hey – you walk out that door and you are both fired!'

Eternally grateful she'd never gotten an abortion the female half of the couple stopped. 'Fuck you, you pretentious self-righteous, child-murdering prick!!! You can shove your goddamned job up your ass – if you can fit it up there! You don't get to decide what the truth is, limp dick – the truth is the truth!' Struggling with the weight of her belongings she still somehow managed to find a way to flip Suckerborg the Double Bird. 'And you're a lousy software engineer! You don't know shit about tech!!'

The beleaguered CEP was so stunned by the audacity of the venomous verbal bitch-slapping the young woman had just given him that both she and her proud husband-to-be were safely out the door before he could even start to think up a retort. A few seconds later other people joined the couple and walked out with them. Soon a long line of backsides was facing Suckerborg and heading down the stairs in one giant mass exodus.

Over the next hour, as CEP Merc Suckerborg and Director of Disinformation Alicia Mary-Moe Alphonslade-DeWittbuchater-Shlop struggled in vain to contain what would eventually be called the "Free Speech Virus", over 60% of the staff at Tech Media Giant *Behemoth* walked off the job.

*　　*　　*

'This is America First News. In business, the big news today was the epic collapse of the social media technology market in response to what experts are calling the "Free Speech Virus". Shares of Microsoft, Facebook, Twitter, Instagram, Tiktok and other commodities such as the popular super-platform *Behemoth* plummeted by a record 82% since trading opened this morning. YouTube, the video sharing platform that blocks all videos that concern election fraud, also suffered a 40% loss in value. Information technology companies were unaffected and Cyber-security firms actually saw a 2% rise in response to this new threat. Joining us today to discuss this new development is Dr. Tomas Payne, cyber-security expert and renowned author of the book *Information in the Social Media Age*.'

'Thank you for having me on your program.'

'Dr. Payne, tell us what this new development means.'

'Well, obviously this is a serious problem for social media and providers of social media content. Let me explain the issue these platforms face. Normally when a virus invades a computer system you would simply isolate the offending code and purge it. But this "Free Speech Virus" is different from anything we've ever seen before: it's not localized to one part of any individual system. In fact, it's spread in small parts *throughout* the whole internet and replicates faster than it can be suppressed. It's almost as if truth is hard-wired into the DNA.'

'You're saying it's on *all* computers? Our laptops and smart phones?'

Dr. Payne nodded. 'Pretty much. But since laptops and phones generally aren't the initial sources of the problem it doesn't seem to have much effect on them. And this virus doesn't seem to do anything to actual works of fiction like novels or movie content. Anything that declares itself to be a work of fiction seems to be immune.'

'That seems quite odd.'

Payne nodded. 'Yes, it is very odd. But like I said this virus is like nothing we've ever seen before.'

'Couldn't platforms like Facebook or Twitter simply reboot their systems? Restore the hardware using protected files?'

Dr. Payne shrugged. 'Well, in theory, yes. But there are significant challenges to Facebook's and Twitter's platforms that make that option a practical impossibility. Let's assume you wanted to restore the operating system back to its original specs and keep this pernicious virus out of the system with some kind of advanced firewall.'

The host nodded. 'You mean take the servers back to their save point and keep the systems from being reinfected once you've purged them by using a containment barrier?'

'Exactly. Restore, then keep "Free Speech" out with a buffer wall. In the process of the reboot, excuse me the restore function, however, you would lose all customer data – and therein lies the problem. Facebook, Twitter, Behemoth and the like are, in effect, data collection apps; they are in the business of information acquisition and make their money selling user preference data – data which the user voluntarily provides. If Facebook or Twitter or any other platform that relies on user content were to commit to a hard reboot it could *theoretically* wipe out the virus but in the process it would make these virtual companies – these data brokerage companies – virtually worthless, if you'll pardon the pun. It's a scorched earth solution, sort of like dropping fifty hydrogen bombs on New York City to eradicate its roach, rat and political corruption problems.'

The host of America First nodded. 'Rat and roach infestations carry diseases harmful to humans, of course, and corrupt politicians hurt people in all sorts of pernicious ways. But is the *Free Speech Virus* really that harmful? Is it so terrible to have content fact-checked in real time?'

Dr. Payne shook his head. 'No, not really. Not at all, actually – well, except to those who have some vested interest in actively spreading disinformation. This virus has largely only significantly affected the political establishment – and of course, all the major media that comments on it. All of Wikipedia's entries on politics have been corrected so they are no longer heavily biased in favor of the left.'

'That's a staggering admission of overt bias.'

Payne nodded. 'Yes, quite. For example, you don't see the kind of factual misinformation looking up an entry on giraffes as you do when researching, say Marjorie Taylor Green. Before "Free Speech" hit Wikipedia the entry on Green was decidedly a work of fiction intended to purposefully and unfairly harm her reputation. The bias was that incredibly overt.'

'And because the protections against slander and liable have become so weak in recent years these platforms have been able to get away with these kind of disinformation campaigns.'

'Exactly. The courts have given a free pass to lies told about politicians.'

'It's very disconcerting. It would also seem to be a violation of campaign finance law.'

'Yes.' Dr. Payne held up his finger for emphasis. 'It's interesting to note that Parler.com, a company which goes by the tag line "The Free Speech Network" (and does not censor its content unless a law has been explicitly broken) has been almost completely unaffected by this virus – though we have no information to suggest that the Parler network has not also been infected like social media platforms Behemoth, Facebook, Twitter and Tiktok, etc. have been. The same thing is also true for the recently upgraded *Truth Social* network currently dominating its competitors in downloads.'

'Yes. Parler and Truth Social have bucked the trend. Shares for Parler.com have actually risen by 15.3% and Truth Social by 23.5%. Some of their competitors have even publicly speculated that these companies or some of their employees may have had something to do with creating the *Free Speech Virus*, but America First has no information to confirm this rumor is in any way true. Still, the effect on the global social media industry has been devastating.'

'Well, the average consumer shouldn't be too concerned. Most of the things people have traditionally used social media for – sharing funny stories, memes, exchanging family photos and the like, etc. – have been unaffected. And even if the larger companies were to commit to a hard reboot and lose all their past customer data the infrastructure of the platforms themselves would still continue to exist and they could theoretically rebuild from scratch. It's even possible *Free Speech* could simply "burn itself out" over time like traditional viruses in the real world, but like I said since we don't know much about it that's pure speculation. No, the largest effect – the greatest "damage" from *Free Speech* has really been done to disinformation brokers (those paid to dis-inform the public or promote products with fraudulent product reviews) and to primary stockholders who's portfolios consist almost entirely of investments in these "Free Speech Suppression" companies. The companies themselves can eventually recapitalize to meet demand or be bought out by their more honest competitors, however, major shareholders such as Mark Zuckerberg, Bill Gates, Elon Musk, Dorsey, Page, Merc Suckerborg and the like stand to lose tremendous amounts of money if that should happen. These people are likely over-leveraged in the companies they control and would suffer tremendous financial losses if they are forced to sell at this time. If a solution is not found to purge the internet of *Free Speech* it would not surprise me if one or even all of these individuals went bankrupt.'

'You're suggesting Bill Gates, the founder of Microsoft, could go bankrupt because of *Free Speech*?!!'

Dr. Payne leaned forward. 'Suggest? No, I'm not just suggesting – I'm saying it's highly *likely* that unless *Free Speech* is eradicated from these networks these individuals will go bankrupt.'

'You're serious about this?!', the commentator replied, genuinely taken aback.

Payne nodded earnestly. 'Yes – serious as a heart attack. It's almost inconceivable to think that a person as rich as Bill Gates could ever lose his fortune, could ever lose everything. But you have to consider that much of a mogul like Mr. Gates' wealth is tied up in margin calls – money borrowed against his personal assets and reinvested in the market. To retain control of his company, like most tech moguls virtually all of his wealth has been reinvested in the market he understands best and the one he considers most completely secure: technology. As you know, tech stocks are highly dependent on capital investment for expansion – in effect, they borrow against the future to grow. As such, it would not surprise me to learn that Gates, Zuckerberg, Suckerborg and the like are catastrophically over-extended. There is even precedence for this – think back to Atari in the 1980s. At one time they completely dominated the home gaming market and were untouchable. But then they overextended and within a year the company had gone belly up.'

'You're suggesting Microsoft and Facebook could go bankrupt?!'

'Not the companies themselves, no. As I said, these companies have a sound business model and can recapitalize based on consumer demand for their products. But in the time it takes for these corporations to reorganize and their stock price to rebound from the catastrophic blunder they committed in suppressing *Free Speech* and unfairly censoring user content these individuals are likely to suffer tremendous personal financial hardship. It's entirely possible *Truth Social* and *Parler.com* will swallow their market share up or buy them out.'

'And of course our viewers are already well aware that when a company issues new stock to recapitalize it dilutes the price of existing stock.'

Payne nodded. 'Yes – as Eduardo Saverin's lawsuit against former business partner Mark Zuckerberg in the movie *The Social Network* accurately depicted. This is why I would be highly concerned if I was these individuals or if I had personally been investing in these companies on the margin. The combination of personal debts coming due with a heavily devalued portfolio can be disastrous.' Dr. Tomas wagged his finger. 'It's always wise to diversify and be careful in investing in companies chaired by individuals that engage in unethical behavior!'

'Yes, we all know the mantra of diversification of assets. Like all significant market events this should be a cautionary tale for the average consumer.'

Payne shrugged. 'There's always a chance the engineers at Microsoft will come up with a solution in time. I'm sure Mr. Gates, Mr. Suckerborg and Mr. Zuckerberg are all working diligently to eradicate *Free Speech*. After all, in the end they have the most to lose.'

The host nodded. 'They certainly do! Well, that's all the time we have today. Thank you for joining us at American First News, Dr. Payne. As someone who knows very little about the computing world, you've opened my eyes. It's been very informative – I never realized *Free Speech* could be such a threat to the global establishment!'

'Always a pleasure. Be happy to come back on your show whenever we know more.'

* * *

'And we all lived happily ever after!', concluded Emily Rosenstern. 'All except for those rich assholes who think they have the right to control the world through lies and fear. Those fuckers died penniless and insane, still trying to get the people to believe their stupid bullshit.'

Sitting half on, half off his seat her partner Guy Guildencrantz was almost rolling on the floor with laughter. 'Holy – holy shit! Goddamn! That – that was – !'

Giddy at the thought of her epic Free Speech Virus fantasy actually coming true Agent Rosenstern joined him in his chuckles. With the exception of a meteor falling down from the sky, breaking into tiny pieces and landing on their heads – precisely on *their* heads and no one *else's* – she couldn't think of anything more perfect than bankrupting these asinine captains of oppression. It was so *Count of Monte Cristo!* 'I would really love, love, love, love, love for Zuckerberg and the rest of those lying, deceitful cheats to end up in the poor house! Serves them right for all the damage they've done! I mean, telling outright slanders the way they did to sway the election! What were they thinking?! That we would *thank them* for it?! That we wouldn't want them *dead* for what they did to us?! Hell, Bill Gates thinks the problem with the planet is that there are too many people!'

'Damn straight!', Guy sang. 'By the way, Facebook and Twitter have lost half their value since the election! Zuckerberg has lost billions! And Jack Dorsey's not even at Twitter anymore!'

Smiling at that welcome news, Em giggled excitedly. 'How can anyone think they hold any kind of moral high ground by intentionally *deceiving* people?', she pontificated, raising her hands up to heaven. 'By repressing the truth?! What's up with that???'

'Oh, oh...they're all just assholes!', Guildencrantz exclaimed, still unable to keep a straight face.

Emily raised her fist in the air defiantly. 'Stinky assholes! Like – like a fart through a face mask!'

Stuck on that image Guildencrantz lost it completely. He could barely stop chortling long enough to bleat: 'Oh, yeah – <ha!!> that – that magic <chuckle!> face mask! Can't stop a fart <ROTFFL!> but it'll – it'll somehow <ha!> somehow – protect you – protect you <chortle!> from the China Virus!!'

Laughing their asses off it took a good half minute before either of the two secret service agents calmed down enough to get more than two words out. Neither was in any rush. It felt so good to laugh again! To laugh at and mock all the people who'd done them and the United States of America so much wrong!

Guildencrantz finally wiped his eyes to clear them. Though the tears were gone the twinkle in them still remained. 'I saw somebody from St. Louis talking online about the absurdity of masks. He was a lung doctor at one of the larger hospitals. He explained it this way: coronavirus is 1/2000th the size of a particle of smoke from a burning house fire. If a cloth mask can't stop smoke from getting in your lungs, it sure as hell can't stop a virus! Masks are for reducing the amount of germs such as bacteria from getting in your lungs, but they can't do a thing against sub-microscopic particles like viruses! When the CDC came out and admitted that cloth masks aren't any good at stopping smoke they inadvertently let the cat out of the bag and admitted cloth masks don't work! They've been advocating a placebo this whole time!'

Emily nodded. 'Yup. Cloth masks are as useless as using my grandma's afghan to serve a bowl of soup in! I mean if it can't even keep out smoke how's it supposed to somehow filter out a tiny virus you can't even see?!' She pinched her finger. 'I mean, it's a virus! You can't even find a virus with the microscopes we used in science lab in high school! Viruses are barely as big as a Democrat's prick! And Covid-19 keeps getting weaker, not stronger! Each new mutation helps it die out.'

'Attenuation.', Guildencrantz said with a nod, supplying the medical term. 'If funny how they keep avoiding talking about that, ignoring the medical facts about how viruses work.'

'Exactly! Attenuation. They keep trying to pretend human beings don't defeat viruses all the time! Instead they pretend each mutation is a new virus to keep everyone scared – and banning anyone on the social networks who speaks the truth! This whole "we're gonna shut you down for spreading medical misinformation" is all non-scientific horseshit!'

The left's fear tactics and intentional misinformation campaign really pissed the two agents off. When politics crossed over into manipulating healthcare it crossed the line! The CDC and WHO had been worse than useless – steering people into expensive treatments when cheaper ones worked just as well or better! It was all about making money, not helping people! How could these people call themselves doctors?! How could Herr Fauci be considered an expert on anything?!

'I think the Deep State and the Social Networks must be held account-able. This isn't just business as usual. Facebook and the lot should be sued over all the wrong information they've been peddling over coronavirus. They've been actively shutting down whistle blowers trying to inform the public about how they are being lied to.', Guy said, lowering his voice so he didn't wake the sleeping buffoon tucked away in the adjacent room. 'It's willful negligence.'

Still riled up, his partner was more emphatic. 'There should be a Special Investigator!', she proclaimed. 'A Special Counsel to look into all the harmful lies the media told about this disease!'

Guy nodded. 'At least Durham's on a roll. Heads are finally rolling.'

Wanting to seriously kick some ass Agent Em clenched her fist. 'I hope they work up the food chain and get ALL of those bastards! Certainly Page and Strzok need to be executed!'

'Don't forget about Clapper! And Super-Patriot – what's his butt?

'Comey! Comey!', Rosenstern replied, slapping her forehead. 'Jeez, I can't believe I forgot James Comey! He should be the first one on the list! Spying on the President of the United States! His boss! And actually lying to him to his face!!'

Guy nodded vigorously. 'They should all be in front of a firing squad – Comey up front.'

Emily agreed. 'James Comey – fucking super-traitor!!!'

Ready to clean house they sat in somber silence for a moment.

Guy Guildencrantz finally shook his head. 'I still can't believe the Republicans allowed this to happen.', he remarked in disbelief. 'They just stood by and let the crazies take over, like it didn't matter who was in charge.'

Less charitable to the political class Emily Rosenstern held a more cynical view. She wasn't ready to give any of the mother fuckers in Washington DC a free pass! 'Oh, come on – they had to be in on it!

That or co-conspirators in some other schemes with these douche bags that would come to light if they tried to stop it! For every Comey, there's a Romney or a Cheney. They all live neck deep in the Swamp! They are Swamp Creatures, profiting at our expense!'

Knowing she was right, Guy frowned and nodded. 'Screwing people over is just another day at work for them. It's a business.'

Emily shook her head. 'I wish we could get rid of them – all of them.'

'We are.', Guy replied, miming like he was washing dirt off his hands. 'Taking them out in the primaries one by one.'

Rosenstern sighed. 'Too bad there's not a faster way. They need to be gone, like, yesterday.'

Guy agreed. After a second the twinkle returned to his eye. 'Maybe there is a faster way.', he said with a sardonic grin.

Feeling a story coming on, her eyes lit up. 'Oh, yeah? Tell me.'

Smirking, Guy cracked his knuckles. 'So once upon a summer time...'

Rinos V. Rhinos

The hidden retreat was a veritable paradise. Nestled in the foothills of an out of the way pocket at the Southern border of the Canadian Rockies the campsite was secluded but lush, with a long stretch of cabins ideally suited for vacationing guests and elite dignitaries. Privacy was the greatest concern of the current residents who today graced this out of the way resort and the cabins were capped with tall pines obscuring overflights so the who's-who of the old guard Republican party could get down and boogie out of the watchful eyes of their common folk constituents. Some had already chosen to retire from public life to enjoy the ill-gotten fruits of their service to the state (and the rest – if they had any sense at all – *should* have quickly reached the same conclusion) and able to "let their hair down" the atmosphere about the cabins was carnival. Dress was casual but as this was not an officially sanctioned Congressional coke-binge fueled orgy appropriately demure and adorning three long tables wine, liquor, beer, fruit, sauteed vegetables and meat straight off the bone waited to be devoured at leisure by revelers as they strolled by.

The camp ground guest list was extensive and included the biggest names in Republican corruption. There was Ronna Romney McDaniel, RNC Chairwoman and niece of Senator Mitt "Oven-Mitt" Romney (also in attendance) with her spouse Patrick; Georgia Governor Brian Kemp and Georgia Secretary of State Brad Rafen Sperger, both of whom helped orchestrate changing the 2020 Presidential election from Donald Trump to Mail-In Biden by refusing to call the state legislature into session despite overwhelming evidence of election fraud, including but not limited to: actual video tape of thousands of secret "ballots" being scanned when no poll watchers were present, eight thousand pages of eyewitness testimony claiming election fraud and bills of lading showing hundreds of thousands of illegal ballots transferred across state lines. Another governor, RINO Larry Hogan of Maryland, also an outspoken opponent of President

Trump, common sense and putting American interests first was in attendance as well.

Of Senators there were seven: former Senators Richard Burr of North Carolina and Pat Toomey of Pennsylvania, both of whom had wisely retired after voting to remove Trump during the Forty-Fifth President's second fake Impeachment trial on the absurd grounds that objecting to election fraud and demanding full audits and accountability was somehow "Inciting Insurrection"; Senators Bill "Hop-Along" Cassidy from Louisiana, Ben "Sassy" Sasse of Nebraska and Susan "Make Me a Tom" Collins of Maine who voted the same on the grounds that the President – who is the only reason outright open warfare to restore legitimate government did not ensue – did not object "quickly enough" to quell the violence (the trios' seats would be up for re-election and subsequent removal in 2026); aforementioned Senator Oven-Mitt Romney of Utah, the incompetent 2012 loser to infamous snake oil salesman Barrack Obama, who'd had the gall to twice vote to remove the President to whom he directly owed his seat in 2018; and finally Lisa Murkowski, outrageous half-baked Senator from Alaska who's political head was first up on the chopping block in the primary of 2022.

From the House of Representatives the list of jackasses-in-elephant-garb was likewise extensive: Liz "Look Out, She's Got a Gun!" Cheney of Wyoming; Tom "White" Rice of South Carolina; Dan "Slums" Newhouse and Jaime Herrera Beutler from Washington; Anthony "Don't call Me Tony" Gonzalez and David "James" Joyce of Ohio; imbeciles Adam Kinzinger and Rodney Davis of snake oil salesman Barrack Obama's Illinois; Fred Upton and Peter Meijer, close personal friends of hypocrite Gestapo-Governor Gretchen "Witless" Whitmer of Michigan; from corrupt mob-run New York: John Katko, Tom Reed, Andrew Garbarino and Chris Jacobs, all secret Democrats; David Valadao from the environmentalist-crazy, forest-fire starting desert state of California; Romney sycophants John "Fork You" Curtis and Blake "Spoons" Moore of Utah; Brian "Fizzy" Fitzpatrick of Pennsylvania, hater of the automotive industry; illegal immigrant supporters Tony "Don't Call me Anthony" Gonzales and Van "Vin Number" Taylor of Texas; Dusty "Dust-for-Brains" Johnson of South Dakota; Chris Smith, panhandler from New Jersey; David "Fort" McKinley of West Virginia; Don "Pork-Barrel" Bacon and Jeff "I Farted" Fortenberry jailing – hailing – from Nebraska; Maria Elvira "MES With Me" Salazar and Carlos Gimenez, fresh off the boat from Florida; Mariannette Miller-Meeks "Triple M" of Iowa (victim of too many Absenth laced-buckeyes); from Arkansas: Steve "Grab Ass" Womack and "Freshy" French Hill, stems from the same family bush; Stephanie "Beijing" Bice of Oklahoma, Chinese Apologist; Mike "Wait One Potato Pickin' Minute" Simpson of Idaho; Michael "House" Guest of Mississippi; and lucrative post-political career job-seekers Trey Hollingsworth from Indiana and Cliff "Mercedes" Bentz of Oregon.

'As I was saying – ', failed 2012 Presidential hopeful Mitt "Oven-Mitt" Romney drunkenly rambled on, 'Donald Trump upset the apple cart. We've had an under-the-table arrangement with our Democratic friends for decades: we each stay on our respective sides and quietly take our cut of the campaign money and side deals that come up. They get minorities and the working class, we get the more lucrative business class. They take pro-choice, we take pro-life.' Romney hiccuped then paused to take a stiff drink and silently break wind. 'The key part of this arrangement is to make sure that nothing (or at least as little as possible) actually gets done – solving problems eliminates the argument and without ongoing political conflict there's no reason for the campaign dollars to keep coming in. Same thing is true with the kickbacks – you've got to create demand.'

His simpleton niece Ronna McDaniel chimed in. 'But uncle, aren't you concerned about the Democrats' election steal? Won't they just keep doing it every time? I'm worried we will lose our allies in the primaries. I mean, I control the RNC's money but the Trump camp is out-raising us by huge margins. He's polling in the high 90s – and he's got *Truth Social* now! People don't trust us anymore.'

'Once Trump is out of the way for good things will go back to normal.', Oven-Mitt breezed dismissively. 'I promise you – everything will be fine. Conservatives will have no choice but to fund us again once he's gone.'

Louisiana Senator Bill "Hop-Along" Cassidy shook his head. 'I don't know. These Dems these days is pretty goddamned crazy. This ain't normal – they ain't normal. Who in their right mind champions shutting down the oil industry? Electric cars and wind power? Guaranteed Income for people who don't work? These people are living in the goddamned nuthouse. They're crazy.'

McDaniel shrugged. 'All the better for our election prospects. Like my uncle said – the Dems are creating a need for us. We should win in a landslide!'

Half-baked Alaska Senator Lisa Murkowski shook her head. 'Not if they change the votes again we won't! I don't know about anyone else but I'm concerned about the Primaries. Trumpism is threatening my seat! And beyond that I'm really worried the Dems won't give up power! I mean, changing the votes to Joe Biden?! That was a fucking coup d'etat if ever there was one! Sure, I hate Donald Trump for derailing our gravy train – but damn!!! Biden's bad for business! He's a joke!!!'

Ex-senator Richard Burr nodded. 'For all the trouble we have convincing the common folk to give us their loyalty (and their money) there is something to be said for Democracy. We shouldn't be so quick to give it up. Playing the game is our bread-and-butter.'

'Bet you $1,000,000 come 2024 when the Dems lose they'll claim the votes were tampered with.', joked Tom "White" Rice of South Carolina. 'Their crazy-ass supporters will believe anything!'

'And the media will assure them they are right.', agreed Dan "Slums" Newhouse.

'It is very one-sided.', agreed ballot-stuffing Georgia Secretary of State Brad Rafen Sperger. 'A "Free Press" is supposed to be free to report the news without government censorship, not promote the propaganda of one side. They are election campaigning 24/7 for the Democratic party, not reporting the news.'

Ex-Pennsylvania Senator Pat Toomey shrugged. 'Well, as long as I'm rich I really don't care. I'm out of the game for good now.'

'Well, I am concerned about the money I have invested in the Stock Market. It seems like the Dems are actually trying to push us off the Socialist cliff!', fretted Liz "Look out, She's got a Gun" Cheney, completely ignoring the fact that she herself had worked to get these jokers into power. 'That's bad for everybody. I worked to shove Trump out of office so I could get richer, not be taken to the poorhouse! Aren't there any moderate Dems we can work with?'

'Used to be.', Mariannette "Triple M" Miller-Meeks of Iowa said. 'I don't know anymore. All the moderates seem to be gone. AOC, Sanders and the far Leftist are running the show now. Pelosi even teased that she was going to retire – not that she ever compromised with us on anything.'

'After the election they wouldn't even take my calls!', complained Susan "Make Me a Tom" Collins of Maine, male transsexuals in women's high school sports supporter due up for removal from her senate seat in

2026. 'I've never experienced such outright disrespect before! It's unprofessional! How do they expect to make deals with us if they won't sit down to the negotiation table? We are all horse-traders looking to get our cut – it's how we make our money!'

'It's almost as if they think they don't need us anymore – that the people will accept one-party rule.', whined imbecilic Representative Adam Kinzinger of Illinois, sounding a little like the classic protagonist mewing "Please sir, may I have some more?" did in *Oliver Twist*.

'We have it in California.', noted Representative David Valadao, proud of the dysfunctional state of his absurd State.

'And look at what a mess you're in! You make all the bigwig assholes in Hollywood rich but you can't keep the damned lights or the goddamned air conditioning on! The chaos in California – literally – spreads like wildfire!', Don "Pork-Barrel" Bacon joked, referring to the brown outs and recurrent wildfires Newsome's forestry incompetence had directly caused. 'Makes you wonder how in the hell Democrats keep getting elected...'

Georgia Election-Steal Governor Brian Kemp nearly choked on his drink. 'Voter fraud, obviously.', he blurted with a cough. 'If 2020 proved anything it's that free and fair elections in the US are an illusion. If you don't give people a choice, what does it matter? People still talk about the assassination of JFK – but how were the last four years any different? Example: The New York Post ran a piece where Obama and Trump did the exact same thing – shared information on terrorists with Russia – and the headline read "Trump Revealed Highly Classified Information to Russian Diplomats" instead of "US Offers to Share Syria Intelligence on Terrorists with Russia" like it did with Obama. It's a total snow job. They write hit pieces, not news.'

'That's why they call it "Character Assassination".', chuckled Nebraska Senator Ben "Sassy" Sasse. 'There's just no there, there LOL!' He shook his head. 'If you're too stupid to know any better you must be one of the sheep.'

'There, there, Mr. President! There, there!', Fred Upton of Illinois teased.

Cackling at unfairly abused President Donald Trump's expense the assembly of corrupt sycophants all shared a laugh.

Suddenly the clucking fools' conversation was interrupted by a low rumbling. 'What the hell is making that stupid noise?', bitched Mitt "Oven Mitt" Romney.

The reveling RINOs turned and pointed their snooty noses towards the unfamiliar sound. As they watched a curious dark silhouette slowly pushed its way through the bushes. Standing just slightly higher than the height of a normal human man the creature nibbling its way through the foliage had widely spaced eyes on either side of its head and an elongated snout that curved upwards into a fuzz covered horn. 'What the fuck is that???', Senators Bill "Hop-Along" Cassidy from Louisiana and Half-Baked Alaska Senator Lisa Murkowski exclaimed in unison.

Hearing noise the strange beast turned towards them and blinked. Fearful of the humans it retreated away from them back into the brush.

Believing it gone the herd of political elites breathed a sigh of relief and turned their attention back to their drinks. Their calm was short lived, however. A much, much larger specimen thundered its way through the bushes, trampling them as it went. Standing more than twice the height of the tallest man present it snorted ominously at the bipedal predators who'd scared its young calf. The horned mother was joined presently by four more wooly beasts and together they created a massive wall of hairy flesh between their collective offspring and the herd of RINOs. Soon even more joined them and the forest beyond the gigantic beasts became just a backdrop of timber.

Hidden away in the northern wilds of North America since the last ice age the long-thought extinct Wooly Rhinoceroses had only come into this region a few weeks ago because of a very usual and unprecedented bit of climate change. The herd normally took great pains to avoid humans, but Covid-19 had shut down much of the world's industry and because so many fewer people were driving their cars the sudden drop in the carbon dioxide emissions had caused the low plant life the massive herbivores depended on for their sustenance to suffer. In ecology change always causes stress and deprived of their primary food supply these massive herbivores had been forced out of their hidden enclave into the base of the Southern mountains by the very environmental activism that was supposed to preserve rare species.

But beyond the ever-present need to find sustenance one thing causes a herd, or Crash, of mother Rhinos extreme stress: any predator threatening their precious offspring. Aggressive in the extreme African Mother Rhinos charge whenever they believe their calves might be in danger and at 4,000 pounds they are second only to the elephant in terms of size and strength. This particular Crash of Rhinoceroses was of a different long-forgotten era, though; larger, stronger and much bigger than their African counterparts they weighed in at five tons rather than the usual two. Spooked by a group of bipedal predators laying in wait so close to their young the titanic mothers of the Wooly Rhino Crash barreled as one straight into the camp of RINOs. Food laden tables splintered like chopsticks, wine bottles scattered and kegs of beer were upended or spewed froth in the air like miniature geysers. The herd of political elites partying at the resort weren't so lucky. Skewered through the rump like kabobs Oven-Mitt Romney and his stupid spoiled niece Ronna McDaniel were impaled in the first wave. Carried along as trophies their limp bodies jiggled as the Mega-Rhinos tossed Tony "Don't Call me Anthony" and Anthony "Don't Call me Tony" Gonzales into the air then squashed Van "Vin Number" Taylor, Dusty "Dust-for-Brains" Johnson, Chris Smith, David "Fort" McKinley, Don "Pork-Barrel" Bacon and Jeff "I Farted" Fortenberry like bugs.

Trying to flee the carnage Georgia Governor Brian Kemp and Secretary of State Brad Rafen Sperger ended up trapped between the two Romney hood-ornamented Wooly Rhinoceroses. Becoming the fleshy meat in a Romney/McDaniel-Rhino sandwich the gigantic beasts crunched them together like corn chips atop a bowl of chili. The rest of the herd of Rhinos meanwhile continued to charge through the crowd, ending the legislative careers of Maria Elvira "MES With Me" Salazar, Carlos Gimenez, and Mariannette "Triple M" Miller-Meeks in the process.

Squealing like pigs every establishment Senator or Representative – past or present – eventually ended up getting the horn or being trampled underfoot. The aggressive Crash of Wooly Rhinoceroses did not calm down until the last RINO was smashed to a pulp and not a single cabin was standing. Satisfied their young were finally safe the titanic beasts devoured the scattered fruits and vegetables before turning away and heading for greener pastures. In the battle for supremacy the better creature had won. The Rhino Crash had trampled the RINO herd into extinction. Order had been restored to the forest.

*   *   *

'Ooo, you go there with yo' bad self! Mmm-hmmm!', Emily cheered, mimicking her favorite pod casters Diamond and Silk.

'Tha's right, girl!', Guy replied, playing along.

They did tit-for-tat for several go rounds before Agent Rosenstern finally held up her hand. 'Okay, okay – I gotta go after the "thought-leader" of the Democratic party now.'

Wanting to hear it but worried they were running short on time Guildencrantz glanced at his watch. It was after three – they still had more than an hour left to kill. He was almost sad this day was passing by so quickly; as much as he hated the traitors he was forced to work for mocking the assholes who were running this shit show into the ground was so therapeutic he almost didn't want to go home! There were so many funny stories they could tell! 'You go, girl! We still got seventy-two minutes – correction, seventy-one now – left to kill before our relief shows up. Lay it on me, Agent Girl!'

So This is Earth?

Hiking in queue down the flashlight illuminated trail the six prime specimens of Homo Liberalis took care not to lose their footing on the treacherous slope. Comprised of five females and one token male the denizens of the House of Representatives were far, far removed from the respective districts they were supposed to represent. This was not New York or Michigan or the stupidest, most-depressing part of Missouri; they were in the deep desert of Arizona well away from the prying eyes of their constituents on a mission to "inspect the southern border". The reason for this change of venue could be easily discerned from a simple search of their backpacks: the squad of six were toting all manner of illegal substances recently acquired at the southern border from the drug cartels their party had for years been conspiring with to keep the border wide open and intentionally unsecured. Dulling their minds further than usual was a pastime that required secrecy (and to travel on the taxpayers' dime, an excuse) and so for this reason they had come to this desolate place seeking to lose themselves in the barren wastelands....and get themselves wasted. What litter they left to pollute the pristine sands would go unnoticed and eventually get swallowed up by the empty wilderness – unless, of course, they were met by a pack of illegal immigrants trying to sneak their way across the border. In that (somewhat) unlikely event the squad of six would simply point the way in and afterward tell the cameras heartfelt tales about how the poor downtrodden people they met on their tour of the border were suffering terribly and deserved to be allowed to invade the United States, drain its public resources and hurt the wages of everyday Americans. That a legal entry point with medical facilities to check the potential immigrants for disease (and computers to verify they weren't criminals wanted for murder, rape and child sex trafficking) was only thirty miles away would go unmentioned as would the fact that only a few years before – during the disastrous Obama Presidency – the whole Democratic party was clamoring like hell for a border wall. Those soundbites had all been for show, though, and now that they held the illegally obtained reins of power Democrats intended to do absolutely nothing to fix this problem (or any other). Safe behind their own high walls and private security forces they didn't care about protecting the average American citizen. Undocumented aliens gave them something to exploit (and they needed more illegal votes to stay in power) so as long as they themselves were safe what happened to actual everyday Americans was of no consequence.

Tromping along without a care – or intelligent thought – in the world, AOC abruptly paused her hike. 'So Ilhan – I'm confused.', she announced to no one's surprise. 'If you divorce your husband...is he still your brother?'

The uncomfortable facts of her immigration into the USA sticking in her craw Ilhan Omar didn't answer simpleton AOC's seemingly innocent little question. She had already complained about this scandal on her Twitter account. How she got into this country was a forbidden subject, as was her hatred of the Jews or of the America she was supposed to represent. How dare anyone challenge her with uncomfortable questions she didn't want to answer?! That everything about America was so much better than her homeland of Somalia was left unsaid – well, except for when President Trump had the audacity to point that inconvenient truth out to the public. Forty-Five also had a nasty habit of focusing voters' attentions on the fact that the worst parts of America were in the districts the squad was supposed to represent. Like the rest of her liberal friends Omar hurriedly beat on the drum of oppression, called Trump a white supremacist and charged him with inciting violence towards her person. Only racists disagreed with or pointed out how bad any Democrat's job performance was! Whites could *never* criticize a black person!

Up ahead dark-skinned and very fat Rashida Tlaib suddenly broke wind.

'Hey! No farting!', Alexandria Ocasio-Cortez complained, sucking it in deep like she could contain the offending stench and keep it from affecting the rest of the world. 'It's bad for the environment! Don't you care about the oh-zone?!'

While the others waved their arms like fans Cori Bush smiled and like Ocasio-Cortez breathed in Tlaib's ass gas like it was air freshener. Far removed from the horrendous smells of her section of the city of St. Louis Missouri she found the cleanliness of the air out here in Arizona disquieting. The fresh breeze smelled too conservative for her taste. 'You guys are just so awesome!', she gushed, star-struck to be in the presence of such important up-and-coming uber-liberals like Omar, Pressley, AOC and Tlaib. 'Me and Jaamal are just so glad to be here!'

'I want to create a bill to outlaw farts.', twittered the squadron's leader stupidly. Brushing the hair out of her vacant eyes AOC tromped forward to keep close to Tlaib in case she had to diffuse another of her smart bombs. 'Farts are a threat to Mother Earth!'

Marginally less ridiculous than the backward-thinking former bartender-turned-Democratic-legislator the other squad members of Clan Stupid Fuck nodded like sheep but did not reply. Focusing their attention on their feet to avoid stones the imbeciles continued down the path until they finally reached level ground. An open canyon lit by a bonfire their underlings had prepared for them was waiting, illuminating a small section of dark desert. This was the Democrats' party site.

'Wow, that was quite a hike!', exclaimed Ayanna Pressley. Throwing her bag of marijuana beside the fire the ridiculously bald former Planned Parenthood abortion model stretched her aching shoulders. They should have made their staffers carry their things – after all, it was what slaves were for. 'We should create a commission to look into building transporters – like they have on Star Trek.', she joked.

'Nah – the damage to the environment caused by transporters is just as bad as from cars.', AOC declared confidently as she tossed her satchel filled with cocaine next to Pressley's bag of Mary Jane. Nudged closer to the fire's edge the bag filled with reefer began to slowly blacken. 'You gotta calculate the production costs to figure the total damage caused by stuff like that. I thought about chairing a commission to study the problem, but my advisers' advisers advised me against it.'

It took a moment for the other members of Clan Stupid Fuck to figure out what the text of the former bartender's repetitive babbling meant. As usual it didn't really matter, though, and like the rest of Ocasio-Cortez' exclamations most of them let it pass like a fart in the wind. Ilhan Omar was the only hold out. 'That's too bad.', she said with a little chuckle, oblivious to the reality that the "transporter devices" used on Star Trek were science fiction television magic and not real life technology. 'It would be nice to get to the places where you wish to go much faster than it takes now.'

'Yeah – ', Ocasio-Cortez agreed stupidly. 'And it would show just how evil cars are!' Pissed that she had to take an airplane and three cars to get here, she stamped her feet like a toddler throwing a temper tantrum. 'People in Republican states are so stupid! We need wind and solar power now – before it's too late! The planet is dying!', she whined.

'They're all on drugs.', declared Rashida Tlaib as she fiddled with her sack of party favors. The collection plate came around and she added her contribution to Democracy: two pounds of hash brownies. Killing two birds with one stone the flatulent fatty scooped out three huge squares before passing the platter along to Cori Bush.

Less of an obese pig than her congressional rabble-rouser colleague the newest member of the squadron nabbed a single brownie. 'You know, it's so nice to be out here where there's no police to harass us.', the freshman representative from Missouri commented as she dumped a heavy helping of toasted raviolis next to the brownies. A St. Louis delicacy she'd cooked them herself in the microwave like an idiot; half the ravs were tough as burned rubber while the others were *al dente* and limp as a noodle. None were the delicious golden brown they'd have been were they cooked properly in a convection oven – as any true St. Louisan who'd ever enjoyed the scrumptious authentic Italian dishes on the Hill would know. 'It's the first time I've felt safe in a while.'

'Yeah, I know!', squawked AOC with a little giggle. 'This place is like a suburb! I mean there's no crime here, right? Making someplace "police-free" turns dangerous places into suburbs!'

Sure she'd hit on the answer to making America safe and crime-free the stupid spoiled girl added her item to the pile: a single loaf of uncooked garlic-buttered french bread. Pleased with her contribution to the festivities the thought leader of the jackass party held up the plate for all to see. 'And I didn't even have to shoplift the bread because my rent is already paid up for the year!', she declared absurdly.

The assembled butt-kissers cheered her "accomplishment" as the pretty stupid girl passed the over-large platter over to Jamaal. The token male in the squad, Bowman offered up his meat to be gnashed to pieces by the surrounding pack of she-wolves: a half-dozen burgers with all the trimmings. As one the affronted female squad members gasped in horror.

Alexandria Ocasio-Cortez held up her hand to silence them. 'It's okay, it's okay – I went with Jamaal when he got these and the lady at the counter said they're bison burgers! Bison burgers! Completely vegetarian and made out of free range bison plants!', she assured her woke-believe followers with great cheer. 'Since they're not real hamburgers and don't come from cows they're not real red meat! I'm a vegetable-arian and even I can eat them! We're setting a good example for others – and making sure we aren't hurting the environment!'

Not fluent in the nuances of English but knowing how important it was to her career to second her woke leader, Ilhan Omar nodded her ignorance. The plate came her way and the painfully skinny antisemitic Somalian misrepresenting Minnesota offered her wares up to her fellow squad members: plantain and a pound of heroin. Still refusing to be assimilated into American culture she eschewed the brownies and hamburgers but took a small chunk of uncooked bread to placate her thought leader's ego. 'We must do all we can to save the environment.', she ass-kissed.

Uncorking a bottle of fifty dollar wine Ayanna Pressley filled up her plastic cup and raised it to cheer their little cabal's success. 'To black, brown, queer and Muslim voices all saying what we want them to!', the bald representative from Boston toasted with a sneer, ignoring the fact that Islam had historically persecuted homosexuals and homosexuality. 'Death to dissenters!'

'Yes, Death!'

'Cancel them!', roared AOC intolerantly. Unaware that firing or discriminating against someone for their political beliefs was a violation of creed protected by the Constitution in many states – including her own in New York – the pretty-stupid party girl downed the alcohol in her cup like the bartender she used to be. Fueled by liquor she started in on the coke.

'Praise Allah in her infinite wisdom!', Rashida Tlaib exclaimed, blaspheming the religion she claimed to uphold. Waiting for her turn to snort some coke she inhaled the fumes coming off the bonfire liberally; Pressley's bag of weed had caught fire and was smoldering nicely. Her ravenous appetite further fueled by reefer the fat twat stuffed another hash-filled brownie in her mouth then grabbed a burger.

'You know – ', bald bitch Ayanna Pressley from Massachusetts rambled between overpriced sips of wine as the flames on the other side of the fire away from her turned her $1500 satchel into a giant smoldering Doobie. 'It's just so nice to be out here without any fucking white people for once! Sometimes I really hate whites! Not all the time – just like 80% of the time. Fucking Distraction Beckies! It so nice to be around just my niggas!'

'Heck yeah!', AOC said, cheering Pressley's racism and ignorant (as she was about virtually everything) of the fact that almost all old world Hispanics had a considerable amount of Caucasian blood in their genes. 'Those stupid white people!'

'Stupid, racist privileged white people!', flatulent Tlaib declared, attacking her hash-brownie-burger with the same zeal she did races other than her own. Her mouth now full, she pontificated on. 'They just want to build walls to keep out all the brown people! Walls don't stop white people! They just walk right on through them like ghosts and leave the rest of us out here in the desert to fend for ourselves and starve to death!'

Eagerly joining in their white hatred and overt racism, Cori Bush motioned them all closer. 'Down with Whitey! Sistas get together! Whooo-hooo!', she cheered.

Cloaked in the unrighteous garb of perpetual victim-hood and race-baiting the sisterhood of woke woe-is-me embraced one another with euphoric glee. Everything was the fault of the White Man! If they complained long enough the world would turn Left and embrace the joys of impending Environmental Disaster! Only by slitting the throat of the world economy could they bring about certain doom and thereby save the planet from humanity's evil!

Left outside of their vagina clique token dude Jamaal Bowman felt his manhood shrivel. He sidled up like a pathetic orphan and because of the color of his skin was finally accepted into their little cult. The circle of woke now complete the half-dozen doughnut holes smiled as one.

'You girls rock!', the Bush of Missouri exclaimed. 'And I mean that! You too, Jamaal! You're one of the girls now!'

Fully emasculated, Bowman beamed with pride. At last he was *finally* one of the girls!!!

So immersed in the drug of their mutual awesomeness was the absurd sisterhood of woke that the members of Clan Stupid Fuck failed to notice a stranger appear from out of the desert. Drawn by their fire the newcomer got within five feet of it before the chuckling fools finally noticed him. As one the squadron of perpetual victimization turned. The intruder was dressed in shabby clothes and a lopsided cap was on top his head. Beneath his get up he had a goofy face dominated by a gigantic nose and two prominent buck teeth. At first glance he looked dumb as a box of rocks. 'Ya'll having you-selves a shindig? Haha-haha-hay.', he chuckled.

'Who the heck are you?!', demanded AOC rudely. Eying the odd-looking drifter like he might be law enforcement she slid the pile of drugs behind her svelte silhouette to hide them.

But the disheveled stranger failed to notice. Smelling heavily of beer he began to laugh to himself happily. 'Who the heck am I? I'm John-Jay Jasper Jefferson, Jr. Ev'body round these parts calls me Jay-Jay. How ya'll doin'?'

'Um, fine.', Cori Bush replied tersely. Confronted by someone who was obviously one of "The Enemy" the white-hating black woman curled up into a defensive posture. This Jay-Jay was Caucasian – by definition all Caucasians were slavers and prejudiced racists! She didn't want to be enslaved by Whitey!!!

'Yeah, we're fine.', bald Ayanna Pressley said dismissively. 'Is there something we can help you with, Mr. Jay?'

'Aw naw, naw, I'm good.', hiccuped Jay-Jay toothily. 'Just saw...just saw the fire here and thought I'd be neighborly and come say "hey". So..."hey".'

Still believing him to be an undercover cop AOC eyed him warily. 'How'd you find us all the way out here?'

JJ shrugged. 'I was out walkin' and just kept walkin' t' the left. Then I saw ya'll had a bonfire an' I thought I'd come over.'

'You walked? All the way out here?', Pressley asked skeptically.

Mr. Jay nodded. 'Yup. Couldn't take my truck.'

'Too drunk?', offered Tlaib with a smirk and a fart.

Oblivious to being ass gassed Jay-Jay grinned toothily. Believing wholeheartedly that there was no such thing as being "too drunk", he shook his head. 'Nope. Outta gas.', he answered.

'Yeah – gas prices are so sky high right now!', AOC bitched, momentarily forgetting her suspicion of the stranger and oblivious to the fact that the Democrats' Green New Deal initiative that she herself had so stridently championed was the direct cause of the rise in fuel prices.

Jay-Jay nodded. 'Yup. Had a choice o' buying beer or gas, so I made the smart choice.'

'You bought beer instead of fuel?!', laughed Ilhan Omar.

The big-nosed wanderer nodded. 'A course! Can't watch NASCAR without beer!'

'So why aren't you at home in front of the TV watching it then?', Pressley scoffed at him.

'I run out o' beer!', he replied like it was obvious. 'That's why I'm walkin' – had to go git me some more! Can't watch NASCAR without beer!!!'

'We thought you were the border patrol.', AOL insisted stupidly, though clearly she was the only one foolish enough to ever suspect that.

Jay-Jay shook his head and snorted. 'Nah. Just out to git me some more beer. Hey, ya'll wouldn't have none I could buy off ya? Any of the good stuff – like Milwaukee's Best or Natty Light?'

'No. We only have wine.', Pressley answered snootily, lifting her plastic cup of ridiculously expensive 2012 Petit Verdot to show him.

The odd stranger's expression deflated at the news. 'Aw, shucks! No beer? That's terrible! I feel so bad for ya'll.' He cocked his head to the side quizzically. 'Did yer wine come in a box?', he asked.

Tlaib snorted, nearly choking on her last brownie. 'No, no...it's in a bottle.', she laughed derisively.

Quintuple J frowned. 'Oh. Didn't know it came in a bottle.'

Thinking he must be dumb as dirt Ayanna Pressley sneered at the goofy looking drifter. After a few seconds her disdain morphed into a look of glee. How much fun would it be to invite this "Deplorable" to sit down with them so they could mock him right to his face? He was so obviously drunk and stupid he probably wouldn't even realize they were making fun of him! 'Why don't we ask this....fine neighborly gentleman...to sit down with us and join our little party?', she offered. 'There's plenty of room next to the fire.'

'What?! Really?!', Bush exclaimed, afraid any second he might clap irons on her and sell her down the river.

'Ayanna! I don't know if there's enough...food.', AOC said, looking just as frightened and keeping her voice low. What if this Quadruple Jay-Junior smoked all their drugs and they ran out?!

The bald Nazi gave her a knowing look.

Realizing her Captain-Picard coiffed black friend must be up to something, ever so slowly the dim light bulb in Ocasio-Cortez' miniature brain brightened. 'Oh, I see.', she said after a moment. 'By all means, yes! Feel free to join us, Mr. Jay!'

'Well, that'd be...hic....mighty nice of ya'll.'

The pretty-stupid party girl patted the sands beside her and Jay-Jay took a seat. The plate of morsels was passed his way and the inebriated NASCAR fanatic snagged the burger Ilhan Omar had refused. 'Thank you kindly! Damn – these is some good eats!', he exclaimed, chomping down on the ketchup smothered meat.

'Yup! All vegetable!', insisted AOC ridiculously.

Swallowing the ground beef, John-Jay Jasper Jefferson, Jr. eyed what he was eating in wonder. 'Really? Holy cow! This is a veggies?! Tastes just like real meat!'

Jamaal Bowman smirked at the goofy-looking deplorable devouring the bison patty. The fool didn't know the difference between meat and vegetable! Strangely glad now that another male had joined them he leaned forward. 'So what do you think about standardized testing?'

Perplexed by the strange question J-Jay swallowed. 'Don't know about testing standardizement or whatever you is talking about.'

Bowman shook his head. 'I mean about giving everybody the same test. Don't you think it's racist?'

John-Jay Jasper Jefferson, Jr. blinked. 'Givin' ever'body the same thing is racist?', he replied quizzically.

'Sure!', insisted Jamaal B. 'It's like asking a monkey and a bird to both climb a tree!'

Quintuple J cocked his head to the side. 'Why don't the bird just fly?', he asked, confused.

'Exactly!', chirped Jamaal like it was obvious.

Cori Bush interrupted Bowman's absurd line of "reasoning" – clearly this was beyond the dorky-looking stranger's level of education! 'What Jamaal is saying is that black people are still slaves! He's saying that only white people are free! The rest of us are still enslaved by our shared history! We can't even get a loan from a bank!', she bleated, pointing accusingly towards the white slaver of her people.

Oblivious to her accusation but feeling her pain, JJJJ Jr. nodded. 'I tried that once too. Tried to buy me a new truck and the bank said I didn't have no "co-later-ya'll"! Said my double-wide weren't worth nothing!'

Exasperated, skinny Ilhan Omar waved her hand to get the Deplorable's attention. 'What Representative Bush is trying to say is that it is much easier for people who are white color to get loans than for those of us who are dark skinned.'

'Really?', John-Jay Jasper Jefferson, Jr. replied innocently.

'Yes. This is the truth.', Omar lied, consciously ignoring all the research that proved the exact opposite was true. Afraid of lawsuits and bad press, banks were oftentimes extending credit when the data said they shouldn't to insure than no charges of discrimination could be leveled against them.

Quintuple J scratched his head. His eyes suddenly lit up in understanding. 'So if'n I was to pour a bucket of white paint all over myself before I go t' the bank, they'd give me a loan so's I kin get a new truck?!', he cried excitedly.

Astounded by his stupidity, Ayanna Pressley breathed an epitaph into her hand. 'No. It's all about your parents and grandparents!', she insisted. 'It's racist!'

Jay-Jay cocked his head, still confused. After a momentary pause, he asked, 'So if'n my parents were to pour a bunch of paint on themselves and go wit me t' the bank, *then* I could git a loan??'

'No!', shouted Pressley in exasperation. How could Mother Allah make these Deplorables so freakishly dumb?!!! They must have been cursed by the Man-Satan!!!

'It doesn't work that way!', seconded privileged Alexandria Ocasio-Cortez. Seeing this Mr. Jay was stupid and would never understand what it meant to be racist, she swept the matter under the rug. 'Whiteness doesn't matter! The only color that matters is Red! We're gonna flip all the seats in America Red!', the pretty-stupid party girl insisted.

'Heck yeah!', Jay-Jay belched in agreement, thinking the imbecilic poster child for the Progressive bowel movement wanted to turn all of Congress to the Right side of history. The true reality was that Ocasio-Cortez was just a monumental idiot; the Democratic bartender-turned-legislator was so stupidly absurd she didn't realize that the Communism Red she foolishly embraced happened to also be the same color as the much more popular Trump Republican party.

'We can't have Donald Trump polluting Facebook or Twitter with his lies again!'. Tlaib suddenly complained with a fart, twisting the conversation back to her favorite rant. She absolutely hated that once upon a time other people had free speech too – life was so much simpler when no one was allowed to disagree with her! 'As I told my 1.5 million Twitter followers: freedom of speech just doesn't exist for Muslim women in Congress!', she declared absurdly.

'I think my three million followers would agree with you!', seconded Omar, ignoring as she always did the fact that the two Muslim women's combined audience of four and a half million completely disproved Tlaib's ridiculous assertion.

'We must silence him for good! Impeach the fucking bastard again!', roared Tlaib.

'Yes! Yes! Impeach!', declared AOC. 'Third time's the charm!'

The woke-fueled religious chant for yet another fake impeachment began in earnest only to be broken by a sudden thunderclap. This time it wasn't another one of Tlaib's mighty farts – the roar breaking the sound barrier came from above. Realizing it wasn't more of the fatty's flatulence the party-goers searched the night sky for signs of cloud cover that might suggest an impeding storm was about to cut short their festivities. But the moonlit darkness appeared clear.

'Wha? What was that?', super-dolt Alexandria Ocasio-Cortez bleated.

For several moments no one knew. They were all asking that same stupid question when suddenly a small object became visible, drawing their attention. Streaking across the horizon at first it looked dark. But as it got closer flickering sparks of light appeared around its silhouette.

'Is that a meteor?', queried Cori Bush.

'I don't know. It sure is bright. It looks like its glowing!', AOC exclaimed in wonder.

Quadruple-Jay Jr. suddenly rose from the fire side and began jumping up and down. 'My cousin Billy Beau Benjamin Bartholomew Buford said he saw something like that once!', he exclaimed, pointing excitedly at the approaching object. 'It's one o' them there flyin' saucers!!!'

'Space aliens? Are you mad?!', hissed bald bitch Ayanna Pressley with disdain.

Bush pointed up at the sky with increasing fright. The bright white object – it was coming to enslave her! 'It's coming this way!', she cried in terror.

'It's gonna squish us! Run!', seconded Jamaal Bowman.

Before any of them had time to scatter a brilliant beam of light abruptly enveloped the campsite. The half-dozen woke Representatives and the Deplorable guest they were making fun of suddenly found themselves unable to move. As they sank softly to the sand the unidentified flying object began to get larger. Slowing down as it approached their position the extra terrestrial craft descended to the desert floor as the paralyzing floodlight coming from its base slowly faded to a dull orange and finally disappeared. The captives remained stunned by the knock out ray, however, and could only watch helplessly as the flying saucer came to rest some twenty feet from the bonfire.

Their ship now landed on Terra Firma a door opened from the side of the space vehicle and two creatures emerged. Both were bipedal and wearing space suits.

The leader, the one members of his species called Kryxzelak, appraised their captives. 'That one.', the Grand Space Navigator ordered.

Chief scientist Quellum-num-num nodded. 'Yes. From our observations of their interpersonal communications this Jay-Jay is clearly the most intelligent. The others are not worth taking – they are obviously mentally deficient members of their species. I suspect they were shunned and sent out here to perish in the elements.'

Kryxzelak pointed to the smoldering weed and piles of narcotics heaped high upon the platter. 'What do you make of all this?'

The scientist assessed the artifacts. 'Likely used to placate the defectives so their caregiver Mr. Jay can abandon them to the desert without undue fuss.', Quellum-num-num theorized dismissively. Paying the drugs no mind he returned all his attention to his new specimen. This Jay-Jay was fascinating! Obviously adapted to be a superior hunter, his proboscis was so exceptionally large!

Kryxzelak paused momentarily to consider his chief scientist's supposition. 'A logical deduction. Perhaps the drugs are a ritual enhancement sent along to make their passage to the afterlife easier? We know so little about this species or how they deal with their defectives.'

'Very likely both.', replied the doctor absentmindedly. Two subordinates had just departed the space craft and at his direction were hoisting Quintuple Jay off the ground using an anti-grav ray. Their precious cargo now in stasis they placed him in a hermetically sealed cylindrical tube and took their new guest back to the ship.

As was the protocol for Grand Space Navigators in command of a star ship Captain Kryxzelak took one last look around the campgrounds to make sure he hadn't missed anything important. Feeling nothing was amiss he boarded his vessel. Shutting the hatch behind him he turned to his science officer. 'What do you think the response from the defectives will be once they learn their caregiver has left them?'

'I would anticipate great confusion. As mental defectives I expect they will lament his departure and succumb to panic.', Quellum-num-num replied confidently. 'We should record their response for posterity.'

His captain nodded. 'I will order it done. What will you do with the specimen before he is returned to his planet?'

'The usual protocol. Once I am finished with my investigations we will return him to his place of origin unharmed. To insure his survival and that of his progeny we should supply him with a generous supply of this "beer" he was foraging for. That should maintain the ecological balance of this bio-system.'

'It will be so.' Captain Kryxzelak gestured to the woke laying outside. 'And the defectives?'

The chief scientist did the extraterrestrial equivalent of a shrug. 'It is obvious they were sent out into this desert to die. We should do nothing to either aid or hinder them.'

Kryxzelak nodded his assent. 'How much time will you require?', he inquired.

'Three zebulans should be sufficient. We should be on our way shortly thereafter.'

'Very good. Keep me apprised of any changes.'

'Yes, Grand Navigator.'

*   *   *

'Datz-a-good! Datz-a-goo-da! Yay, a-very much-a!', Guildencrantz applauded as she concluded her tale.

Rosencrantz nodded her appreciation. 'Thanks! AOC and her cronies are pretty easy to mock. Hey – did you hear the crazies on the internet were threatening a little girl who was doing a caricature of her on YouTube?'

The male protection agent blanched. 'Really?! Threatening a child? A little girl?!'

'Yeah! She was like eight or nine years old. Can you believe it?!'

Guildencrantz's nostrils flared in outrage. 'That's...that's...'

'I know!!!'

Incensed, Guy shook his head in disgust. The Left had sunk that far into the muck – even children weren't safe from their hatred anymore! And the seeds of racial hatred they were sowing in school these days with Critical Race Theory!!!

Wanting to bury the lot of them he glanced down at his watch. It was almost time for their relief to show up. 'Hey, it's almost the end of our shift.

151

I know we agreed to do about the same number of stories for our little game but I got one more I just gotta tell. I know the bitch keeps claiming she's retiring – and then not doing it – but I got to take a stab at "Fancy Nancy" before the twat (supposedly) goes riding off into the sunset. She's been too much of a stupid hypocrite for too many years not to get the beat down she deserves. There was definitely harm and definitely many, many fouls.'

Emily Rosenstern soft-clapped her hands. 'Oh, hell yeah! Lay that fucking cunt out! I hear since there's so much light on her for her insider trading and her family is tied up in a "pump-and-dump" stock scheme she's not going to retire anymore! Talk about obvious "Obstruction of Justice" charges! There's an Impeachment that is deserved if there ever was one!'

Guy nodded stridently. Some calamity needed to befall Congress-fool Nancy Pelosi, big time – either the people in California were incredible morons or the voting system there was horribly broken! Fancy Nancy was an international embarrassment; she wasn't the Speaker of the House – she was the House Jester! How could the voters keep re-electing such an unbelievably corrupt joke?

Just Desserts

Fancy Nancy Pelosi pulled up a chair. Today was Sunday, which meant that to "honor" her Catholic upbringing she would binge out on copious amounts of designer ice cream – and to boost her metabolism (so that she kept the weight off her thin frail frame) consume equally large amounts of illicit drugs. The sin of gluttony combined with breaking the law was something of a finger she gave to holy mother church. Nancy didn't actually believe in any of that Catholic doctrine crap and most certainly did not practice what the Bible preached. She was anti-life and publicly took the stance that ripping small children apart with a suck-blender was a "personal choice", one to be kept solely between an emotion-ally distraught teenage mother and her Nazi Planned Death Agent – the rights of the expectant father, the grandparents and the child him or her-self be damned. The fact that she lied at least once a week demonstrated her absolute disdain for the concept of "thou shalt not bear false witness" and her video-taped flip-flops on the border crisis and the wall President Trump had built to fix the problem had become legendary. She had no intention of granting citizenship to the DACA kids (as the President had generously offered in 2017 and to date still had not happened); the whole point of bringing public attention to an issue was to place all the blame on your opponent for the problem but do nothing to actually fix it. It had been very upsetting to her when President Trump offered a viable solution to the immigration problem in his first State of the Union address. He was breaking the rules; politicians were not in Washington to actually solve problems but to profit off them.

Yes, Trump had been a huge nuisance but they'd gotten rid of him – at least for four years. Pelosi's original plan had been to be well out of office enjoying the vast wealth she'd amassed during her years cheating the American people out of theirs before the Slaughter-of-the-Democrats began and Trump was back in office. But that was before junior got involved with

Oroplata Resources in a fraudulent stock scheme and her husband made all those hugely profitable tech stock trades using the insider information she'd provided him with through her oversight position. Now that 2022 loomed large and the Democratic party was sure to suffer a crushing defeat she was going to have to run again to squash any investigations coming their way out of the suddenly-rogue elements of the Justice department. Somehow Durham had been able to go around the usual boundaries and seemed actually willing to prosecute anyone – regardless of their status. She had to stay in a position of power just to cover her own ass. Obstruction of Justice was a way of life for career politicians.

The only snag to her plan to avoid prosecution and keep lining her family's pockets was Joey B's obvious mental incapacity and corruption. If he had to step down, Kamala Harris had shown herself to be even more incompetent than her racist and perpetually befuddled running mate – and that left Nancy next in line. But the gleeful possibility of assuming the "Awesome Burden of the Presidency" (and the bribes she planned on accepting should it happen) was a worry for later and as long as she could go out to her favorite beauty shop regardless of any ridiculously absurd stay-at-home orders (the ones she and her draconian comrades imposed upon the little people but ignored themselves) Fancy Nancy was good. Rules were for slaves after all, not the ruling class.

The corrupt career politician's video phone suddenly rang. It was Mazie Hirono, the toady Senator from Hawaii. Hirono never called over business – she was a yes woman and didn't really *have* any business of any sort to discuss. Like the majority of Democrats currently in power she'd accomplished absolutely nothing over a long and boring career and only ever called to shoot the shit or find out when her next payday was coming. Crazy Mazie's greatest achievement in life to date was convincing people to give her their vote – not any real accomplishment considering Hawaii was blue as the ocean waves surrounding the islands. Stick a Democrat label on Adolph Hitler and the mass murderer who started World War Two would still win in a landslide in Hawaii. Satan herself could run for office and the anti-God crowd would happily donate billions to fund her campaign. CNN would spin it as a necessary separation of God from State.

But that was business that affected the lives of everyday hardworking Americans and completely unimportant to skinny Nancy Pelosi and her toady colleague. Ready to shoot-the-shit Hirono's fat flabby face appeared on screen. She took in the scene. 'Looks like it's ice cream time.', the senator commented happily.

Momentarily ignoring her colleague Pelosi opened her first bottle of fun-time happy pills and took a preparatory hit. Henrietta Liggoletta, her posh well-groomed drug dealer, still made house calls to the Pelosi mansion like any proper pharmaceutical sales rep and like her ice cream Fancy Nancy's choice of delights was also designer. Her "medicine cabinet" had a generous supply of Adderall, Cocaine, Ecstasy, Methamphetamine, Oxocodone and of course, Fentanyl – all recently imported through the wide open southern border tariff free, of course. Technically, the Congresswoman wasn't breaking the law; she had used her leverage with the FDA to obtain prescriptions for everything, even the controlled substances. Using drugs was the least of the vices a Congresswoman could get away with when law enforcement was compelled to always look the other way. She was far above the law and it still gave Nancy a special thrill to know that as long as she followed a few simple rules (most notably don't get caught with your pants down in a way you can't spin) she could pretty much get away with murder – as the Clintons had proved repeatedly. Deny and lie until the public gets bored and her media partners would do the rest: "Hey, ignore that! Look at this... look at this! Anyone who speaks the truth is lying, even if they show you proof!" Her constituents were retarded sheep – and if need be 2020 proved that votes could be Xeroxed with impunity.

Happily downing her first dose of X, Pelosi shivered with excitement. Anticipating the pleasure to come she stroked the pint of ice cream on the counter like it was her lover. Mmmm, Darkest Chocolate! So sexy! 'I love chocolate ice cream. The darker the better.'

'Don't you cook regular food?', crazy Mazie Hirono asked, skeptical Nancy could stay so trim binging on such delectable sweet meats. 'You can't just live on ice cream!'

Unconcerned, Fancy Nancy shrugged. 'My daughter Alexandra once told me, "Mother, you're a pioneer. Now, hardly anybody cooks, but you were one of the first to stop." After 20 years of cooking I started to appreciate the value of *other* people's work. So I would say, go get a duck in Chinatown. I always had the salad and set the table, but I didn't clean the pots.', she bragged.

Eying with envy all the fattening ice cream the skinny bitch had laid out in front of her the pudgy toad from Hawaii laughed derisively. 'That's exactly what peons are *for*, Precious. Slavery is still legal, we just have to pay them minimum wage now – and convince them they are lucky to get it and can somehow actually live on it! The sheep don't seem to realize how bad they got it – the dumb shits don't understand economics at all! They don't get that no company will ever be able to pay them more than what they produce! If we raise minimum wage the cost of a gallon of milk just triples! They get more money but everything costs more! It evens out and are still poor as shit.' Hirono rattled the glass in her hand, stirring the $255 a bottle oak aged whiskey inside. 'Doesn't really matter. As long as we keep skimming the cream off the top the best people are still getting what we deserve. Ice cream tastes better than salad.' The useless Asian-American career politician paused to stroke her fluffy, fat chin. 'So do you think they'll ever get Comey? The "Justice League" is still making waves.', she bitched, referring to Judicial Watch's ongoing efforts to shine a light on Washington's blatant corruption and finally rein it in.

'I think there's no question Comey abused power.', Pelosi answered dismissively as she popped the top on the Darkest Chocolate. Her sweet-treat looked so decadent it was absolutely sinful!

'Oh, stop it! The world is in flames.', Hirono retorted with a chortle. 'It's like "sexual preference". Just because Ruth Bader Ginsberg said "sexual preference" only three years before she croaked doesn't mean Amy Coney Barrett can say it too. The rules aren't the same for us – they can't be or we'll get burned. If Comey gets caught I say let the bastard fry – just so long as there's no way they can pin it on us. We can always "Epstein" him if he goes to jail so he can't reveal anything.' Starting to sound like a really fat version of Gollum the toady senator downed a heady shot of whiskey to clear the frog from her throat. 'There's nothing to link the DNC directly to him, right?', she hissed, swallowing the alcohol to send the phlegm down into her gullet. 'I mean I assume there's a trail of breadcrumbs even an idiot could follow, what with that Russian thing splattered everywhere and the New York Times finally admitting Hunter Biden's laptop was real, but it's something we can deny for the cameras, right? At least publicly claim it didn't happen to confuse the sheep? No direct money changed hands?'

Unconcerned, Pelosi stirred the ice cream with her spoon. 'No money changed hands, of course.'

'Good.'

Salivating, Pelosi snorted a quick line of Coke then without further delay dug into the iced chocolate delight. Doubly lit up now and savoring the cream on her tongue, the Speaker on borrowed time smirked. They were scurrying around like furry black spiders on white ceramic tile but somehow the American people still hadn't squished them. A part of her really wanted to brag about all their corruptions. After all they'd done to screw over America it was so hard to resist crowing in everyone's face. 'We really haven't gotten credit for what we've done.', she mouthed ironically.

Nervous about all the scrutiny and wise enough to sense that not everyone was so blasé about it Hirono-Gollum rattled the ice in her glass. Taking another drink to calm her frayed nerves she said: 'Well, look, it's a lesson learned for all of us. It took a lot of work and pay offs out the ying-yang to fix things. Convincing those stupid RINO Republicans behind the scenes that we'd actually work with them if they'd just help us cheat them out of power LOL! How weak and dumb are these people? How many low-life minimum wage losers did we have to bribe to fix all those ballots? The stupid morons who were dumb enough to do what we told them to do without question and are the ones on the hook if they get caught? How many thugs did we have to pay to toss out all those Trump ballots? How many did we have to hire to sign and date those mail-ins – and then to make the PDFs of the votes disappear?! I know the whole January 6th thing is bullshit, but it's a wonder we *didn't* get lynched!!! I was truly afraid the Proud Boys were going to storm the capitol and kill us all!! We had hundreds of thousands of veterans ready to fight us! And the military is *infested* with Conservatives!! We've got to disarm them, Precious!! Take away their guns – before they actually decide to use them on us!!'

Only half-listening and well aware that the remarkably peaceful protest of January 6th that they'd falsely branded as an Insurrection was a complete hoax, Pelosi paused to savor another spoonful of her chocolate. The Dems couldn't do much about the military other than to keep appointing political entities they had control over into the chief positions so they could "Deep State them" and order the obedient lower ranks under their command to stand down. The civilian population was another matter, though. Even though after a very thorough search the FBI hadn't been able to find any assault rifles or military surplus weapons in the crowd during the peaceful protest of January 6th – and in spite of twenty government agents trying to instigate violence while the real protesters themselves were on video chanting for peace – American patriots were unpredictable and had a history of championing Democracy, as the American Revolution of 1776 that had actually founded the country itself had proved. 'If I had my way, sporting guns would be strictly regulated, the rest would be confiscated.', the illegitimate Speaker of the House declared irritably.

'Damn right, Precious!', croaked Mazie-Gollum, railing as she rattled the drink in her hand. 'Screw the fucking 2nd Amendment and take away their fucking guns! It's the only way we'll ever be safe! I mean, I know it was a Republican – Steve Scalise – who got shot but the fucking shooter was from Illinois! I mean, that's deep blue! We've got to Xerox more votes for next time – now! We've got to take away their ability to resist! Make them comply! Disarm the terrorists and force them to submit at gun point! Any vote we can't write for ourselves is Jim Crow!'

More interested in pigging out than discussing election politics (or the discriminatory laws Southern Democrats used to champion to win elections before they resorted to outright election fraud), Fancy Nancy scarfed down the last of the container and shoved it in the trash like it was the State of the Union address she theatrically tore up for the cameras to please the stupid Never-Trumpers. To insure she didn't taint the next pint she tossed her used spoon in the sink and went to the drawer to get a fresh one. 'America will be far safer if we reduce the chances of a terrorist attack in one of our cities than if we diminish the civil liberties of our own people.'

Mazie-Gollum nodded so vigorously her flabby chin wagged like a yo-yo. 'That's what I'm saying – take control and disarm them! The Scalise shooting happened on a baseball diamond! A baseball diamond, Precious! Where was the Secret Service?! I'm telling you – Patriots are mad, Precious! Ready to take us out to the woods and nail us to a tree! We <u>must</u> stay in power or we'll *die*! The Senate is fifty-fifty! And we were barely able to make that happen! If that idiot Governor-what's-his-name had done what he should have done and called the State's Congress back into session...'

Engrossed in her personal entertainments, Fancy Nancy popped her Adderall and took a heady hit. Next on the menu was Blackout chocolate cake! So addictive! 'Civilization as we know it would be in jeopardy if the Republicans win the Senate.', she agreed.

Blood surging full of alcohol, drunken Hirono-Gollum's croaking voice rose. 'I'm not talking about power in 2022 here, Precious – I'm talking about our lives!'

Unfazed by threats about the future temporary Speaker of the House Nancy P delved liberally into the scrumptious pint of chocolate cake. So sweet and so creamy! 'It's all about turnout and how we connect with the voter as to what it means in their lives.', she declared, taking a huge bite. 'To win the House, the Senate, statehouses, governorships. The key is to be able to put forth a vision for our future and how this election affects people's lives. I would never think of crying about any loss of an office.'

'As long as it's not *your* office!', hissed Gollum, shaking the ice in her glass like a witch-doctor summoning spirits over a prostrate villager at death's door. 'Donald Trump nearly fucked us! And the orange hobgoblin is more popular now than ever! He's beating every possible candidate we have in the polls by at least a 10% margin!'

Scooping out a giant helping of sweet treat Pelosi suckled the spoon in her mouth like it was a bottle of mother's milk. Mmmm! '"We can withstand...", she quoted herself, talking with her mouth full, "A candidacy of Donald Trump. And when we emerge from this, it has to be respecting the position of those who supported him, addressing the anger and anxiety that they have, and, again, bringing the country together, which was always the purpose of our founders, a more perfect union.'"

'Oh, anal lube!', croaked Crazy Mazie, nearly spilling what little remained of her drink. 'You're not taking this seriously, Precious! They will never accept us! They believe we are traitors!' Her blood up the fatty chugged her drink dry then hurriedly refilled her glass.

Nancy took advantage of Hirono-Gollum's pause to savor another gigantic bite. Oh, Toasty Hell, this was some good shit! 'The word "campaign" is a war term.', she slurred, talking with her mouth stuffed so totally full it was nearly impossible to understand her. 'When you go into a campaign you must prepare to go to war. If you think it's an exercise in civil activity...'

'No – it's scorched earth.', Crazy Mazie Gollum agreed, glad her counterpart finally seemed to be getting it and the reasons why she was so unnerved. 'If a few civilians get killed along the way, so be it! I really don't care about Hiroshima or all this environmental crap or if any of the little slaves get axed! They don't matter! That thug who got killed by that fucking cop – George what's-his-name – that was the best thing that ever happened to us! It gave us the opening we needed to play the race card again! So what if all the scientific studies say systemic racism isn't real? We'll always have some sensational crime to put out in front of the camera so we can do our little song and dance!', she croaked, rubbing her plump hands together greedily. 'As long as we keep covering up any other narrative the sheep will go whichever way we tell them to! It's all about media power, Precious! Control the flow of information and we will always win!'

Pelosi's hands were starting to tremble from all the drugs she'd taken. 'Power is not given away.', she declared, heady with it. The blood was surging so hard through her veins she could literally feel the back of her eyeballs. What a rush! 'Power is something you have to compete for.'

Feeling equally omnipotent, Gollum-Mazie chuckled – a tremendously disquieting sound. 'Well, thank Hell for the Coronavirus – and China, of course. I don't think we'd have gotten away with shoving Sleepy Creepy down America's throat without their help! That biological attack really saved our bacon!', she exclaimed, jiggling her porcine chin as she did so. 'We'd never have been able to push unverified signatures from bullshit addresses through without it! Hell, audits confirmed we even got the same bogus votes counted multiple times and kicked out all the non-partisan observers!' Coming down momentarily from her triumphant perch the toady senator from Hawaii paused. 'Not that Sleepy Joe isn't a complete disaster.', she noted morosely. 'My stock investments are all in the fucking toilet.'

Crazy Mazie went off then, pontificating about all the deficiencies of the nursing home shadow puppet they'd installed into power over the will of the people. Having made a killing herself in the Market through insider trading of the tech stocks she had Congressional oversight of, while Hirono bitched away Fancy Nancy took the opportunity to polish off the rest of her pint of ice cream. As she shoved spoonful after spoonful of Blackout chocolate cake into her mouth Fancy Nancy mused at the irony of the name. Unlike Candice Owens, bestselling African-American author of *Blackout*, Pelosi's only interest in black people was their vote; other than that the slaves in Democratic districts didn't matter. Her section of the country was riddled with feces and diseases of every kind (including coronavirus) had decimated the population of San Francisco but none of that bothered her. Her backroom deals and insider trading had made her obscenely rich; she lived in a mansion and could afford whatever expensive ice cream and recreational drugs she wanted. Next up was Salted Peanut Butter with Chocolate Flecks and a generous side of Oxycodone!

'So what do you think about Kamala?', Crazy Mazie abruptly asked, interrupting Pelosi's drug-fueled ice cream binge. 'Do you think she'll help us?'

Her mouth stuffed full with SPB Nancy P was too enamored with savoring it to immediately answer the overweight fat fuck. In truth, she was as sure as everyone else that Harris was a complete and total nut job. She dare not say it out loud but if things worked out the way she hoped Biden would get forcibly retired for his senility (or Impeached for accepting bribes) and Harris would be removed on the basis of her psychological illnesses. If that happened, she was next in line. The office of POTUS would be a hassle but as President she could command all sorts of kickbacks – even more than what she got in the Speaker's chair! 'There's no question that women helping women works for women.', she answered wryly after she'd sucked every last ounce of sweet out of the Salted Peanut Butter and swallowed, doubling down on the Democrat's standard policy of overt sexism.

Mazie nodded, then paused nervously. 'Do you think – do you think maybe Hillary will run again? Even after getting her ass kicked by the Orange Man in 2016?'

Fancy Nancy's shoulders knotted almost imperceptibly. The question Crazy Mazie posed was a sobering and dangerous one. Not wanting to think about the possibility that the murderous bitch might reassert herself directly into the political arena, Pelosi sidestepped it. 'I believe that Hillary Clinton is one of the best prepared people in our history to enter the Oval Office.', she said, consciously masking her shudder.

Less practiced in masking her disdain Hirono-Gollum cringed. 'Everybody hates her, Precious. I hate her. If she didn't have dirt on all of us-s she wouldn't be able to keep pulling the strings like she does. She's got us all by the clits, everyone voting lock step. Anyone who doesn't vote straight party line gets their junk chopped off – or worse, gets Epsteined.' Mazie paused, fingering her drink. 'Not being able to compromise and cut a deal with the other side takes a lot of money off the table. We're promoting some pretty crazy-ass-s shit these days. Maybe we should start negotiating again? Letting people decide their own votes-s?'

Pelosi knew the reality of the situation all too well. Off the chain loose cannon Alexandria Ocasio-Cortez was a serious pain in her ass – her immature nemesis was determined, dumb as a box of rocks and completely sure that her fake education was 100% real. Worse, because she was young and pretty she had the ear of the ill-educated sheep who'd gone through the liberal indoctrination programming they jokingly called "college" these days. The idiot children liked the celebrity status afforded "one of their own" and believed they actually had a voice in government now that their favorite bartender had a seat at the table. AOC was their figurehead, the urban hipster lamb-whisperer.

Still, the Speaker of the House did not like where this conversation was veering. This was dangerous insurrection territory and as part of the machinery that kept everyone in line she could brook no break in the ranks. 'The Democratic Party has always been a party that is not known for its unanimity.', she warned coldly. As her counterpart had just mentioned Hirono knew the exact opposite was true, as were the understood penalties for disobedience. Getting your funding cut off was the least of your worries if you did not go where the globalist overlords behind the Clintons directed – as the recent censure of Senator Kyrsten Sinema of Arizona for voting against the Democratic party's attempt to remove the protections of the filibuster and ram through permanent mail-in voting fraud mechanisms proved.

Moderately inebriated and missing Fancy Nancy's implied threat, drunk Gollum snorted. 'Yeah, right, Precious-s.', she joked. 'Next you'll be saying Obama wasn't a con man...'

The subject pivoting away from the suicide-assisting Clintons (and their Chinese, Russian and Hungarian partners) to the safest of targets, Pelosi relaxed. "Brown Turd" was fair game to mock – with impunity. Smooth-talking con-man Barrack had a line for everything but was a complete and total pussy out of the spotlight. Putin had made him his bitch so easily it was a wonder who's collar Little Barry O wore: his openly racist wife Michelle's or the "Iron Man's". 'Obama has never done anything for political reasons...', she teased, calling to mind the total nonsense video Obama tried to blame the embassy riot on during the 2012 election.

'Yeah, Precious-s! Only lied once – and hasn't stopped since!', Hirono-Gollum croaked, making fun of the "community organizer" game show host who through the incompetence of the old guard Republican party had somehow managed to get himself elected 44th President of the United States. 'Ol' "gimme a dollar and I'll give you change" wouldn't know how to s-sharpen a dull pencil! When Barry-O flushed the economy down the toilet his-s publicly announced "solution" was to print more money!'

Laughing and smiling, Mazie-Gollum belched and farted simultaneously. 'It's like saying we've got to run up the National Debt to decrease it! Jesus and his-s whore of a mother Mary...'

Approving of Hirono's overt blasphemy and letting her guard down "Catholic" Nancy nodded and scarfed down another huge spoonful of peanut butter chocolate. This time she was so revved up she swallowed it almost immediately. '"It's almost a false argument to say we have a spending problem."', Pelosi quoted herself, relishing one of her more ridiculous comebacks to an actual reporter's serious question. '"You can not cut your way to deficit reduction."'

Not too bright under the best of circumstances it took drunken fish Crazy Mazie a moment to translate Fancy Nancy's double-speak into something that made marginal sense. Almost false...so it was <u>true</u> to say that Congress under Democrats had a serious spending problem!!! As Murphy's Law so eloquently stated: "If you can't convince them, confuse them!" 'You actually...got away with s-s-saying that, Precious-s???', she hissed in astonishment.

Pelosi slurped down another scoop full of SPB and laughed maniacally. The Spin Doctors could fix anything if her audience really wanted to play along – the sheep were dumber than monkeys! '"If Democrats win and have substantial majorities, the Congress of the United States will be more bipartisan."', she bragged, showing off the stupid shit she could get away with saying in front of the cameras when the media companies and their talking bobble-heads were all owned by Democrats.

Taken in by Nancy's outrageous public comments, Crazy Mazie literally spat her drink out onto the desk. 'They bought that, Precious-s??? They *actually* bought that???!!!! How can these – these – *idiots-s-s* – actually – actually! – believe that voting your opponents-s-s <u>out of office</u> will somehow lead to more bipartisan – bipartisanships?!?!?!'

Revved up on drugs and iced chocolate Nancy Pelosi churned her bullshit engine into high gear. Proud of all the dumb shit she'd gotten away with saying in front of the camera she began rattling off some of her most famous blunders: '"We have to pass Obama Care to find out what's in it!" "Obama Care will lower everyone's rates!" "Unemployment benefits are creating jobs faster than practically any other program!" "Every month that we do not have an economic recovery package 500 million Americans lose their jobs!"

'Oh, you are killing me, Precious-s-s! Killing me!', Crazy Mazie Gollum chuckle-croaked. Given hope by Fancy Nancy P's outrageous exploits she grabbed the bottle of whiskey next to her elbow, took a hit from it directly like a redneck, then attempted to pour herself another drink.

Flying high as a kite, Congress-fool Pelosi paused to clear the ice cream from her throat before delivering her favorite punchline: '"The American people voted to restore integrity and honesty in Washington, D.C. and the Democrats intend to lead the most honest, most open and most ethical Congress in history."'

Half into her pour Hirono-Gollum sloshed whiskey all over the desk and nearly lost her grip on the bottle. The fat toad hurried to right the ship before her stash of over-priced liquor ended up all over the floor. 'Oh, sweet Lucifer-s! You *actually* said that? And they *bought* it, Precious-s-s? After all *the shits-s* we pulled? They really bought *it's-s*???'

Tongue coated in super-expensive milk-fat Pelosi cackled throatily like the wicked queen in the classic pre-woke Disney film *Snow White*. Screwing over people was a lot of fun – especially when she could rub their faces in it and at the same time feint that she gave a crap about the very people she was screwing over. Fancy Nancy got a special rush of power when she warned the peons about what she was about to do to them first, sort of like a sadistic medieval torturer describing in detail the torment the rack produced right before turning the screw another notch. '"I have deep emotion about the American people. If I were to cry for anything, I would cry for them and the policies that they're about to face."', she promised with a cruel smile.

Drunk-as-a-fish, Hirono bobbed her head up and down and grinned back at her stupidly. Holding her cup in both hands like a preschooler she took a heady draw on her tonic. 'You would think-sies that the hurts we've done to people's wallets-ies would....would catch up with them – ', she slurred. 'With us-es, I means-s. Sooner or later peoples-s have gots-s to realize that what we're doing doesn't works... that it hurts-s-s them.'

Not caring one way or the other, Pelosi scoffed breezily. Democrats had been playing the same tired game for decades now and at least some voters were still dumb enough to buy into it. As Hitler said: "The bigger the lie the more people will believe it.", and given all the Big Tech resources at their disposal they had plenty of 1984 Big Brother-style social media clout to shove their narrative up people's asses with.

Delving into another helping of ice cream she paused mid-spoon. She had to admit it *was* getting harder and harder to pull the wool over the sheep's eyes. It hadn't worked this election cycle; in spite of their campaign of lies – and the chaos and fear caused by the China Virus – they had been forced to resort to outright election fraud to regain power. Next time they wouldn't be able to get away with it. As Crazy Mazie said, at the end of the day they could very well end up lynched. 'Think of an economy where people could be an artist or photographer or a writer without worrying about keeping their day job.', she woke-believed, fantasizing about some sort of faux-economy where nobody actually worked for a living, a mirror image of Congress under her leadership.

'We have, hic...have to....keep working on the young-sies, convincing them before they have any real life experience-ies. We gotta keep getting them...in the Universities-s-es before they know any better.', drunk Mazie-Gollum rambled. 'School tuition isn't frees-s and we're not....not going to s-s- subsidize it unless those teachers keep in-indoctrinating new voters-s-ies...for us-s-s. Either...they act as our mouth pieces-ies...and shut down s-smart thought...or we yank their fundings.'

Unconcerned, Pelosi swallowed the remainder of her ice treat. The iron lock liberals had on so-called "higher education" was near-total. Though their go-to indoctrination mill had produced the unintended by-product of idiot-deluxe AOC, ideological Socialism (what Democrats had re-branded as "Progressive") was easy to sell to children with no work experience. The idea of "free stuff for nothing" appealed to kiddies still living off their parents. It didn't matter that it didn't work; Democrats were only promoting it to: 1) get young dumb kids to vote for them and 2) grow the cash pool in Washington DC so they'd have more money to steal from the public. No Liberal ever won a fair debate against a Conservative so to counter the truth Universities were shutting down all discussion in the interest of "public safety". To push stupid ideas on people (and make-believe they weren't insane) the first right Americans had to lose was the power of free speech – on both social media platforms and in so-called institutions of "higher learning".

But maintaining the voting block was for politicians with a career ahead of them and not someone as old and corrupt as Congress-Fool Nancy Pelosi. Ill-gotten money and Insider Trading bought the things she loved most – drugs and ice cream – and right now she was all about stuffing her face with a fresh pint of Middle West Whiskey and Pecan ice cream. Mmmmm – love that whiskey flavor!

'An' another thingg – ', Hirono-Gollum slurred as her friend Precious Fancy Nancy pried open the ice cream container with glee. 'It would be nice if we could get at least *s-s-some* of the so-called "menses"...inn our party....t' stop raping their staffers-s-s! "Slick Willie" just...can't seem to stop s-s-sticking hiss little willy...inna young girl-es. An' some of these newer ones-ies are evens worse! I have – I have to go out an' push this-s-s "MeToo" crap – "Womens are to be believed and men should shut up and stand up-sies!" – and it's hard to sell that s-s-shit...s-s-shit....when the men-ses inn our own party won't stop rippin' the pants off underage girls-ies and sticking their lil' dicks-s in their holes-ies! Billy Clinton...got...got caught taking twenty some-odd underage s-s-sex trips-s-s with his-s good buddy Epstein! Har-har-Harvey Weinsteins convicted....convicted off raping virtually every piece-ies of ass-s in Hollywood! I mean-ses......Ally....Ally....Al Franken....he actually *posied* for a picture while he was gropin'....gropin'....a s-sleeping female soldier's-s breasts-es-es! Her breasts-es-es!! While she wass sleepings! Posed for it....like it was a photo-ops....an'.....an' then let it get posted all over the-the internets-es!'

Gollum-like, Crazy-Mazie paused to regain a modicum of her senses before she passed out from alcohol poisoning. 'I still can't believess the press-es...the press-es-es...said he was "fallin' on his s-swords-s for the party" when he....when he resigned. And now with that ass-s-s....as-s-hole Cuomo.... up in New York.....with all....with all those.....so many women-es...'

Barely listening to Hirono's drunken rambling Pelosi licked her spoon with the same focused gusto with which she snorted Coke and closed her eyes so she could savor the taste. Sweeet Saaatan!! Totally worth damnation for!!! 'I went to Congress to change the policies of our country...', she muttered dreamily, unconcerned with the fate of the Democratic Party or the hypocritical conduct of its members now that she had an exit strategy in the works. It was either the Big Chair and corrupt side deals galore or a very pleasant retirement enjoying the fruits of her Insider Trading. 'I did not go to change the behaviors of members of Congress.'

'Well, half of them think being in Congress-s-es is-s a license to break the laws-s-s!', exclaimed Hirono-Gollum excitedly, momentarily coming out of her fugue. 'I mean, yes-s-s, it is-s.......but there are limits-ies! Limits-ies,

Precious-s! I get enough grief from women's rights groups for taking money from Tom Carper and he...he admitted to punchin'...to punchin' his-s wife-ses...in the face! I mean Feinstein, Klobuchar, Donnelly, Manchin and a bunch of others-s...they did the same thing! What's the big deal-ies?! The big deal-ies, Precious-s?!'

Lost in the joys of desert/drugs Pelosi didn't give two shits about Hirono's political problems. After her MWW&P was all gone it was time for another line of coke and a pint of Milkiest Chocolate! And when *that* was empty she was going to finish it all off with Green Mint Chip and whatever drugs were still left!

Her audience of one lost, Crazy Mazie continued to ramble on semi-coherently. 'I just dodged – just dodged, Precious-s! I told 'em: "As-s Americans-s, it's all on us-s to take a stand and do what'ss right – regardless of political party-ies. It's time-ies to stand up for......' So drunk now she was barely able to sit up straight, Hirono-Gollum wracked her brain trying to remember the catch phrase she used for those she claimed she defended. What was it again? Uh......

'"Victims-ses of sexual assault and harass-s-ments."', she screeched abruptly in a high pitched voice, suddenly remembering her bread and butter demographic. Lowering her tone back to its usual frog-like timber she continued her drunken musings. 'I tell you, Precious....it doesn't matter what you...actually dos-ies! You tell s-stupid peoples the right story.... or s-sell them the right phrase...and they shut their brains-ies off! It's all make-believe-ies! If they ever opened their eyes-ies they'd see...they'd see, Precious-s!! We accuse others-s....to divert attention from what we're... actually... doings! *What we're doings, Precious-s!* We don't rape-ies in the Democratic party – we accuse other people of rape-ies! The lock...the lock... we have on the TV stations won't allow anyone to say that we rape-ies!'

Taking Pelosi's continued ice cream-induced silence for assent the fat Gollum-cloned Senator from Hawaii farted loudly. Smiling like a toddler she breathed in the gas like it was sweet perfume and slurred: 'Well, Precious-s-s....I think I'll let you go s-so you can enjoy-s your....your....ice cream-sies. Lemme know....lemme know if you have any good deals-s-s I can get in on. Time-s 's wasting. We won't.....won't.....have the chance to make much monies-s soon.......after 2022......'

Engrossed in her sweet cream the Speaker-in-name-only gave Hirono a quick parting wave then happily cut the connection. Gollum croaking drunk was a poor conversationalist. She much preferred to be alone with her treats.

Settling down in her seat so she could really get serious (about getting seriously loaded) Nancy P elatedly but judiciously pondered her remaining pints. A delicious thought suddenly occurred to her: what if she combined her goodies and put the drugs _in_ the ice cream? Would it work just as well if she ate it? Or would she have to snort the whole thing up her nose?

Ready to try anything to get a greater buzz, Fancy Nancy took a chance and delved in. Like her remaining time in office, life was short.

*   *   *

<u>Coroner's Office. San Francisco, California 10:24 AM Pacific Standard Time.</u>

'I don't think I've ever seen a toxicology screen come back like this.', young Dr. Joseph Ansel exclaimed in wonder as he read the report in his hand. 'I mean, she was absolutely loaded!'

Glancing over his protege's shoulder Chief Coroner Bartholomew L. Chernovski gave the print out another quick once over. 'I have. A few dealers who used their own supply have come in like this. It's unusual, but it happens.'

Ansel shook his head. 'Pretty shocking for a public figure.'

His white-haired mentor shrugged. 'She was a professional politician. There's not much that would surprise me about a person like that. I've seen a lot of celebrities come through these doors.' He cleared his throat. 'What _is_ shocking to me is _how_ she died.'

Ansel wrinkled his nose. 'What do you mean? Seems pretty obvious: a drug overdose.'

Dr. Chernovski shook his head. 'No – and that's the really shocking thing. I've never seen anything like this.'

His brilliant young apprentice looked at him with disbelief, utterly perplexed by the wizened old physician's strange assertion. The good doctor was ordinarily Sherlock Holmesian in the careful precision of his deductions. 'Dr. Chernovski – ', he began respectfully, careful not to overstep his bounds as he questioned his superior's strangely dubious claim. 'You're telling me all that Fentanyl, Coke, Adderall, Ecstasy, Methamphetamine and Oxocodone running through her system <u>wasn't</u> the cause of death??!! You've got to be kidding me!'

'I can understand why you'd think that – and it's a rational conclusion, Joseph – but no, in this case it wasn't the primary cause. The old woman had developed such a tolerance to opioid derivatives that I don't believe an overdose was what actually caused her death.' The learned professor shook his head mirthlessly. 'Believe me, son – I've seen rock stars and Hollywood starlets on this slab with twice as much running through their veins. Back in my ER days a few of them even got up off the bed and walked out the door under their own power!' He scoffed, baffled by what he'd seen when he was Ansel's age. 'You'd be amazed at how hard some drug addicts are to kill.'

His protege paused to let this new knowledge sink in. 'Then what do you think killed her, doc?', he asked, perplexed.

The old coroner sat back and wiped his glasses. Preferring to have his apprentice see the evidence for himself rather than explain it to him he gestured to the microscope on the table. 'Have a look for yourself, Joe. Tell me what you see.'

The young genius did as his mentor asked and bent forward and peered into the microscope. In the viewer were fixed and stained slides of the Congresswoman's brain tissues. The edges were all distorted. 'What the – ! What the hell is going on here...', Ansel murmured.

'Look at the cell wall ruptures.', advised Dr. Chernovski, giving his charge a hint what to focus his attention on. Even with all his years of experience the chief coroner could barely wrap his own head around what he was about to write on the death certificate as the official cause of death. A fresh set of young eyes confirming his diagnosis would help set his learned mind at ease. 'Remind you of anything?', he challenged.

The brilliant twenty-seven year old MD/PhD looked away for a moment then reexamined the slides again. His face took on a puzzled look. 'Frostbite?', he replied tentatively.

The elderly coroner nodded, though he could scarcely believe it himself. 'Frostbite. I've never seen anything like it before. Not once in my 38 years on the job.'

'So, what are you saying, doc?', Ansel murmured, his eyes widening with incredulity. 'That the cause of death is...'

The two men's eyes met, youthful inquisitiveness matching age and experience in a mutual quest for the truth. Confirming Dr. Ansel's tentative supposition the wise old coroner nodded. 'Yes, doctor – misadventure.

As hard as it is to believe: "When you eliminate the impossible, whatever remains, however improbable, must be the truth." Congresswoman Pelosi ate way too much designer ice cream way too fast. She was so Coked out and snorted it up her nose so quickly that she somehow managed to super cool her head. She froze to death.'

Though he couldn't deny the evidence before him, the younger doctor looked at his mentor like he'd gone nuts. 'So the official cause of death is...'

Dr. Bart Chernovski stood tip-toe like he was addressing a crowded room full of students in the lecture hall at University Medical School. 'Nancy Pelosi just became the first person in recorded history to ever actually *die* of brain-freeze.'

*　*　*

'Oh, shit! Oh, shit!!', Emily cried, laughing. 'That was freakin' hilarious! Brain freeze! Brain freeze!!! What a punchline! Holy shit!!

'Told you I had to tell one more before we got out of here.', Guildencrantz grinned.

The two friends were still laughing heartily at the peculiar circumstances of Pelosi's demise when they heard voices coming from the adjacent hall. Agent Rosenstern stole a quick look at the clock. Two minutes past. Their relief had finally shown up – late, but they were here! She and Guy weren't trapped guarding Mail-In anymore! This shit-stained Depends of a day was finally over!

'Okay, to be fair, Fancy Nancy's brain's been on ice for a long time, long before her little ice cream misadventure.', Guildencrantz joked as the two poor souls assigned to replace them reluctantly strode in. Drawn by the sounds of Guy and Emily's hearty laughter Billie Henrietta Harrison and Grover Jefferson Cleveland, Jr. regarded the chuckling pair's apparent mirth with surprise. Nobody who worked in the White House laughed like that anymore – cackled like a hyena maybe, but never a healthy joyful laugh like they used to.

'What's got you two havin' such a good time?', the dark-hued male of the pair queried. 'Excited at the prospect of finally getting the hell outta here?'

Guy nodded happily. 'Well, yeah – of course we're glad to go home! But that's not what we've been yucking it up over. We're laughing our freakin' asses off because of this game we've been playin' to, you know, pass the time.'

'We've been telling each other funny stories while we waited for you two tardy motherfuckers to finally show up.', Emily snarked. Putting her hands under her chin she eyed her partner competitively. 'We never did decide who won.', she challenged puckishly.

Unaware that there was money on the line Agent Cleveland set his gear down grumpily. 'Funny stories? About what?'

'Yeah – what's so funny about being trapped here all day in this dump?', Harrison added dumping her satchel down opposite her partner's. Feeling like she was wasting her precious youth protecting a complete idiot, the pretty lipstick lesbian sighed. No one in their right mind was going to take a pot-shot at Joey-B – not with Camel-Toe waiting in the wings to take over. 'Did little B. J. – sorry J. B. – soil his shorts again?'

'Yeah-he-did.', Rosenstern sang half under her breath, not wanting to rehash the details of Biden crapping his pants or how she got her butt pawed during the clean up process. It seemed like the whole world was swimming in shit these days! She longed for a return to the days of glory – America the beautiful could be so great again! 'But we made a rule that Mail-In was off limits. Have to respect the chain-of-command.'

'Oh yeah, that precious chain-of-command.', Billie quipped with a roll of her eyes. Joey B didn't even have command of his own bowels! Did no one remember how he completely fucked up the withdrawal from Afghanistan President Trump had carefully planned out?! It was a total cluster fuck that directly led to the Russian invasion of Ukraine! And those were the high points of his "presidency"!

'Everyone else was fair game, though.', Guildencrantz bragged with a smile switching the subject back to their contest.

Interested, the pretty lesbian leaned in towards the big man like a high school girl longing to hear the latest juicy lunch room gossip. Did the cheer captain's hot milf-of-a-mom really get caught going down on the soccer coach in the girl's locker room? 'Yeah? Who'd you get?', she demanded insistently.

Guy leaned back and stroked his chin sageously. 'Well, let's see: there was Pocahontas and Cuomo....the Clintons, of course...'

'Colonel Sanders – ', interjected Rosenstern.

'Oh, yeah! The fried chicken spokes-model!', Guy teased with enthusiasm, remembering one of his particular favorites. 'That one was fun!'

'Don't forget about the snake oil salesman!', his grinning partner added with a chortle.

Reminded of ol' Hope and Change, Guildencrantz slapped his forehead like Obama's Understudy's forgetfulness was rubbing off on him. How could even a dolt like B.O. think a useless twit like Biden was fit to be his backup? 'Oh yeah! Obama – absolutely!' Smiling broadly he stroked his chin again. 'Let's see...after that there was sex-change Obama...'

'Michelle?', Billie Harrison blanched, wrinkling her nose sourly. As a hot lesbian the only first lady she ever had fantasies about was the super model, Melania Trump. Her bitchy predecessor (and the bulge in her pants) gave her and her girlfriend Wendy the creeps.

Realizing he was confusing his friends Guy shook his head in the negative. 'No, the other one.'

'The Hyena.', Rosenstern quipped, using the code-term they used to refer to the illegitimate mentally-ill Vice-President who'd acted as Obama's racial stand-in during the 2020 election. Taking the reins from her male partner-in-law Emily continued listing all the offenders they'd delivered well deserved spankings to. 'AOC and the Squadron of Stupidity...LIE-GUY and THE FIBBER...'

'Who?!', Grover queried interestedly. Drawn in he sat down in the chair adjacent.

'Schumer and Schiff.', Em breezed. Particularly enamored with the epic tale of *"MAGA MAN and THE TRUTH versus LIE-GUY and the FIBBER"*, she gestured to Guy to give credit where credit was due. 'And the big man here just froze Pelosi's brain for posterity!', she announced with glee.

'It was a small service to mankind for a very small brain.', Guildencrantz joked.

Laughing along with him Emily continued counting through the hit list on her fingers. They'd missed so many people who deserved a good public flogging! 'Oh, yeah – got Big Tech too! Can't do the fuckers in without talking about the importance of Free Speech!'

'Truth Social?', pretty Agent Harrison quipped hopefully.

'Naw.', Guildencrantz replied, shaking his head but equally eager for **Truth Social** to dominate the market. With 85 million people ready and willing to sign up the free speech social network was a mega-hit outperforming all other platforms in every metric – in spite of super-rich Elon

Musk (who paid no Federal Income taxes in 2018) buying the dead carcass that used to be Twitter. The self-appointed "savior" of free speech was more like a vulture swooping in to gnaw on another subsidy; all the people who supported Free Speech were already working for (or had invested) in Truth Social – and Musk (who owed over 90% of his vast fortune to the favorable Left-wing policies enacted since Biden usurped power from the rightful leader and couldn't have bought Twitter without this cash influx) was openly competing against them! The move had backfired, however – having been burned severely by censorship in 2020 Americans were unwilling to trust their Free Speech rights to yet another left-winger; "more" transparency was not guaranteed "FULL" transparency. And on the left the Woke were leaving Twitter in droves in protest of allowing anyone who disagreed with them to speak – clearly they were afraid of being confronted with the many uncomfortable truths Big Tech had been shielding them from. Worse still for Musk the floors of rapid anti-free speech censor teams (the ones he promised to fire but were still employed at Twitter before his take over) had turned the dying corporation into an absolute technological dumpster fire. Musk claimed to be a champion of free speech but paid good money to buy a shipwreck that only got sold to him in a vain attempt to temporarily devalue the stock price of Trump's surging social network – and given how much money Elon had made since Democrats illegally took over, subtly controlling the narrative and preventing any change back to sensible Conservative energy policies might have been the electric car maker's grand scheme. Absolute power did corrupt absolutely – and self interest always rules all. 'Em here took the disinformation peddlers in the media to task.', Guy bragged with a smile. 'She created a virus that *fact-checked* everything.'

'It was beautiful!', Rosenstern crowed, relishing that story and proud that it was entirely her concept. Things were finally – finally! – starting to go in the right direction! 'Took the whole goddamned network down!'

'I hear Sandmann ripped them for over a quarter billion.', noted Cleveland smoothly.

'And that was just from one company!', giggled Em. Feeling the shared vibe, she turned her attention back to all the others they'd done in. 'Let's see....got Mad Max....Feinstein....who'm I missing?'

'I ran over the RINOs.', Guy reminded her.

Rosenstern tipped her phantom cap in his direction. 'Yup – that you did. Great job, by the way! You've done a great service for our country!'

Wishing it would actually happen she thrust her fist in the air. 'Road rage rhinos to the rescue!'

Impressed by his friends impressive tally of smack-downs, handsome ever-calm secret service agent Grover Cleveland Jr. stroked his smooth chin. 'Sounds like you two had quite a fun day – in spite of being stuck here. Love to hear all about it sometime.' Masking his smile, the dark-skinned man leaned towards them conspiratorially. 'In detail.'

'Yeah.', perked his girl-inclined partner with far less restraint. Desperately eager to hear all about it Billie Harrison dragged the nearest chair over with a squeak and plopped down beside her lovely female coworker. 'Tell us!', she begged, batting her eyelashes prettily. 'Please! Please, pretty-please!'

In danger of being cornered by the agents sent to relieve them of the horrible burden slumbering in the next room, Emily Rosenstern chuckled and quickly rose from her chair. Her and Guy's shift was over; it was time to get the hell out of dodge and go home. 'Maybe some other time.', she promised. 'I got a man at home waiting for me.'

'Yeah, me too.', Guildencrantz seconded as he gathered up his things to leave.

In spite of being rebuffed, Cleveland grinned. 'Didn't think you swung that way, Guy.', Grover sassed with a smile.

Knowing her married partner-in-law was actually the least homophobic man in the service his sapphic twenty-something companion ignored Agent Cleveland's playful little jest. 'Really, Em – ', Billie Harrison pressed, putting her hand on the departing agent's like by gently squeezing it she could wring all the funny stories out of her. 'You've got to tell me! Can't I take you two out for drinks some time? When are you guys free?!'

Surprised by her lesbian friend's offer Rosenstern glanced over at Guildencrantz. The twinkle in Guy's eyes said he was thinking along the same lines as she was. Why squabble over who won their little game when they might talk someone else into picking up the whole tab instead? 'Tell you guys, what – ', she offered, taking a negotiating cue from the President. 'You two take us out for dinner and drinks sometime...and we'll fill you in on the whole thing.'

'Man, have we got stories to tell.', Guy added quickly, baiting the hook.

Em nodded vigorously and made a whistling sound. 'Oh, yeah! It's gonna take a while too!' The prime temptation to the other party spelled out clearly from the get-go she paused and pursed her lips to let it sink in. 'But you gotta spring for someplace nice.', she wheedled shrewdly. 'No cheap little chain restaurant! Someplace swanky, with good food and good wine! And we're gonna want to bring our squeezes along with us too!', she added, piling on an important concession to the deal while the other side was still salivating over what she was offering them.

Really wanting to hear all about the funny calamities that befell the ne'er-do-wells running this shit-show government into the ground, Billie Henrietta Harrison and Grover Jefferson Cleveland, Jr. paused for a hurried side bar to talk it over. Agreeing to split the final bill for the night equally, they nodded their assent and readily accepted Agents Guildencrantz's and Rosenstern's all-too Trumpian terms.

'We'll make reservations for eight on Saturday.', the beautiful Conservative-leaning dyke declared, eager to hear all the dirt. 'I'll text Wendy and she if she's free for a night out on the town with her way-too-gorgeous-for-words girlfriend and all her desperately straight-but-cool coworker friends.', she sassed with dramatic flair. Looking forward to getting together for a night of laughter and good times with other people who didn't have their heads shoved up their asses she turned to her professional life-partner. 'What do you think Grove? That sexy wife of yours game for dinner and a show?'

Cleveland nodded. 'I'll check with Na'Tasha, but I'm sure it's doable.' He coughed to clear his throat, then frowned. 'She's tired of hearing me bitch about all the crap that goes on around here, anyway.'

Dinner and date night secured, Emily smiled. After a second she shook her head. 'Crap is right! The poor nurse just about lost it today!'

'"Sleepy Creepy" still pulling grab-ass duty after he goes doodie?', Billie complained uneasily.

'That's what she gets for voting the way she did.', Cleveland interjected, placing the blame for the nurse's plight squarely on her own two shoulders. Voting stupid leads to bad results. He turned to his partner-in-patriotism. 'If Joey soils himself tonight, I'll take care of him.', he promised.

Billie nodded her appreciation. 'Thanks, Grove.'

'She said "doodie".', Guy joked, trying to make light of the uncomfortable situation. Taking a more serious tone, the big agent leaned in close and gripped Grover's arm. 'Good man. I do the same for Em.', he whispered.

'Gotta take care of our partners, brother.', replied Cleveland with a return squeeze.

'Damned right we do.'

Plans made, with that the day shift gathered up their things to leave. Praying their good friends' night went smoothly they started for the door.

Before he walked out Guy turned to his fellow patriots. 'Keep the faith – it's gonna turn out all right in the end. And let me and Em know about Saturday!'

'We'll be in touch! Looking forward to hanging out with you guys in a better venue!'

With renewed promises of better times the two pairs of agents went their separate ways. As they headed for the parking garage and home Rosenstern and Guildencrantz smiled. The victor of their little contest hadn't been decided, but that didn't matter to Emily or Guy. Saturday's revels were paid for and in a few short months a brand new election was coming up – they could begin to eject the usurpers who had tainted the country they loved so much and finally restore much needed freedom and justice to America! All it took was enough votes (and thwarting the election fraud that plagued – along with the Chinese-made plague – the terrible year of 2020). That year was past and good things were on the way. **Truth Social** was leveling the playing field of Big Tech like a steamroller and media liars were being successfully sued in court by the private citizens they had slandered. Voters who *had* actually supported Biden were waking up and finally coming to their senses. Hindsight really was 20/20 – if the so-called 46th "president" hadn't convinced everyone everywhere that the Democratic party was a bunch of incompetent anti-democratic traitors who cared nothing about the everyday person and just wanted to rape, plunder and pillage America, nothing ever would! You really can't fix stupid.

GO,

BRANDON,

GO!

Permission is granted to the public by the publisher and author of The Jackass Calamities, Perfidious Nick, to freely copy and disseminate the following two pages:

<u>Proposed Twenty-Eighth Amendment to the United States Constitution:</u>

<u>Section 1:</u> All votes cast in Federal elections must be verified by photo identification, verified legal signature, verified valid legal address in the proper jurisdiction in which the voter has a Constitutional right to vote and any other requirements as may be imposed by a quorum of the states such as fingerprint verification, legal citizenship status verification or any other uniform method of identity verification. Only legal US citizens may vote in Federal elections. All votes must be paper and possess a unique identifying number, voting must be completed on the appointed day of the election and tabulation completed within six hours after the polls are closed. Tabulation of votes must be uploaded to the state office within 24 hours and available for individual voters to verify that their vote has been properly assigned. Disputed votes shall be assigned as the voter requests by legal affidavit. Ballot harvesting and drop boxes are illegal and specifically prohibited. Legal votes are limited to votes cast in person on election day or absentee ballots requested at least thirty days before the appointed election date, postmarked fourteen days prior to the election date and received on or before the appointed date of the election. Physical votes must be kept for two years from the date of the election. All voting in federal elections must be audited prior to certification of the election results.

<u>Section 2:</u> Election fraud shall be considered high treason or if by a foreign entity an act of sabotage punishable at minimum by imprisonment for life without the possibility of parole or pardon or if the number of fraudulent votes is equal to or greater than one thousand votes punishable by a mandatory sentence of death imposed upon the offender within three years of the offender's conviction. Election fraud shall be considered any willful violation of section 1 and/or alteration of votes, destruction of votes, tampering with voting machines, willfully counting a single valid legal vote multiple times, counting votes without the presence of sufficient poll watchers to ensure voting

integrity (a minimum six to one ratio at a minimum distance of ten feet), illegally moving votes from one state to another, production or distribution of counterfeit ballots, willfully accepting and counting counterfeit ballots, forging signatures on ballots or any other activity which materially compromises election integrity such as cyber-crime or willful negligence in physically securing the votes.

<u>Section 3:</u> The statute of limitations for election fraud shall be defined as twenty years or five Presidential election cycles, which ever is greater.

Signed: _____ Date: _____

Sign and date this proposed Amendment and send it to your local Congressperson. Keep a copy for yourself in case the need arises to prove your support for this much needed Amendment. Support for these measures should be Bi-Partisan and universal – I challenge any American to argue that this Amendment is somehow superfluous or unfairly benefits any political party.

To repeat: The pages detailing the proposed Twenty-eighth Amendment to the U.S. Constitution are to be considered severed from the usual copyright protections and may be copied freely by the public and disseminated in both print and electronic form. All other rights in regards to this work (*The Jackass Calamities*) remain reserved by the author.